THE PRINCE OF PIRATES

A Story of Love, Loss, and Lots O' Loot

A fictional novel based on events from the life of Black Samuel Bellamy

By: E. H. Casteele

Most names, characters, and places are products of the author's imagination. Any references to historical events, real people, or real places are used fictitiously and should not be construed as factual representations.

ISBN: 979-8-9904183-0-1 (ebook)

ISBN: 979-8-9904183-1-8 (paperback)

ISBN: 979-8-9904183-2-5 (hardback)

Editor: Kara Travis

Beta Reader: Cielo Bellarose

Front Cover Image: Nicholas Raymond (www.boldfrontiers.com)

Printed and bound in the United States of America

DEDICATION

Thank you to my husband, Rob, who answered all my weird questions asked at odd times. I am super proud of your military service and the insight it gave me for some of the scenes in this book. You are my best friend, and this debut novel wouldn't be possible without you.

Thank you to my children, Kaitlyn, and Alan, for supporting and indulging my history stories and out-of-the-blue random facts. You never cared if I took the time to overexplain something of historical significance. It is wonderful to be able to pick your brains now that y'all are grown and able to outsmart your mama.

PROLOGUE

Off the Coast of Wellfleet, Massachusetts, October 1985

Sunlight glinted off the ever moving surface and choppy waters off of the coast of Wellfleet as sea birds played among the waves in search of food. Swirling sediment and other detritus flowed under the waves, causing the water to be murky and reduce visibility. Lobsters pistoned their tails and swished through the current, pulling themselves backward and passing various reefs covered in mussels. Crabs scuttled between the turbulent sands in search of their next meal.

Divers swam in the obscurity with only flashlights and compasses to guide them and kept a wary eye out for sharks that inhabited the deeper waters off the shallow shelf. Fish darted in and out of the reefs, escaping the predators that lurked above and below them.

The daily antics of sea life were quickly disrupted when a large, artificial tube descended from above. A loud *thump* sounded and reverberated through the waters as a sudden rush of forced air caused them to swirl and move out in a large circle from the epicenter, open a pit, and widen it below on the sea floor. Each *thump* moved more sediment, revealing mysteries hidden for over three hundred years.

Several extensive reefs remained anchored to the sea floor, connected as if by concrete, and stuck fast. Odd-shaped and unnatural, these reefs were odd and long cylindrical shapes and very large concealing cannons underneath. The *thumping* subsided, and the crabs and fish gradually returned to the area and flitted around the newly revealed reef structures and down into the pit. Light pierced the darkness as it rotated around the sea floor before focusing on the pit.

A large, triangular-shaped rock lay in the pit as the sediment moved around it, and inhabitants scuttled to find new housing. The bottom of the rock was a large ring that flared out and was the most prominent part. A long bar shape stood on top with a half circle at the very top and on the center of that bar. Bits of coral covered it, and bottom-dwelling inhabitants awakened with the sudden illumination. Soon, hands touched the object crusted with the ocean's concretions, gestured excitedly, and left briefly before returning with a rope and tied it around it.

The rope lifted the strange rock from its salty home and took it to a research facility where electrolysis would find the object hidden within it. A few weeks later, chunks sloughed off, and the process revealed a ship's bell and its corresponding nameplate, confirming the discovery of one of the most significant historical finds in pirate treasure and history. Once cleaned and detailed, the writing was indisputable and helped cement the ship's fame and confirm its location.

A swipe of a hand across the broad span revealed they had found their treasure as it read:

The Whydah Gally 1716

PART ONE: A HERO'S BEGINNING

"He told me it was men of desperate fortunes

on one hand, or of aspiring, superior fortunes on the

other, who went abroad upon adventures, to rise by

enterprise, and make themselves famous in

undertakings of a nature out of the common road."

— Daniel Defoe, *The Life and Surprising Adventures of Robinson*

Crusoe, Mariner 1719

Chapter 1: A Storm Brews

Wellfleet, Massachusetts, Present Day

Seabirds flew in lazy circles, calling out their raucous calls around the beach where tourists walked looking for any treasures dotting the shores. They tightened their jackets against the late October breeze as winter released its last gasp on the region. Based on folk stories, the waters were rich with sunken treasures and other flotsam and jetsam. There was hope of finding "that one thing," so the tourists continued to search while their children played in the sea spray and watched tide pools teaming with life. After all, a famous wreck was just hundreds of feet from this particular beach.

Loyd Jones strode across the deck of his lobster boat, checking traps and ensuring lines weren't tangled. The lifted bow, made to part the waves easily, bounced and bobbed with the influx of motion, but Loyd developed his sea legs long ago. Putting his right hand up to shadow his light blue gaze, he looked around to ensure no more buoys indicated his traps. The radio crackled with static between the reports from the local weather station. A brief tone sounded, and the tinny voice of the announcement reached Loyd's ears. There was a storm blowing in fast and furious and a possible nor-easter.

Loyd swore softly and quickly began winding up the ropes and stowing things correctly. In his fifty-four years, he had learned the consequences of letting salt set in on the ropes and not rinsing off the boat once in the dock. Luckily, he had a small berth nearby and didn't have to worry about loading it onto the truck.

Once loaded, Loyd kicked on the single-engine and pointed his bow towards the docks near Marconi Beach. Looking off to the side, he could see Nauset Lighthouse and the light rotating on it, so he knew it was getting to be late afternoon since he could see where it illuminated the treacherous waters below.

Breathing in the salty air, he could taste the impending weather, confirmed by his aching knee from an old sports injury when he was younger. *Damn*, he thought, *it sucks getting old*. Even at his age, he still possessed an athlete's physique with a build over six feet tall and muscles honed from decades of seamanship.

Pulling into the docks, he could see others sailing in and trying to get things battened down and home before the storm hit. Various people called out to him, and he waved back and muttered under his breath with the authentic tones and sounds of Boston interlacing it.

Yeah, hey, how are ya? Next time, don't come zooming in like you are at NASCAR trying to park in the pit.

Here's a wave for ya, dumbass. You wouldn't know a bow from a stern from your asshole.

Okay, that's not a bad sight, he thought, nodding and waving towards a boat carrying a bridal party having their night out on the town and already well into the drink portion of the evening. One of the ladies fumbled with her shirt, attempting to lift the hem, but only succeeded in knocking her friend's drink out of her hand; pushing and hair-pulling ensued. *This ain't Mardi Gras, but I appreciate the thought.*

It took another hour to get his catch out of the holds, sell it to the local vendors, and then back to clean and batten his boat. As he walked towards his truck, he saw the clouds darkening and casting a deeper gloom on the afternoon for his drive home. Drumming his fingers to the 80's music station, he thought, *Yep, this storm might be a wicked one after all.*

Tourists streamed out of buildings lining the road out of the marina carrying various sea-themed or Halloween knick-knacks and clothing. Soon, they would probably head north for historic Salem, about three to four hours away, depending on traffic. Some children wore costumes of witches, with many of them being the Sanderson Sisters from the Disney movie, to get into the spirit of the holiday and as a reflection of the state's history.

Loyd was glad such a dark time in Salem and Massachusetts's history from 1692 to 1693 was still recognized in modern times. The paranoia was intense back then, and you never knew who to believe. It wasn't until the governor's wife was accused that the clamor for the death of witches finally began to die down as he declared an end to the ridiculous trials.

How could so many people believe the tales told by children?

Or even believe that a slave named Tituba could possess powers such as those detailed in the witch trial histories. *But*, he thought, *is it any different than cyberbullying today? Now, keyboard warriors and trolls could tank someone's life and career with just a few posts.*

His thoughts changed back to the storm as the wind whipped the trees lining the road to his neighborhood. Pulling up to his house, he saw his neighbors readying their property.

His house, a historic clap-board-sided structure with steeply pitched roof lines and large dormer windows, had been updated throughout the centuries since it was passed down through his family. His late wife, who hailed from The South, had ensured a porch was added to the front for "visiting and just being nosey," she told him when she gave her reasons. It was also her wish to have it painted a light blue favored by historians in Williamsburg and for whom the name of the paint was derived.

Calling out a greeting to the neighbor on his right and good friend, Josiah Bentley, Loyd entered his house and prepared for the incoming storm. Luckily, he had surge protectors on most of his electronics, so he didn't worry about lightning strikes as much as when he was a kid. Part of the warnings by grown-ups of adult perils was lightning striking your television. That was in addition to quicksand and booby traps. They could happen and did sometimes, but not nearly as much as Loony Toons and The Goonies had warned him. Now, his biggest worry was if he could sneeze without having his back go out.

***

"Breaking news: this season's first nor'easter is approaching the Massachusetts mainland with estimated landfall projected over twelve hours. Residents are urged to secure all loose items outside and to have emergency kits and supplies ready. We will stay on the air and continue coverage of what is looking to be a rough one. Remember, if you lose power, we also broadcast on the local airwaves, so keep batteries in your radios!"

The very polished and calm television anchors talked about emergency measures, ways to prepare, and all the usual things given during exciting times of impending doom before breaking into a commercial about how artificial intelligence would significantly enhance your cell phone.

Loyd stood near the window, surveying his earlier preparations to his property to ensure things were storm ready. He twirled the golden beads on his lucky bracelet and mentally ran through his storm checklist. His wife teased him that it was just a "fidgety clicker" of a different type.

Although the morning had been sunny, an oppressive, muggy heat increased as the day went on while aboard his lobster boat trawling along the coast. Loyd turned a weathered eye to the horizon, knowing how these storm events usually went. He mentally ran through a checklist to ensure he and his family prepared accurately.

Joining him at the window was his ten-year-old grandson, Charlie, who took Loyd's hand and looked worriedly outside. "Think it'll be bad, Grandpa?" he asked.

"Naw, kid, but it will be a little more than most, I reckon," he replied. People in the rest of the country would recognize the blending of the "r" and "a" sounds in a unique lilt and cadence special to the Boston area. Crouching down to a head with hair as black as his, he looked Charlie in the eyes. "Are ya scared?"

Charlie, his hair pulled back in an ebony waterfall that girls would flock to once he was grown, nodded once, then caught himself.

"But just a little bit," and bravely lifted his chin, worry in his hazel eyes.

Loyd glanced over to the tv and noted his granddaughter, Clarissa, playing on her cell phone, watching short videos that were popular on social platforms, as most sixteen-year-olds do these days. She twirled her raven hair streaked with its red stripes as her freckled face peered closely at the screen, dark blue eyes narrowed in focus. Loyd was sure an apocalypse could occur, and she would be none the wiser. From the furious typing and flying thumbs, it appeared she was fighting, once again, with her boyfriend, Reggie.

Loyd, still holding Charlie's hand, went and sat by Clarissa, and she glanced up to watch the news anchors. "Wow," she said, "that woman has a wicked cool glow-up happening."

"A what?" Loyd asked, definitely feeling over a half-century old. He had always enjoyed caring for his grandkids as his son and daughter-in-law worked in Provincetown nearby at their comics and games shop. His wife, Julie, had passed soon after Charlie was born, and Loyd was glad she could hold him in her arms before the cancer eventually took her from him.

"Like, she has lots of contouring enhancements and stuff, right? See how the camera captures her at all the right angles and shows off her profile?" Clarissa hoped to be a make-up and costume artist for the movies someday, so she put her phone down (*miracles happen!*) to inspect the make-up work.

Loyd couldn't believe it. She parted with an appendage. She launched into her critique of the anchor woman's attributes and why the glow-up was above average from what she was learning in her classes in school.

"Okay, look at her face. Usually, camera-ready means a lot of make-up applied so it shows on the screen. Here, you can tell she has on the basic layers of primer, foundation, and concealer, making her skin flawless without lines and wrinkles. Next, see the contouring used?"

"Umm, sure?" Loyd had no idea but wasn't going to tell her that.

"It takes special tools to get to this level of lines and blending. Take her eye liner, for instance, I know of cosmetologists who use scotch tape to create the angle and ensure the lines are straight and there's no bleeding over. Kinda like painter's tape."

"Ah, that I understand!" Loyd agreed.

"See? They put the scotch tape on the edge of the eye, angle it diagonally, apply the eyeliner, and then remove the tape, leaving a clean cat-eye look." Clarissa pointed to her own eyes. "See? That's how I did my eyes this morning." Pulling up a video on the internet, she showed a quick clip to Loyd on the process as he sat between the two kids on the couch.

"Wow, interesting, thanks, kiddo!" Loyd was proud, Clarissa was excited, and that was all that mattered. She knew what she wanted in life and was jumping in with both feet.

Charlie, kicking his feet next to Loyd, stiffened as a peal of thunder sounded about five miles away. Two minutes later, lightning flashed, lighting up the living room. Charlie gave up trying to be brave and snuggled into Loyd's armpit. Loyd laughed softly and pulled Charlie and Clarissa closer.

"Ya see, the gap between lightning and thunder is thought to be a good way to judge the distance of a storm," Loyd told them.

"What do you mean, Grandpa?" Charlie asked.

Clarissa attempted to pull a face like she already knew but leaned closer to hear his reply. Her phone sat in her hand, ready in case she had an emergency, or her boyfriend apologized for the hundredth time. No one called anyone anymore, it seemed.

"Well, kids, the calculation is that for each second between the time you see a lightning flash to when you hear thunder is a mile. So, that was about five seconds or 'five Mississippis,' which means…" he stopped and stared at them.

Clarissa answered, "five miles!" and then looked at her phone. Loyd could see she was scrolling through the web browser function, trying to prove or debunk his theory. He could also see the pleading texts from her to her boyfriend asking him to stop ignoring him, plus lots of emojis and memes.

Another lightning flash lit up their front yard, and Charlie started counting Mississippis. He got to two when the roll of thunder washed over and shook the house gently as a warning.

"That's two miles away!" he expressed excitedly.

"Correct, kiddo," Loyd said, smiling.

The sky darkened considerably, and then the lights flickered once, twice, then went out with a sharp sizzle and pop as electronics gave up their lives. Clarissa loudly exclaimed displeasure when the television cut off and then calmed down as she realized she still had a few hours of battery on her phone. Charlie jumped off the couch and ran to check all the rooms to see if there wasn't at least one thing that still glowed with life. Soon, he returned looking glum.

Loyd asked both kids to help him find battery-powered candles and flashlights he kept stocked for this purpose. Storms weren't uncommon here. They placed the candles around the room and then settled by the fireplace. Loyd lit the fireplace, and then joined them on the floor.

"Are ya both too big for stories?" Loyd asked.

Both kids shook their heads and settled in for one of their grandfather's famous tales. He had regaled them with stories of daring-do on the high seas and local folk tales since they were born and never spared the gory details. He believed that nothing should be romanticized and should be told honestly. He always said these stories were passed down straight from the mouths of those who lived, but who knew if that was true since their grandpa also liked to embellish.

"Let me tell you the tale, as was passed down to me, of a young lad who believed he would be rich and famous even though he started in the slums of England."

"Wait, Grandpa," said Charlie, "Can this be told *Princess Bride*-style where you promise fencing, giants, monsters, and true love?"

Loyd laughed softly and said, "I'll give it a try and you can also ask me questions as we go. I will tell you this much to start. He met his lady love in a tragic tale, not unlike *Romeo and Juliet*, as her parents didn't approve of him, and he was forced to leave her. Kinda like Westley leaving Buttercup to get enough money to support her. Our hero fathered a child he never saw and lost his ships full of loot and his motley crew in a horrific storm worse than the one outside. His is a tale of love, loss, and lots o'loot which was not kept but given to the sea as payment for repentance for his actions, some believed. Some would later call him The Prince of the Pirates and likened him to a Robin Hood of the time."

"I'm listening," said Charlie. "Color me intrigued."

"Let me take you back to March 1689 in the small town near

Plymouth, England. Imagine growing up and literally fending for yourselves day to day, without", he paused dramatically, "electronics, as our young lad did in this story, Samuel Bellamy."

Loyd began narrating his tale with the storm as the backdrop.

Chapter 2: A Rough Beginning

Devon County, England 1689

Various farm life huddled together in the town as the gusts of

wind carried a hint of warmth for the spring, but residents still

shivered in their cloaks during the later part of the Baroque period.

Paths of mud mixed with other undesirable things carved their way

around and between tenements and rookeries where the poorest

population of the town lived. The smell of different types of bodily

fluids and other odors to a modern person would be overwhelming, but

having lived in it all their lives, these people did not notice.

In the previous two years, the English monarchy was embroiled

in their usual fight over who got to sit on the throne and claim a vast

amount of land as their kingdom. The British kingdom is England,

Scotland, and Ireland and there has always been a slight divide between Catholics and Protestants. In the 1960s, some objected to John F. Kennedy as president of the United States since he was Catholic, and protestors felt he would put the Vatican and the Pope's word over the people of the United States. That was the same feeling during this time, so let me give you a quick background.

At the time, there were two main parties: the Whig and the Tory parties. The Whig party wanted James II (a Catholic) excluded from the right of succession to the thrones of England, Scotland, and Ireland. The Tory party wanted him included, and he eventually won the three thrones. This turmoil would lead to The Glorious Revolution in 1688, also known as the Bloodless Revolution, between those who supported James II who firmly supported Catholics or his daughter, Mary, and her husband, William III (William of Orange), who supported the Protestants. James II ended up abdicating and was exiled to France, where his cousin, Louis XIV, ruled. The thrones were now jointly ruled over by William and Mary. They created William and Mary University in 1693, which still stands today. They also influenced the Bill of Rights that America would draft later. James II would die while still exiled in 1701. Queen Anne would pass away in 1694 leaving King William III to rule alone.

This royal kerfluffle was the world into which Sam was born and affected relations between Britain and the New World. Seeking adventure, Sam would seek adventure in the New World and would be the wealthiest pirate ever recorded. They say he amassed as much as $140 million when his piracy ended. It's not too bad for a lad who grew up on a farm but that's getting too far ahead. Let's pick up with the story of Sam's birthplace and his beginning.

Outside the town, a small farm lay nestled in a valley and was home to Stephen and Elizabeth Bellamy and their five children: Rose, Hirana, Elizabeth, and Joan. Elizabeth was extremely pregnant and due to give birth soon and was starting to have lower back pains. They had lost their toddler son, Solomon, a few years before having Joan, so Elizabeth secretly hoped this babe would be a boy, although none could ever replace a child in a mother's heart.

On this particularly blustery winter morning, Stephen left to tend to the farming chores as Elizabeth cared for their children and the household work. After having five children, she was well aware of her pains and told Stephen, as he left early that morning, that he may need to keep an ear out for her. Stephen had given his usual crooked grin and kissed her soundly before telling the kids he was heading out for the day.

Elizabeth used cloth scraps to grab the vat of tallow made from their livestock animal fat, where she had let it melt over the fireplace and took it on the table where she kept her candle-making supplies. She hoped one day to use beeswax, but it was very costly, and none of their neighbors were into beekeeping. The girls waited, and each knew their role, even down to the youngest, only three. Elizabeth placed the vat at the end of the table so there was an assembly line type of production and then stretched her back, placing her hands on the lower portion, and kneaded the muscles. Her oldest, Rose, gave her a questioning look as she knew what the motions meant after having so many siblings.

"Rose, prithee, could thou go ahead and set a vessel of water to hang within the hearth, that it may commence warming?" Elizabeth said, motioning to the pot near the basin where they washed dishes.

Rose, in the manner of pre-teens everywhere, sighed quietly

and dramatically as she knew this meant multiple trips out to the well and then hauling the heavy buckets back inside. After telling her sisters to wait for her before beginning, she snagged the two buckets and shoulder carrier for them as she went out the door.

Elizabeth checked the supplies and the cooling rack, which waited for the dipped candles to hang so they could dry on it. She chuckled and told the other girls they would not be waiting on their sister and began the process by lining up the candle molds passed down by the women in her family each generation until they had a well-worn patina of gloss.

Tallow was very smelly due to its composition of animal fat renderings, so Elizabeth learned early in her life to add salt to the pot while rendering the fat to lessen the smell. It didn't work a hundred percent, but it made it less smelly and helped with the smoke the candles produced. Elizabeth told the girls they need not wait for Rose, and she could catch up.

Rose returned as Elizabeth finished showing her youngest, Joan, how to place wicks made from linen into the molds. With a huff and dramatic sigh when she saw her sisters had begun without her,

Rose petulantly set the buckets down, filled a pot, and put it on the pot hook in the fireplace hearth. Once Joan was happily engaged, Elizabeth gave Rose and Hirana rods with wicks hanging from them to make hand-dipped candles. Young Elizabeth's job was to help her mom pour grease into the molds, ensure they filled them evenly, and then place the top on them so the candles had a round form.

The sun had just approached its zenith as Elizabeth and the girls finished the candles and cleared the table so work could begin on the evening meal. By this time, the heat boiled the pot holding water in the fireplace. Elizabeth judged she could start adding the vegetables she had canned in jars previously in the fall, along with strips of beef she had cured. She hoped the winter would soon diminish as her stores were getting low.

Before starting the meal, however, she took out the bread and cheese, made a small sack lunch for her husband, and asked Hirana to take it to her father. Once lunch was on the way, Elizabeth turned to the counter and felt a strong pang that caused her to gasp and grab her back. Always alert to her mother's health, Rose ran over to Elizabeth and placed a hand on her back, gently massaging.

"Rose, verily I reckon 'twould be best an' thou didst make haste to thy father and let him know his help may be needed ere the hour is through," she said while going to their feather mattress on the floor that served as their bed. All her children had been born here, and it appeared time for this one to join them, though this one appeared feistier than the others.

Hirana returned as Rose ran out the door and, knowing what it meant, ran to her mother's side. Young Elizabeth stood to the side, and her mother bade her to find the cloth linen she had in a chest by the bed that had served for each of their births. She kept her mood light for the girls' sake, although she felt as if she was being torn in two as the contractions began in earnest.

"It appears we shall be using the water for linens instead of stew, my darlings," Elizabeth told them as she quickly cleaned up the candle supplies.

Turning to the younger Joan, she bade her to start counting, then beginning again after each contraction to keep time. She sent Hirana went to the midwife who lived close by as Rose barreled into the house with Stephen.

Stephen's face was white, and he attempted to smile and keep everyone calm. Elizabeth told him that Hirana had gone for the midwife, and Stephen could hear the younger Elizabeth counting softly, so he asked her how the count was going.

"Father, you interrupted me," she pouted, her lower lip jutting out, then stated, "I was saying '14' 'ere I had to commence anew for the past twain attempts."

Stephen stilled, then looked over at his wife for confirmation. Elizabeth nodded her sweat-drenched head, and her eyes showed the first signs of panic.

"This one doth approach with slight swiftness, doth it now, love?" He dropped to her side and used the linen supplied by Joan to wipe Elizabeth's brow.

"Aye, seems to be in a hurry to grow up," she panted between contractions, "must be a lusty lad."

"Now, love, mayhap it doth be a girl with her mother's fire," he said, chuckling while trying to cover the fear attempting to creep up his spine.

Hirana ran into the door shouting that the midwife was on the way, and she took a pail from beside the door and hurried back out to the well. She returned with cool water and poured some into the bowl held by Stephen as it was nearly dry from the sweat running off of Elizabeth.

For the first time since her first birth, Elizabeth was worried. There were always some complications, as was the norm for births during this time; however, this one felt very different. This babe had not dropped like the others before the contractions began, and she worried it was too soon.

A plump, round-faced, matronly woman stepped through the doorway and immediately took charge.

"Here now, love, don't you worry, Goody Tate will help you," said the woman as she proceeded to take command like a naval commander.

Martha Tate was a phenomenon, giving birth to twelve children, and all but one survived. She was addressed, as most women of the time (most times married), as "Goody," which was short for "good wife."

Goody Tate set each girl to a task and told Stephen it was time to take the younger girls outside and "get out of her way, you handsome man." Stephen looked to Elizabeth, who panted and nodded her agreement as she did not want anyone to witness her in this state. She was not keen on her oldest two daughters staying, but, in this world, it was good for them to see what lay ahead of them and learn these skills.

Goody Tate told the girls to keep Elizabeth's brow dry and talk to her to take her mind off the pain. She crouched down on a stool, looked under the bedsheet, and then inhaled sharply. Elizabeth, by this time growing more delirious with pain, did not hear it, but the girls did and looked at Goody Tate sharply. Goody Tate returned their look and, with a pale face, told the girls to prepare the linen cloths as it wouldn't long now.

Goody Tate removed the bedsheet and saw blood tinging the blankets. Typically, there is a small amount from the plug of the womb giving way, but there was more than usual. Elizabeth gave a small cry and arched her back.

"Now, now, love, thou art well-versed in this matter. Thou must not arch thy back, for it shall not bring ye naught but distress. Let us guide ye to the birthing stool and bring this babe into the world."

Goody Tate assisted Elizabeth in standing and shuffling over to the

stool in the corner where it usually held kitchen items.

The birthing stool looked almost like a modern kitchen chair,

however lower to the ground and with a rounded bottom cut out in the

middle to allow the birthing process. It kept women upright so gravity

could assist, and women could bear down to push out the baby.

Once Elizabeth was situated, Goody Tate set to bring the baby

into the world while keeping the girls busy getting washcloths and

soothing Elizabeth.

Stephen continued to wait outside with the two youngest,

pacing in front of the livestock enclosure while trying to answer the

hundreds of questions posed by his children. He answered them while

staring at the house, waiting for the sound of his new baby's cry as had

happened in the past.

He was worried that this one was different, and he dropped to

his knees and began to pray silently. The girls, unsure of this

movement from their normally easy-going and happy father, dropped

beside him and bowed their heads similarly, although they did not know what to do.

"Father God Almighty, I beseech thee to watch over my wife and helpmate, Elizabeth, and guide her through this birthing. Only ye know what lays in the future and I trust in ye for all things. Guide the hands of Goody Tate as she assists in bringing our child into this world. I have been naught but faithful to ye and to thy will and I ask this in the name of your Son, Jesus Christ, Amen." After closing the prayer, Stephen hugged both children tightly and hoped the prayer would help.

Five hours after it began, Elizabeth screamed as she felt she would be pulled apart at the seams. Goody Tate spoke in a soothing voice like you would a child as she tried to coax the baby from Elizabeth's body. Since the birth had not progressed as usual, Goody Tate told Elizabeth to hold a moment as she checked the baby. Reaching into the canal, Goody Tate found out quickly the baby was attempting to come out sideways.

Goody Tate had encountered many difficult births, even some of her own, and knew that this meant she would need to intercede. Goody explained to Elizabeth that she needed to try and turn the baby, but Elizabeth was too far gone in pain to understand and just nodded to anything Goody Tate said.

No one knows in modern times what exactly happened during Sam's birth, but this situation wasn't easy, even by today's standards. Goody Tate reached into the canal and used her strength to push the baby back into the womb to attempt to turn him, thus causing even more pain to Elizabeth. She tried to be quick, but it was slippery going and hard to get hold of the baby. Finally, Goody Tate turned the baby, so its head was down.

Blood and mucus poured from the canal as the baby slipped down quickly, and Elizabeth gave a final push, expelling it. Goody Tate caught the baby, a boy, and began cutting and tying off the umbilical cord, then slapping the babe's back to expel the mucus in the nostrils to start the lungs working. She handed the baby to Rose and Hirana to clean and then turned to help Elizabeth expel the afterbirth.

Goody Tate stopped short, however, when she saw Elizabeth's eyes opening and closing and staying closed longer and longer. Hurrying back to Elizabeth's side, she attempted to help her sit up but Elizabeth resisted.

"Nay, nay, my good friend, see to the babe. I shall be better in a moment, I am but tired from these exertions to give life," Elizabeth murmured to her.

Goody Tate finally relented and helped Elizabeth lay back onto the pallet. In between one breath and the next, Elizabeth's blood and life left her just as quickly. With a smile for her baby and daughters, Elizabeth closed her eyes and exhaled her last breath which rattled out of her chest.

Goody Tate stared at the face of the woman who had been one of her closest friends, and tears slid down her face. She bent over and hugged Elizabeth's cooling body and silently sobbed. Wiping her tears after a few minutes with her sleeve, she then turned to face the pale, wide-eyed girls holding the squalling baby.

"Your mother has gone to be with God and her son that preceded her. You shall need to help thy father during this time as life must go on."

She put a hand on Rose's shoulder, noting the girl stiffened her spine and then nodded to her in assurance. Glancing over at Hirana, she saw Hirana glance at Rose and straighten. These girls would be okay, although it would be dark days ahead, and she'll need to ensure her husband helped supplement their food until Stephen could think clearly again.

Goody Tate, with the girls' help, was able to lay Elizabeth on the bed, running a hand over her friend's head, before cleaning up the afterbirth and all it entailed. She moved slowly and reverently, reciting Bible scriptures, and crying softly as she went about with a pail gathering linens to put into the water on the fire. The new baby would need them for swaddling. She then took time to clean her friend as best as possible so Stephen would not have to do that himself.

Taking the baby boy from Rose and Hirana, Goody Tate swaddled him and went outside to find Stephen so he could greet his new son. She found him and the younger girls kneeling by the watering trough near the small stable. She stopped just short of their sight line as she wanted a moment to herself before breaking the news to the father.

Bowing her head, she sent a silent prayer to God to give her the words and the strength she would need. "I pray to ye, Great Comforter, God of all and Father Almighty, be with this family in these dark times to come. We know not of thy will but follow thy bidding.”

The baby started to squirm, and Goody Tate knew he was probably hungry. She would need to put out the word they would need a wet nurse, but until found, she would show them how to dip bread in milk for the baby to suck.

As she approached, Stephen lifted his head and opened his eyes. Seeing it was her, and she was holding a bundle, he quickly stood and approached her with a joyous face. For his sake, she plastered on a smile.

“Goodman Bellamy, my dear friend, I would like you to meet your new son!” she said brightly, hoping he would mistake her shining eyes for happy tears.

Stephen’s smile encompassed his face, and Goody Tate wished she could let him keep it. He stared at his son’s face as the baby began to cry. Goody Tate waited as he let the little girls look at their brother, and then Stephen looked up and asked her the question she dreaded. He knew by how her face was clouded that it was not good when he asked how his wife fared. Fear and confusion quickly replaced joy.

Tears began to fill his eyes as he handed the baby back to

Goody Tate, mumbled for her to watch the girls, and sprinted for the house. Luckily, the younger girls stayed with Goody Tate and did not follow him. He would spare them this moment for as long as possible as he knew what awaited him.

He entered the house and saw Rose and Hirana crying softly, lying beside their mother on the bed. He closed his eyes and put a hand over his mouth, stifling a sob, he gathered his emotions and pushed them way deep down into his soul before joining them on the bed. He gathered Elizabeth in his arms as he had often done during their marriage and laid his head on hers as tears slipped into her beautiful black hair.

Softly stroking a hand over her sweat-drenched hair, he softly began crooning a ballad called "Greensleeves" they heard from a troubadour that passed through the village one day as they were courting. He would sing it to her when they lay in bed, almost like this, with her head on his shoulder. She would hum it to their children, sleeping in the cradles and pallets around them to help them sleep. The moonlight bathed Elizabeth's face in its glow as if imbuing her with its radiance as her own had dimmed. Rose and Hirana's heads joined his, and Goody Tate entered with the baby, young Elizabeth, and Joan as

he sang.

> *"Alas, my love, you do me wrong,*
> *To cast me off discourteously.*
> *And l have loved you oh so long,*
> *Delighting in your company.*
>
> *Greensleeves was my delight,*
> *Greensleeves my heart of gold,*
> *Greensleeves was my heart of joy,*
> *And who but my Lady Greensleeves.*
>
> *I have been ready at your hand,*
> *To grant whatever thou would'st crave;*
> *I have waged both life and land,*
> *Your love and goodwill for to have.*
>
> *Greensleeves was my delight,*
> *Greensleeves my heart of gold,*
> *Greensleeves was my heart of joy,*
> *And who but my Lady Greensleeves.*
>
> *Thy petticoat of sendle white,*
> *With gold embroidered gorgeously;*
> *Thy petticoat of silk and white,*
> *And these I bought gladly.*
>
> *Greensleeves was my delight,*
> *Greensleeves my heart of gold,*
> *Greensleeves was my heart of joy,*
> *And who but my Lady Greensleeves."*

It was a moment forever etched on Goody Tate's memory, with

Stephen and the girls all resting with Elizabeth and crying softly as he continued the song until he finally trailed off at the end of it.

For a moment, it seemed all was silent inside the little house and outside as if even the animals mourned the loss of such a good person. The youngest two girls joined the rest of the family on the pallet as Stephen softly explained to them, in terms they could understand, that their mother was now in heaven. Slowly, Stephen laid Elizabeth's head back onto the pallet and rose to stand before the fireplace, with his back to his love as if he could bear her colorless face no longer for the moment.

Goody Tate found bread and then bade Rose to please get some milk in a cup. Rose, sniffling loudly with a splotchy face, got up from the bed, taking one more look at her mother's lifeless body before doing as Goody Tate asked her.

Goody Tate approached Stephen, and he ran a hand over his face before turning to look down at her. She explained to him quietly what had occurred and how it was one of those things that no one could know until it happened. Glancing back, it looked as if Elizabeth merely rested instead of sleeping the last sleep.

"Stephen, your love for her was truly God-sent, and He has

plans that none of us know, although I know that provides little comfort at the moment." She waited for him to turn towards her and then handed him the baby. "What will you name your son at his baptism? We can set that up for next week as his soul will need nourishment and protection just as much as his body."

Stephen stared down at the baby and felt a flash of rage that was there and then gone just as quickly. Grief and loss promptly replaced it as he held his new son and looked over at the pallet. Elizabeth would never know her sacrifice brought the son she had desired so many times and prayed for almost daily during her pregnancy.

He could not blame this innocent child for taking his wife's life from her body. He could take solace in the fact that she was now with Solomon until they could all be together again. Indeed, she knew her child's soul, at least, before she rose to meet the Father at the Pearly Gates. He sent up a quick prayer seeking solace as he moved on and cared for their children and that Elizabeth would be waiting for him when his time came.

He told Goody Tate, "His name will be Samuel, which means

'God has heard' since Elizabeth very much wanted another son. I doubt she knew the cost, but I am sure she would not change it since it means she had her wish."

Tears slid down his face again, and Goody Tate showed him the process of feeding the baby with bread and milk. She informed him that she would send a wet nurse once they located one and how she and her husband would help them until he could recover from his grief. Stephen thanked her, stood by the door looking out over his small farm, and turned back to her.

"I doubt I shall recover from this grief, but I must care for our children." He turned, once again, towards the doorway. "I hope this child likes farming."

***

"Oh my God, how horrible!" Clarissa exclaimed, interrupting.

Charlie's eyes were wide as they stared at his grandfather. He subconsciously scooted closer to Loyd on the couch.

"I mean, what the heck, Grandpa? What kind of freakin' story is this?" Clarissa moved a little further away until there was a space between them.

"I'm just setting up the background so you understand how our young Sam began his life so you might understand his later choices." Loyd put an arm around both children and pulled them close. "If you don't think you can handle it, then I'll think of something with a little more frills and fluff."

"Greensleeves is pretty famous, though, right? It sounds familiar," asked Clarissa.

"It is said to have been written by Henry VIII as a response to Anne Bolyn's rejections during his courtship of her even though he was still married to Catherine. None of that had been verified, though. You probably recognize the tune because, in 1865, a guy named William Chatterton Dix wrote a Christmas carol called 'What Child is This' based on it."

"Oh, yeah! Mom likes that one!" Charlie said.

"No, no, Grandpa, keep going you just caught us by surprise, I think," Clarissa said, ending her struggle to detach from him. Charlie nodded his agreement and laid against Loyd again.

"Very well, let me tell you about his childhood." Loyd continued the story.

Chapter 3: The Scalawags

Devon, England 1701

"I hate farming." Samuel Bellamy, Sam to his friends, threw rocks at the buckets on the brick wall, knocking each one off. The day was already trending towards warm, but a cool breeze played with his raven hair that escaped from under his capotain hat. His friend, Jacob Tierney, tried to throw one at a bucket farther away but missed it by a large margin.

***

"Wait, wait, wait." Clarissa's fingers flew on her phone. "His what hat?"

"Capotain." Loyd peered over her shoulder as she looked at

images.

"Oh, the Pilgrim looking hat things." She looked at Loyd, and he nodded.

"Carry on," she said, smiling.

***

Stephen Bellamy was very busy trying to care for his family and depended on the community for the resources for all the mouths he had to feed. This situation only increased the opportunities for Sam, a young, precocious dreamer, to find mischief instead of helping around the farm.

His sisters were moving on with their lives and had married and moved on, though they remained close in distance as their homes were not far from their childhood home. His father re-married a few years after his mother passed away, but they had no more children. She was a comfort, however, and a companion for his father, which Sam appreciated. He did not appreciate it when she found chores for him to do. She assumed, rightly so, that he was planning mischief.

Sam was a few inches taller than his friend and loved lording the fact over Jacob every chance he got. However, the voice cracking was embarrassing. The girls in the market twittered at him and laughed whenever he tried to impress them, and his voice betrayed him.

Jacob agreed as he also wished for adventure that farming was dull, unlike the tales they heard of pirate-turned-privateers like Sir Francis Drake, the first person to circumnavigate (go around) the world. Sir Drake sailed the waters around the West Indies, plundering the ships from Spain, some say in revenge for an attack off the coast of Mexico. Later, under the order of Queen Elizabeth I, he became a privateer (sort of a legal pirate) and would become a scourge against Spanish military ports. Sir Francis Drake grew up in Plymouth, near Sam's birthplace, and was considered a local hero even though his life was over a hundred years before Sam's birth.

Sam's father was already maneuvering him towards a life as a farmer, which Sam fought like a badger in a barrel. Please do not ask how he knew what that was like. He just knew that he needed to be faster next time after kicking over the barrel.

They walked along the narrow alleys between buildings in the "nicer" part of the town until they arrived at a sheet-covered door near the docks that housed the stable. Both boys looked around, gauging if any followers or spies were around, and then Jacob knocked on the wooden post frame. Shortly, a small boy of about nine moved the sheet aside and asked for the passphrase.

Sam grinned and said, "Fight smart, harm few, score big," then he raised a hand, bending the thumb and pointer-finger in an "o" shape so it made the "okay" sign. The hand gesture was used for ships while sailors were diving to indicate everything was good to go, and the boys adopted it as part of their signals for danger. When Sam made the gesture, the petite boy knew it meant Sam and Jacob were not followed and allowed them entrance.

Sam rubbed a hand over the more petite boy's head, saying, "Well met, young Jib!"

No one used their real names in their small pirate crew they called "The Scalawags." Sam was known as "Helm," and Jacob was "Stern." There were two other boys in their crew, "Port," who was on the larger side and fourteen, and "Rudder," who was very tall and thin for an eleven-year-old.

Each time the boys met, they planned their next adventure, usually "borrowing" some type of treasure or capturing a flag. As you can imagine, there was not a lot of actual treasure to find at that time, but sometimes things have sentimental value more than monetary value.

Today, they planned their "attack" on an imaginary "island" to loot, plunder, and capture the enemy's flag. The make-believe island was a field behind the monastery near the cemetery bordering the river. They had to be careful to avoid the local monks to spare them from the monks spouting about the wrath of God and indolent children. Then, they would make them scrub something. Stealth was key.

"Listen closely, fellows, 'ere I thrash ye soundly," Port said as the leader simply by age. He moved his large frame around on the haystack.

Using farm implements and wooden tools, Port situated the pieces around in an attack strategy against the guards at the "fort." Those guards were just another gang of boys with headquarters near the blacksmith's forge. They called themselves the "The Hammers".

"Beyond yon mound which lies beyond the monastery, fair companions, is where we shall lay at the task. Together we shall best the others at their own pursuit." Port moved pieces across the top of the hay bale. "Prithee, attend me well or face me wrath."

The area they were to attack was characterized by woods surrounding the river on the west side, the church on the east side, the entrance to the field to the south, and the blacksmith's forge (situated with a waterwheel in the river) to the north. This typography was with the understanding that the Hammers would be in the middle trying to secure their "fort" as well as they could with whatever materials they could find. Usually, it was cast-off broken and unusable barrels from the town cooper. The cooper and the blacksmith tended to work near each other to share parts and labor easily.

Port pointed to Sam, "Helm, thou shalt approach from the west on the riverside, but take heed of the bulky stones near the curve. Those treacherous scoundrels are known to have set traps beforehand." Sam stood at the hay bale for a minute, his eyes taking in all the details and planning all his options.

"Stern, thou shalt approach from the east behind the garden wall of the monastery, but beware the wrath of the Kraken lying in wait in the shadows." Jacob grinned and nodded, knowing Port referenced the monk who ministered to the sick they called "Friar Cox-comb" as he was constantly rubbing his hand over the tonsure on his head as if wishing the hair back in the bald circle.

"Rudder, hie ye hence to the north and maintain stealth as that is the land of our treacherous foes." The thin boy smiled and pulled out an old blanket he would use as a cloak.

"I shall come in from the south at the entrance; they will expect some type of frontal assault, which will confuse them as it will only be me that approaches." Port puffed up his chest. "Besides, I am more intimidating than you."

Sitting on his knees beside the bale, Jib exclaimed, "But what of me, Port? What part shall I play when I am so small?"

Port smiled at Jib and laid a small round rock on the middle of the bale in the middle of all the other pieces. This rock was right amid the Hammers. Jib's face paled, and he swallowed. "Fear not, young Jib, for you are our Trojan horse, and just as Odysseus used it to conquer Troy, so shall we use you!" Port pointed from Jib to the stone. "For you shall hide aforehand in one of the barrels they set as barricade!" He began to laugh loudly, and Jib's smile lit up his whole face.

Jacob's right eyebrow rose as he looked at their plan and asked Port, "Wait, what type of plan is this? Everyone knows the battle is fought face-to-face as is civilized."

Port smiled as if he had a secret and expounded that it was a type of battle that he had glimpsed in messages to his father, the town's mayor, based on some of the reports from the "lethal and lawless lands of America" where the Pilgrims colonized. The boys exclaimed loudly, and Port preened in the attention.

"'Tis the truth! The colonists sought to build a life somewhere they named 'Cape Cod,' and my father received the tidings from the Lord at their last council meeting. The Lord was recently at Court, where he visited with the king, William III, and learned of this style of fighting from the native peoples of the land as they sought to hold to keep the English from settling. 'Tis unnerving to think you could be slayed by something in the shadows!"

Sam sometimes dreamed of running away on such adventures there as he imagined it was a glorious new land full of riches. The occasional news brought to them stated the lands were rich in resources such as tobacco and cotton, and the lands were ripe for the Europeans to expand to them. These routes also formed the early Triangular Trade, bringing goods from America to Europe. The colonists, however, stated there were not enough of them, even with their indentured servants, to work the massive number of lands needed, and they needed help. During this time, enslaved people from Africa were transported in the other leg of the trade through the Middle Passage (Africa to America), thus completing the triangle.

***

The day of the battle dawned with a blush to the horizon and yawning soon-to-be fighters readying themselves. The Scalawags sought fortune and glory this day with grim smiles upon their faces and sturdy courage in their chests. At least, that is how they hoped to remember it.

The battle began as soon as the church's rooster crowed, announcing the dawn of war. The Hammers gathered in a circle with sticks and rocks lined up on the tops of the barrels for ammunition for their ranged attacks. They banged their sticks on the barrels, but it was not a very loud cacophony as they did not want the local populace upon them complaining to the constable.

Hidden among the river rocks, Sam held up a long stick he made from a local tree's shed limbs. He imagined it to be a heroic sailor's cutlass, and he, the hero, was about to wage battle against insurmountable odds during an attack by Spaniards. He moved it in a swishing pattern, envisioning enemies falling to his sword master's prowess. He also used a smaller stick as a pistol for those who did not fall to his swishing.

He spotted Jacob creeping up behind the garden wall, holding a stick low so its movement didn't attract attention or that of the friar on the other side. Rudder slipped by the blacksmith's building and threw some bread pieces to the dogs that wandered near so they didn't alert to his position. Port was approaching the entrance slowly, intentionally drawing the attention of the Hammers.

Standing proudly, puffing up his broad chest, he gave them his terms. "I have come to face you and take your lands and riches for my own!" Port brandished his stick in front of him. "I shall take it by force if needed!"

One of the tallest of the Hammers shouted back, "Where is

your army, you putrid excuse for pig slop?" The other Hammers laughed as the leader crossed his arms and glared.

"I need not the help of my hardy crew, for I am an army unto myself!" Port gestured to his large and wide girth, puffing out his chest even more and thrusting back his shoulders, looking more significant for the benefit of the ruse. "I can trounce ye, and ye're scoundrels meself!" His language fell back into what they heard from the docks and sailors coming through town.

While Port expounded all the ways he could conquer the foes, the others of the crew crept forward, keeping low and slow so they were not noticed. Eventually, Sam and Rudder drew almost abreast of the barrels in a large circle around the Hammers and crouched. The enemy boys, however, mainly gathered near the ones closest to the field entrance to taunt Port some more so they did not notice them. Their flag, a piece of ragged and dirty linen, was mounted on a barrel in the middle of the circle behind their backs.

As fate is a fickle mistress and loves a good laugh, it was at this point the friar came around with a basket of vegetables hanging on his arm and noticed Jacob creeping steadily towards the barrels with his stick pointed towards the Hammers. Not understanding the meaning, as he never had any imagination in his whole life, the friar assumed Jacob was going to hurt someone intentionally.

In a loud voice, the curate yelled, "Pray tell, what art thou young lads doing? I have much to keep ye busy if ye find yourselves without toil!" The friar walked swiftly, monk's robe flapping, towards them, and chickens ran around clucking and flapping their wings so vigorously that feathers began to fly. Jacob, shaking off his surprise and laughing hard, ran towards the entrance and joined Port.

The Hammers, caught off-guard, only then noticed the two other boys who had been so close to the barrel ring they could have touched the barrel barricade. Sam and Rudder made faces at the enemy boys and ran to join Port and Jacob at the entrance.

The friar was closing in on The Hammers inside the barrel ring, so they also made a run for the entrance, dropping their sticks and laughing as only young, mischievous kids would do. Dust and feathers flew all around them as the field erupted into motion from the fleeing boys and the startled livestock.

As the friar changed direction towards the entrance, dropping his basket upon the ground to better grab delinquent boys, The Hammers turned back to look towards their barrel circle just in time to see Jib's head pop up from the middle barrel, reach up, and grab the flag, then tip the barrel over and crawl out running towards the entrance waving it proudly.

The Hammers groaned in defeat, and then all the boys ran back into town to their respective hideouts to plan for another day. Today, victory was for The Scalawags, and they planned to celebrate with some cheese and bread Port had pilfered from his kitchen.

Later that day, Sam laughed as he lounged again among the hay bales before returning to his father's small farm, thinking life could get no better. Little did Sam know that later that same year his life would change dramatically. He would find a way to leave his small town and friends and join the royal navy for their part in the War of Spanish Succession.

***

"I have questions," Charlie said.

"Do these questions involve barrels and badgers?" Colin asked. "If so, it might be better not to think about such things."

In the background, Colin heard Clarissa playing a video singing about badgers, snakes, and mushrooms.

"I withdraw my questions," Charlie replied. "But I would like to know what an indenta…indenti…," he started to ask, stuttering over the unfamiliar word.

"Indentured servant," continued Loyd, "was someone who owed a debt of some type to society back in England or just wanted a new life, which was the only way to afford passage. They signed a contract stating they would give four to seven years of service before being released and given a small amount of funds. They also had some rights, so it wasn't quite slavery."

"Somewhat interesting, Grandpa, but also boring as I learned all this while talking to Reggie, um, learning in Social Studies at school." Clarissa rolled her eyes and pulled her knees up to her chest. "Definitely not lollygagging and being distracted by talking to him during class."

"True, but it is something that formed the land on which you now live and roll your eyes at me," Loyd said, smirking. "This is good to know because it will come up later in our story."

"Man," said Charlie, "he has a tragic backstory, so I'm guessing he's gonna be like a superhero or supervillain or something."

Loyd laughed, "Oh, it's something like that, but you'll have to wait and see."

"He joined the navy when he was, what, 12?" Clarissa asked.

"Yes, he was probably around 12 or 13 when he joined, but, at that time, it was a better life than that of a peasant farmer, and he would be able to quench his adventurous desires, hopefully", Loyd explained. "Never fear, though, as it only made his longing worse for riches and fame, and he thought he could find both when he left the navy and made his way to the New World. That war was from 1701-1714, so he had quite a bit of seasoning at sea, so to speak before he could return home."

"Farm life wasn't that bad, was it? I mean, I know people were poor, and there weren't a lot of bathrooms." Charlie shrugged his shoulders. "I'm not young enough to think it was all rainbows and daisies and had modern sanitation. Too bad he didn't have a 'brute squad' like in *The Princess Bride*. That would have helped him take out The Hammers!"

Colin chuckled and told him, "Nope, no indoor toilets, and most people didn't bathe very often. Some of them thought sitting in the water like that would lead to a plague or some type of disease. And I don't think anyone was waiting around to knock heads together and announce themselves and their intentions to kill someone like Inigo Montoya and Fezzik."

Clarissa reached over and gave Charlie a knuckle noogie on the head before he shook her off. "You know what he means, 'eau de medieval times', which was poop and pee and mud. Dad let you watch *Monty Python and the Holy Grail,* so you know what I'm talking about."

"Hahahaha! Oh yeah! That whole bit of 'She's a witch!' and the difference in sparrows is still my favorite part of the whole thing other than the killer rabbit," he confirmed.

Colin joined them in laughing, then said, "The count shall be three…" referencing another part of the movie. All three of them collapsed against each other in laughter as they recited various other parts of the movie.

Wiping tears from his eyes, Colin sat back up and hugged each of them. "Okay, let's get back to the story."

Chapter 4: New Land, New Friends

Provincetown, Cape Cod, America 1715

Twenty-four-year-old Sam Bellamy disembarked from the cargo ship, and the air around the docks was heavy with the odor of salt and unwashed bodies from the dockworkers laboring alongside the ships unloading cargo. The journey was long, almost two months, but the weather had remained calm. He could handle anything after serving in the Navy for twelve years. He might have stayed in except when the war ended, and there were too many mouths to feed on board the ships and no wars to fund the resources needed for them.

He stood not quite six feet tall and his broad shoulders filled the gangway as he carried his belongings to where the docks met the main boardwalk. The wind tousled his ink-black hair and pulled back in a sable ribbon at his neck. All around him, merchants bellowed orders to their workers to hurry them along, and Sam side-stepped many as they focused only on their task and not their surroundings.

The town was composed mainly of clapboard buildings and muddy, rutted roads. The mixture of the sea air, animal droppings, and lack of sanitation would offend a sensitive nose; however, Sam was used to it, and he proceeded towards the main thoroughfare to find his uncle. His father had written to a female cousin of the family living in America and her husband, Uncle Israel Cole, months before Sam left the Navy to inquire if Sam could stay with them. His uncle was a farmer, and his wife was a chandler who made candles and carried on family knowledge of those things, such as Sam's mother did for her children. His uncle finally replied, and Sam was now here waiting to start this new adventure.

A shout drew his attention towards waiting horses pulling a small two-seater buggy, often called a dogcart. The driver stood and could be none other than his uncle who waved at him to join him. Who else would greet him thusly? He put his trunk into the back storage area of the buggy, strapped it down, and then joined his uncle up on the driver's seat.

"Hadst thou a pleasant journey, nephew?" His uncle asked while clucking to the horse and starting their movement.

"Aye, uncle, indeed I did. No storms accosted us, and our path 'twas clear." Sam leaned back on the bench and took in the surrounding area as they traveled to his uncle's home. "How doth your farm fare?"

"'Tis most profitable, at times, yet lean at others," his uncle replied. "My wife hast cultivated a colony of bees and has greatly increased our funds as beeswax burns cleaner and smells better than tallow."

"Truth as tallow smells like the underside of a muddy cow," Sam laughed. "My sisters hast knowledge of the craft from learning at my mother's knee, but I hast no yearning to learn such a thing."

His uncle pulled the reins to turn the horse's head towards home, although the horse knew the way through Truro, Wellfleet, and finally to Eastham, where the house was located. It was only a few hours to reach their destination, and then the horse was heading towards the opening of the gate. The house, also clapboard, was dingy from the sea air and consisted of two stories with a walkway to the front door but no porch. No one had time to sit and gander at the locals. Glass, expensive, so his uncle truly was doing well, lined the windows in lead panes. Shutters on either side of the windows were necessary for the storms Sam knew were harsh in the wintertime here so close to the coast.

"Hie ye into the stable and let young Ephram know of our return." His uncle directed Sam's attention to the small outbuilding close to the rear of the house. "I shall bring in thy trunk."

Sam told him, "I can carry my own weight, Uncle, but I appreciate the offer." He did as he was asked in regard to informing Ephram of their return. He was soon ensconced in the kitchen near the fire after a brief tour of the home. The kitchen's hearth has always been the lifeblood of a home and perhaps resonates from the early man when a fire was vital to survival. His aunt bustled around, ensuring the evening meal would be ready on time and getting Sam settled.

"Didst thou find your accommodation adequate, Nephew?" She asked, inquiring about the room he would share with the oldest child, Ephram, who was almost a man at seventeen.

"Aye, Aunt Dorothea, 'tis most acceptable, and I hope it doth not inconvenience you."

"Nay, Nephew, we look forward to thy stay with us and hope thy back 'tis strong as preparations be underway for winter's approach." She juggled the baby on her hip while stirring the pot over the fire in the hearth.

Sam laughed and said, "Aye, 'twill be fair for the work and my thanks for thy hospitality."

"The Lord doth declare that we must always minister to those hearts in need of His divine influence and guidance, and thy hast a great need, indeed," she said emphatically, brandishing her ladle towards him.

Sam ducked his eyes and looked everywhere but at her. "Aye, 'tis apparent my father hast informed ye of my adventures in the navy."

"Aye, and well he did! Godless mercenaries bent on sowing strife and misery where thy didst land. Relations between man must consist of piety and Divine law, not who hadst the bigger weapon."

Sam choked a bit on his tea and biscuits and kept his eyes

down. He knew that she only spouted what most of the colonists, consisting of Puritans, proclaimed, although he was sure they found it hard to be pious when trying to take over the lands of the native people. His uncle and the family were not so strict in adherence as they were mainly of peasant stock, but it appeared they still held on to some of the more rigid beliefs that spoke of influence from the Puritans.

He would not inform her that life aboard a ship was not the pleasant adventure he had once dreamed it would be. The captain was very strict, and food was in short supply. What food was available was just something salted: Salted pork, salted chicken, salted fish, maybe some cheese. Oh, and more salted meat. He was surprised that more sailors were not more well-preserved from the amount of salt in their diet. Their captain, however, was a bit more knowledgeable and tried to include some variation of citrus every other month or so when available to stave off scurvy.

***

"What's 'scurvy'?" It was Charlie this time who was curious.

"You've read old pirate stories where they call each other 'scurvy dogs' and things, right?" Loyd looked at Charlie, who nodded.

"Okay, scurvy happens when a person doesn't eat fruits or vegetables or anything good for them for months. It involved bleeding gums, teeth falling out, blood under the skin, and other weird places. In other words, it was not pleasant."

"Gross," was Clarissa's reaction.

"Yep, so captains of ships finally wised up and ensured they got some type of citrus fruit or made landfall where it was plentiful."

"I bet they were thirsty with all that salted stuff," asked Charlie.

"Oh, yeah, and the water wasn't always very drinkable, which led to other problems, so now you know why a pirate's life wasn't as glamorous as the movies show them. The ones you know on Pirates of the Caribbean were actually in good health, whereas in real life, they were most likely plagued by all the same diseases."

"I don't know, Johnny Depp did a pretty good job of looking dirty and like he smelled bad, but dang, he was 'dashing' as Captain Jack Sparrow." Clarissa got a dreamy look in her eyes.

Loyd cleared his throat, "Yes, well, he definitely made the part, and so did all the others in those movies. Just remember, Hollywood is not real life."

Clarissa looks at Loyd and asks, "What is the difference between a Puritan and a Pilgrim? I thought all the first settlers were Pilgrims."

Loyd answered, "The Pilgrims were first, and the Puritans came over later. They both wanted a different type of church, but there the difference begins. The Pilgrims broke from the Church of England after King Henry VIII wanted a divorce. The Pope didn't give it to him, so he replaced the Pope as the head of the church and created the Church of England. This action angered a lot of the Catholics.

"Simply put, they were tired of all the rituals and long sermons and wanted to serve God simply without all the ceremonies. They called themselves Separatists rather than Pilgrims, though. That term came later."

"So, that's what started his long line of marriages?" Charlie asked.

"I saw that play! It was called 'Six' on Broadway," Clarissa stated. "He had, like, six wives or something like that. Great music and choreography!"

"Yep, it's good to be king, I guess," Loyd replied. "Puritans, also wanting to change the Church of England, chose to do it from within the church instead of separating from it. They also didn't like all the pomp and circumstance and wanted to tone it down but understood it would take growth and fresh congregations to do it. So, they came to America to bring their religious beliefs and cram it down everyone's throats, including the Native Americans."

"I thought the Native Americans taught the settlers how to farm and stuff, and now we have turkey and lots of food to celebrate the first Thanksgiving," Charlie asked thoughtfully.

"That's another difference: the Puritans thought of the Pilgrims and the Native Americans as less than them. Puritans came over with their wealth, resources, and ideas on profit, whereas the Pilgrims and others were friendly with the Native Americans and came over with mostly the clothes on their backs." Loyd informed them. "So, basically, the main wealthy peeps of the town were of Puritan lineage, and Sam's uncle and family were middle class, so to speak."

"Yikes, that had to be hard. Bullies existed way back even then," Clarissa stated.

"Yep, humans doing human things," Loyd replied. "Anyways, let's continue."

***

"We should celebrate your arrival, so we encourage ye to visit The Tavern with me, where ye will meet people of thine age," his uncle informed him. Dorothea got up and took away the dirty trenchers.

"It doth appeal to me, and I shall endeavor to attend, my thanks." Sam stood up. "Doth ye require assistance, Aunt Dorothea?"

"Nay, Nephew, 'tis a woman's work here, and the menfolk doth need to attend to their diversions in the front area of the house." Dorothea shooed him away.

Sam followed his uncle and oldest cousin into the front room, where there was bare furniture, another fireplace, and a table with a Bible on it.

"As soon as Dorothea finishes, then she and the younger children shall join us for our nightly scriptures," Sam's uncle advised him and sat in a chair near the fireplace.

Ephram stoked up the glowing embers in the fireplace and took another chair closer to the window. Sam sat on a bench near the wall facing his uncle and cousin. His eyes were starting to burn with exhaustion, and he longed to head upstairs rather than make small talk; however, pleasantries needed to be observed.

"Nephew," his uncle began, "thou hast arrived at a most auspicious time! The first harvest has begun with the area farms, so soon we shall have corn and other fruits of the land to hold us through the long winter months."

Sam couldn't wait to try it fresh after eating foods stored on a cargo vessel for months before arriving at the port. His uncle droned on about what crops were expected and which did not fare well. Leaning back, he felt his eyes close until Dorothea entered with the younger children. His uncle began to read from the book of Isaiah 43:18-19, and his voice's cadence washed over Sam and brought him peace.

"Remember not former things and look not on things of old. Behold I do new things, and now they shall spring forth, verily you shall know then: I will make a way in the wilderness and rivers in the desert."

Sam smiled to himself, thinking he was about to put away his past and begin a new future. Later, as he lay on his pallet, he heard the soft sound of a door opening and closing as sleep claimed him.

Chapter 5: Clandestine Dealings

The Tavern, Cape Cod Bay, America 1715

The Tavern was located on a small spit of land off the western portion of Cape Cod and in Cape Cod Bay. The building was hewn from rough lumber and pieced together to form a rectangle with doors on all sides. The decorations were sparse inside, and the walls were darkened by years of smoke from the hearth and pipes; however, plenty of cider and beer were available. Some men were seated at the tables while others were lined up around the bar and the fireplace, discussing harvests and other aspects of their lives.

It was here that Sam ended up the next afternoon at his uncle's request and prepared himself for more social interactions. It's not that he did not like social interactions; quite the opposite. It's just that after spending so much time on a ship, the loud chaos of many people sometimes overwhelmed him.

Sam's uncle introduced him to Paulsgrave Williams (Paul for short), the local goldsmith and jeweler, who looked around his thirties and had a wife and children living nearby. Paul's father, John Williams, had been the attorney general and passed away a few years ago. That did not stop Paul from trying to impress his father's memory, as Paul was considered the black sheep of the family.

They were the same height, but Paul's coloring was lighter, and they looked like a yin and yang of each other's appearance. Where Sam was darker of hair and tanned from years in the sun, Paul was paler with wheat-colored hair left loose on his shoulders.

Sam and Paul spoke together and discovered their souls were alike in the want of adventure. Sam felt it was like having his friend, Jacob, with him. He missed his childhood friend, but Jacob had moved on and was married with two children to work on his farm.

His uncle introduced him to several men involved in the local agriculture and allowed his mind to wander a bit after what felt like the hundredth rendition of "What news from His Majesty?" Finally guessing they would not leave him alone until he answered, he turned to them.

Sam replied to them as a group, saying, "Upon my departure, King William III had passed, and then his sister-in-law, Queen Anne, who was the daughter of James II, took the reign. Unfortunately, Queen Anne had also passed, and her son, George I of Hanover, sits on the throne. The queen only held reign a short time before a stroke took her ability to speak, and it was not long after she departed this world."

Many of the men murmured, "God save the king," while shaking their heads. They knew it mattered not to them who ruled from across the ocean since all royalty wanted was their taxes. The men dispersed into various corners and tables.

Israel consulted his watch and motioned to Sam towards an alcove in the back. Glancing around, he pressed his hand against Sam's back and moved him towards the alcove, where a door was hidden beneath a large rug. They moved inside the opening, closed the trapdoor quickly and quietly, then walked down a few steps into the basement of the building.

Sam was very bewildered but trusted his uncle and let him lead him into the room lit by small candles in various places. Crates and barrels lined the walls, and multiple bits of ship's rigging hung on the walls.

Men sat on stools in a circle around a low table, tankards of beer foaming around them, and Israel led Sam to two empty seats. Paul came down a few minutes later and joined them. Once they seated themselves, one of the men, a man of about fifty years and weathered hands, spoke to them.

"We have assembled as requested, Israel. What news hast ye?"

Speaking low, Israel regarded the men around the table and told them of a new development. "My friends, 'tis rumored there is a French frigate foundering near the coast south of us laden with furs and whale oil from the frozen country to the north. With winter coming, those furs and oil would be of great need to our families and would fetch a good price from the merchants. I say we liberate this ship of its bounty!" Israel exclaimed while lifting his tankard in the air to emphasize his thoughts.

Several of the men began to murmur amongst themselves, including a man who held a gold-tipped cane he used to emphasize his points to his peers. Wearing the powdered wig favored by many, which sat slightly askew on his head, he gestured around with his gloves, using them and his cane to press his point.

While discussions carried on in fervent whispers, the man who had spoken first looked around the table and then nodded. "We do not take from those who cannot afford it, but we will take what we can use, and it seems this ship has more than an ample supply. I vote aye!"

Others chimed in with "ayes" around the table, except for a smaller man with sallow features and eyes that shifted constantly between the two speakers. He almost whispered in a small voice, "I say nay…'tis too dangerous, and then where would our families be with us in the stocks or the cell? Who would be left to look after them if none of us were to escape the authorities?"

Some of the men lowered their heads in embarrassment, and Sam could tell they were beginning to change their minds. His uncle, however, remained firm and stood. "I tell ye, aye, there 'tis a danger, but methinks the danger from authorities is lesser than the one posed by the winters here." Israel paused to look around and singled out one man. "Josiah, ye have prospered this year, but ye must admit it was due to the last cargo taken of foodstuffs and linen that fed your family and others."

Israel eyed another man and pointed a tankard at him. "John, did ye not use part of the last cargo smuggled that was full of medicine sorely needed? Your daughter, Eliza, is still with us as God's approval of our deeds." John smiled and nodded his head in acknowledgment.

"Aye," John said, "'twas a miracle, indeed, the cargo taken comprised of medicine just when needed. I still vote, aye!"

Israel took a moment to close his eyes and pray for the words to motivate these men. "I know ye are all scared, yet the rewards are greater than the fear. Lesser men may cower in front of danger, but ye have braved many a danger in recovering items from other wrecks. I beseech ye to think about your families."

Sam's interest greatly intensified with the rising pitch of the arguments. He knew any loot obtained would put the men on the hangman's gallows if caught, which would help none of them. Remembering back to his days with The Scalawags and his naval experience, he had an idea he put forth to them.

"My good fellows, ye know me not but I am here by my Uncle

Israel's recommendation fresh from the Royal Navy. Having spent many a year thwarting Spanish incursions, I can tell ye that subterfuge is the way to gain these things for our community. My plan is simple: we create a diversion while a small team goes in to grab what they can, and then we meet up at a gathering place on the knoll behind the mill."

More murmuring as they disputed Sam's right to be present. Finally, Israel put out his hands and made a shushing movement. "My friends, my nephew's plan is not without merit and must be discussed. I know it is different, but stealth has served us in the past. True, we would simply wait for the ship's crew to abandon the ships, and then we took what was offered, yet this ship is still manned. This ship is the largest we have encountered and requires a great deal more planning."

The rest of the men finally agreed to the plan, logistics were discussed with changes made to the plan, and they all dispersed at staggard times so as not to alert anyone of a large group coming up from the basement. After exiting, Sam and Paul stood near a window, questioning Israel about how long the group had been leading raids and smuggling cargo. Sam had many questions and was always a curious man.

"Uncle, how long…are you…where…" Sam sputtered.

Israel put out a consoling hand and rested it on Sam's shoulder. "I know ye have questions, Nephew, and I ask that ye keep them close to you until we can leave this area. Not everyone here is supportive of our activities. Your plan is remarkable, Nephew, and I thank ye for the ideas."

Paul could not stop staring at Israel as if the man had grown another head.

"I just need to know one thing: does Aunt Dorothea know?" Sam asked.

Paul continued to stare at Israel.

"Oh, aye, she doth know. Who do you believe sewed the sacks we use to carry the goods?" Israel patted Sam's shoulder.

Sam started to ask more questions despite his uncle's wish to wait; however, a voice carried through one of the open windows that faced the orchards. The sound was like an angel singing just for him, and he turned from the men and walked to the window to find the source.

The late afternoon sun shone through the leaves of the apple trees and gave the area a surreal feel, like a dream. Sam could not stand it and had to find the source, so he started to walk towards the door.

***

"Okay, now it's getting good," Charlie said beside Loyd. "Finally, some action, and I bet it's ghosts. So far, it's just been a big old history lesson…so boring!"

Clarissa rolled her eyes, "No, it can't be ghosts. I bet his one true love is waiting for him since Grandpa mentioned true love."

Charlie scoffed and said, "Okay, Buttercup."

Smirking at both kids, Loyd said, "As you wish."

Both kids groaned at the references to Princess Bride. Loyd told them it was a good time for a break, and the storm sounded as if it was lessening. Charlie commented on it, and Loyd replied that it might just be the "eye" passing over and the storm would return. It was literally the calm before the storm, so to speak, but Loyd didn't believe it would be as fierce.

As they moved around, the door opened, and William and Laura Bellamy walked in drenched and flapping coats and umbrellas.

"Mom! Dad!" Charlie yelled and ran to hug them, ignoring how wet it made his shirt.

"Oh man, I'm glad you guys made it home!" Clarissa ran and did the same to them.

"What's all this," Laura asked, spying the mugs on the table and the blankets in a cocoon shape around the couch. William hung up both their coats and then said he would go change.

"Grandpa was telling us a story about some type of hero, and he's telling it *Princess Bride* style, but it's just been kinda boring so far," Charlie said.

"Oh, I bet I know the story, and it really is a good one," Laura said, heading back to change her clothes.

Loyd continued his story once everyone returned to the living room and settled in.

"Okay, so now Sam heard an angelic voice and was going to find the source of it." Loyd began.

Laura smiled, stopping at her bedroom door, and said, "Oh yes, this is definitely a good part!"

***

As Sam walked towards the door, his uncle intercepted him.

"Turn ye not towards that sound, Nephew, for it will lead you towards temptation. It is a siren that inhabits that orchard in the person of the youngest daughter of John Hallett, and that family has long felt we are naught but dirt beneath their heels. She is sixteen, and they have planned for a prosperous match for her. Their family is one of the wealthiest and holds Puritan beliefs. Their farm feeds many, exports much of their corn to England, and curries the crown's favor. I beg, ye, Nephew, do not ye go into that orchard tonight." Israel put a hand on Sam's arm and gave him an imploring look.

Sam, entranced by the sound, handed his uncle his tankard without even looking at him, shrugged off the hand, and started towards the door.

Paul stepped in front of Sam and crossed his arms. "Nay, my friend, 'tis not an enigma ye must solve for now. We have plans to lay, and they were of thine own doing so off we go to yon table for victuals and schemes."

Sam took one last look towards the door but knew his friend was right, and they had other things to do right now. He resolved to find the source of the music the next day. After seating themselves at the table, Israel used objects found nearby, much like Port did back when Sam was younger, to show the topography of the coast since Sam was unfamiliar.

"See, here is the curve of the coastline where there is a small canal further south of us known as 'Jeremiah's Gutter,' which connects to Nauset Bay, where the ship has foundered. I believe they tried to cut through during high tide and found themselves running aground when the tide pulled out further than they anticipated. If we time it right, we can run to the ship, grab items, and then run back before the water returns.

"According to my sources, the ship is only a few hundred feet inside the canal, so it should only be a few hours to reach it. We can get there shortly before sunset if we leave soon." Leaning back, Israel asked Sam, "What was the plan ye conceived?"

Sam stood to lean over the table and moved some of the pieces, indicating the men and their places. "If we have some of the men dress as fur trappers, we could have them move close to where the ship has foundered, and the men aboard will think nothing of it as they are primarily fur traders themselves. They may even hail the faux trappers,

thinking they could give assistance. If nothing else, they can provide

some type of diversion while the rest of us sneak aboard dressed only

in the blacks like those of the pious people to cloak us in the

darkness."

Israel ran his hand over his mouth a few times as he

contemplated the situation on the table. At last, he nodded as if coming

to the same conclusion. "Aye, that might work as long as the ship

traders are focused on their own predicament and do not look closely

at our men."

They stood, Israel replacing the items he borrowed, and they

left; Israel to inform the other men and Sam and Paul to gather

supplies and clothing. They arrived at Israel's house later, where

Dorothea gave them linen sacks to carry their supplies and to bring

home their loot. After things were gathered, they all left to meet at the

pre-determined place where a small boat waited to take them down the

coast.

The journey in the small boat down the coastline was quiet, and

only the *whooshing* of the waves running onto the beaches and back out again was heard. The crescent moon gave them enough light to navigate but still hid them from prying eyes. Insects buzzed around them, and they slathered themselves in a mixture of tallow and tobacco. The odor would also help them blend into the foliage and not spook any of the animals as they moved inland.

Reaching the bend before the canal's entrance, they disembarked and moved silently into the trees, making their way to where the cargo ship lay tilted on the silty sandbar. The captain must have been new to not know the way the tides flowed in this area. They could hear panicked shouting they deduced must be him as he berated and cajoled the crew into digging around the ship. The crew probably knew the herculean task was fruitless, but it was better to be down there than up on deck with that lunatic.

Splitting up, half of the men who were dressed in fur trapper gear moved closer to the front of the ship where most of the men were located as they dug at the sand, which only closed back in again with each shovel full. Israel, Sam, Paul, and the rest of the men dressed in black moved slowly towards the stern of the ship to look for netting or lines they could use to hoist themselves up and enter the holds.

Sam heard words such as "porc," "vache," and "mouton" as the captain tried to motivate the crew. From the context and his years of sailing, Sam gathered the captain was calling his crew various types of barn animals and describing the sexual acts the men could perform with them better than digging out the ship as they were.

Finally, Sam heard the faux fur traders calling out, asking if the men needed assistance. The captain stopped his tirade long enough to question them in stilted English. Sam and his team took that as the signal to proceed and ran out the boards they brought with them to make a small walkway wide enough for just one man at a time but out of sight of the crew.

Reaching the side of the ship, they used their laced fingers to help each other up to the rope dangling. One man was left on the ground to retrieve things lowered to him. They made their way towards the holds and down the steps with no one the wiser.

Sam laughed silently to himself as he heard their men asking truly ignorant questions as if they had never boarded a ship in their lives. He swore one of them asked where the "anchor contraption" was, suggesting it would help pull them out of the sand by tossing it out front and dragging it backward. Sam distinctly heard the captain swear at the man, calling him *boeuf stupide*. Apparently, this captain dealt with a lot of animals.

Mink, beaver, fox, and other types of skins were sitting in boxes on the hold floor, and barrels were full of different types of liquor. Sam and the men spread out to quickly look through and grab what they could of what they needed.

Israel motioned Sam over to his area and showed him the inside of an oddly shaped box. Inside, Sam noted several flintlocks and various types of long guns. Sam whispered to Israel, "Looks like they are fresh from trading with their Iroquois allies to the north, aye?"

Further inspection of the goods revealed various medicines and dried goods which were quickly shoved into the sacks Sam's aunt had made them. Sam stopped Paul from "rescuing" anything that was too large for a new home.

Quickly grabbing what they could carry, they went back up to the deck and lowered the larger items over the side before rappelling down themselves and running towards the safety of the woods, picking up the wooden planks as they went. Sam and Paul were the last ones over, and, unfortunately, it was then that the tide began flowing back in, and the ship rocked a bit as it tried to right itself. Paul let out an involuntary yelp as he fell back onto the deck, alerting the captain to their presence.

The captain turned, saw them, and began shouting at his crew to intercept them as they scampered down the side of the ship and ran towards the shore. The crew, already on the ground, quickly gained on them as Sam and Paul ran. The faux trappers had already made their way to safety, so now it was up to Paul and Sam.

Sam was startled when Paul pulled up next to him, grabbing Sam's arm and stopping his momentum. Paul shrugged, grinned, and then tossed an object towards the front of the ship.

An explosion blew sand, silt, and various debris outwards at the bow of the ship. The resulting vacuum caused the bay's waters to flood in and grab the ship, yanking it towards the outlet. The ship's crew scrambled to grab onto the ropes hanging off the hull and hoist themselves aboard as the ship picked up speed.

Sam stopped on the shore, put his hands on his knees, and bent over, trying to catch his breath. "Damn my eyes, Paul, what was that?"

Paul started laughing, raising his hands and arms above his head to better open his airway to catch his breath. He told Sam, "Well, you see, there was this little round object with a fuse sticking out in one of the barrels, and it just looked forlorn and bereft. I hate when things are forlorn and bereft, so I liberated it and gave its life new meaning by using it as was intended! Did they not break free?"

Sam, astounded for a moment, started to chuckle and then broke down into guffaws as Israel and the other men approached, and Paul told them the same story. Shaking their heads, the men carried their goods back to their boat and to home.

***

Charlie was perplexed. "But, Grandpa, there isn't a canal that goes out onto Nauset Beach."

"You are correct, my boy, but there used to be before the land changed and the water receded out, closing the canal way. You can ask your geography teachers, but that is what I was told, anyway. It was also called 'Jeremiah's Dream.' They figure it was because a man named Jeremiah Smith owned the land near there."

"Dad, pull out the map you have, and we'll show them,"

William told Loyd.

Once it was laid out on the coffee table, William pointed out Nauset Beach and then trailed his finger straight west to the shore of Cape Cod Bay. "You can almost see where it ran by looking at the location of the river and the marsh here. Progress and construction pretty much closed it and filled it in."

"Wow, I was today-years-old finding that out, Grandpa," Clarissa told him.

Loyd looked at her and then shook his head. He wasn't going to ask.

"Okay, so Sam and his men got away with phat lewt, and now what?" asked Charlie.

"Fat…what? Nope, you kids are killing me. I'm just going to move on. They got what they needed and went back home with the tale of Paul and the Forlorn Grenade to tell their families. So, let's move to the next afternoon after they are back at The Tavern, celebrating."

Chapter 6: Shakespeare Makes a Good Wingman

The Tavern, Cape Cod Bay, America 1715

Sam listened to conversations as they buzzed around him like bees in a meadow. The families benefited greatly from their nighttime foray, and he now knew why his uncle and the men risked so much. Winter was coming, and land would hopefully yield what they needed, but they would not know till they gathered the crops at fall harvest time. As the voices rose and fell around him, he heard the siren's song again.

With his uncle distracted and no one to stop him, he rose, slipped out the door, and made his way out into the orchard. The afternoon summer sun was setting, and the sliver of the moon shone low on the horizon as it rose and cast a hazy glow on the ground.

Walking into the orchard, he saw the source of the angelic music. A girl was picking apples from the ground and singing as she went. Her cornstalk yellow hair fell forward as she bent down, and Sam wished it would move so he could see her face. Finally, she stood upright, and he could see her eyes were the color of a blue sky over an ocean, and her face was very comely. Her voice was a rich soprano and sounded like the sirens to which his uncle first compared her. Sam took an involuntary step forward, and a twig snapped beneath the heel of his boot. The girl, startled, turned quickly towards him, and Sam felt a moment of intense pride and then humor as he noted a small dagger in her hand.

***

Maria was taking a very needed moment away from her parents, the expectations upon her, and finding any reason she could to remove her linen coif and let her hair down. She knew her parents were arranging a marriage with a neighbor who possessed land next to theirs so they could expand their holdings. Maria just wanted to make her own decisions. Was she nothing but another commodity to sell? However, she knew in this land, and this time, women were naught more than brood mares and housekeepers.

Her sisters were already married and started their own families. As the youngest, she believed the duty to "go forth and multiply" was satisfied by her siblings, and there should be no need for her to follow their path. Much to her mother's chagrin, she sought little ways to flaunt tradition, even going so far as to show her ankle when she entered the local general store or not cover her head when she went outside. She grinned, remembering doing so as recently as this morning. Her mother pled the vapors and nearly swooned when a woman looked at them scornfully while *harrumphing* and prodding her husband to move along.

Now, this man had intruded on her sanctuary. *He is not unfortunate in appearance, but he will think twice if he wishes for a dalliance with an unsuspecting maid.* Holding her basket closer, she hid the dagger she palmed that she always carried for situations like this.

* * *

Entranced by her beauty, Sam did not notice the danger in her hand and moved towards her as if in a dream.

Digging deep for courage, Maria met his eyes and confronted him. "I dare ye, come closer, for I will skewer ye upon this dagger," she said.

Sam was surprised as most women he encountered would have dramatically cowered or fallen, crying and begging. He walked towards her slowly. The world seemed to slow as he neared her, and he felt as if the sun grew brighter to bathe them in its light. The colors of the orchard were more vivid, whereas before, they had been drab and gray. Birdsong faded into the background as he felt the lure of her eyes staring so intently into his own.

Sam could not take his eyes off hers as his mind raced with what to say that would put her at ease. He slowly walked forward, ignoring her shaking hand holding the dagger, and spoke to her.

"What matter of nymph be ye, for ye cannot be human with such a voice and beauty as ye possess," he told her.

"Ye may take thy flattery elsewhere, goodman, for it shall not work its spell upon me. I am not a wanton strumpet to simply throw myself on your mercy," she replied, lowering the dagger until it was the same height as his crotch.

Sam looked down, still in a haze, not fully comprehending that she was threatening him. He was awestruck and felt his soul had met its match in her.

***

"Told you so!" Clarissa exclaimed.

"Ugh, gag me now. There really is going to be kissing and stuff," Charlie moaned.

"We'll see," was all Loyd said mysteriously.

***

Sam's thoughts touched on the plays by Shakespeare he had viewed before leaving England, so he used them to approach her.

"Thou doth speak to my heart as the plays from the Great Bard, Shakespeare, speak to life. I am reminded of one from *The Tempest*," 'Mine ear is open, and my heart is full; The very instant that I saw you, did my heart fly to your service'."

She lowered her dagger, still wary, but something in his eyes spoke to her. "My name 'tis Maria Hallett." She put the dagger away and stared at him before speaking again. "I am familiar with the plays of which ye speak, so I shall answer ye in kind. 'I beseech ye, do not let affection's snare entwine, for I am falser than oaths proclaimed over wine.'"

I believe Sam smiled and said, "From *As You Like It*. My name is Samuel Bellamy, but ye can call me Sam. Are you secretly a man, then, as the character in that play was pretending to be a man?"

"Nay, I am false in that my life does not mirror that of what it should for a woman of my station. I should be learning to sew perfect lines, direct servants of the household, and yearn for a husband and children to make my life complete. I am none of those things goodman. Look not to me to be a pious and dutiful helpmate." She placed the basket on the ground, unsure why she told a stranger such things, then straightened to find him even closer to her now.

Sam closed his eyes and breathed in the scent of her: ripened apples and fresh grass accented with sunshine. He chuckled softly and approached her until he stood directly in front of her, so she had to look up into his face.

"Ye should also not look to me to provide a safe and comfortable hearth, gentle lady, for my soul yearns for adventure and fortunes found." He ran a hand over her long hair, which flowed down her back.

Jerking her hair from his hand, she told him, "I pray ye to look elsewhere your momentary pleasure for anything with ye will surely ruin me," she told him, once again trying to remain strong. "Ye have the look of a man with wings on his feet and cannot be settled. I do not believe ye look for a helpmate and companion."

"Are ye not ruined just by standing with me in the orchard? Is that not how it is for the hen-minded women in this town? I tell ye truly, I have never felt my heart jump at the sight of anyone the way it has for ye. I could live forever sustained only by your voice and the curve of your face." He placed his palm against the side of her face.

Maria remained stiff to his touch but then relaxed and slowly turned her face towards his hand and closed her eyes. Sam lowered his hand but kept his eyes on her as if she was water, and he was dying of thirst.

"I would plight my troth to ye here and now, in nature among God's creations, if it would put your heart to rest. We will find Reverend Treat as soon as I can secure your father's approval of the match and be married in the eyes of God, your family, and this town."

"Oh, do ye have a rich farm, as well? For that will be the only way to win my father's approval. I did not see a cow trailing behind ye, so I guess it must be some type of produce. Perhaps turnips?" She could not help her cheeky reply, but fate's sheer audacity to hand her this like-minded soul when she was to be pledged to another was preposterous.

"Nay, but fear not, I will speak to my uncle and see if there is a bit of land from which he will part." Sam's mind raced furiously like his aunt's beehive as he planned how to keep this intelligent, witty, and beautiful vision with him forever. "I will protect ye and care for ye."

"I do not need tending, goodman," Maria told him and returned to the blanket that lay upon the ground holding her things and sat upon it. Sam joined her and took her hand in his, gazing intently into her eyes. Maria could see his heart as his dark sapphire stare captured hers, and the world around them seemed dimmed. "I cannot pledge to ye, goodman, for I am promised to another.

"No one can put aside their destiny and we are fated to be together, fair maiden," he told her. "I pledge my heart, body, and soul to ye, Maria Hallett the Fair," Sam spoke the words that could only come from deep inside. "My heart to yours, my soul to yours, my body to yours, in the eyes of God the Father Almighty, and nothing but death could keep me from thy arms."

Maria, caught in the moment and feeling the bonding of their hearts, repeated the words back to him. "My heart to yours, my soul to yours, my body to yours, in this life and in death, in the eyes of God the Father, the Son, and the Holy Ghost."

So pledged, they sealed their oaths with a kiss, tentative at first but deepening as they settled against each other. The air was chilled with breezes from the bay, but it did nothing to cool the heat as Sam slowly disrobed Maria, and she did like-wise to him until they were both fully entwined upon the blanket and cloaked in the darkness of the trees. Each touch was a new discovery, and each taste a delicacy upon which they feasted. The fire built slowly inside them as desire soon overrode inhibitions.

And the next morning…

***

Clarissa threw a pillow at Loyd as Laura laughed. Clarissa

asked, "What do you mean 'And the next morning…'?"

Laura *tsked* at Clarissa and said, "No sex ed for you during Grandpa's story, young lady. You'll have to look elsewhere for bodice-rippers."

"Oh no, nope, nope, nope, gross," Charlie said, "just kill me now." He put his finger to his head and mimed shooting it.

Loyd told them, "In a way that was described later by Elizabeth Reynard in her 1934 book, 'The Narrow Land,' Sam then 'made masterful love, sailorman love that remembers how a following wind falls short and makes way while it blows'".

Charlie plugged his ears with his fingers.

"There is no way that's how it was!" Clarissa exclaimed. "I don't care how much you are making up this story; it is just not how life works. Plus, she's just a kid! Isn't that like some perverted thing he's doing?"

"That's not how it works now, no, but back then, you pretty much had your life planned even before birth, and sixteen was quite a marriageable age back then," Loyd explained. "If you were a female, then that's the life you led. Even if you were a female royal, then that's the path you took. For Maria to not want to fit into a mold was refreshing and fits Sam like a glove, wouldn't you say? He's not looking for a woman to stay home and raise babies; he wants a partner. Fate, it seems, has guided him to his soul mate."

"There's no such thing as soul mates, Grandpa. I don't care what romance movies and novels all say. Everyone has emotional baggage and their own insecurities. You can't possibly know from one meeting that you are fated to be with a person," Clarissa said. "Isn't that just lust and momentary attraction?" She could feel herself losing ground but refused to back down.

"Are you sure?" Loyd asked, looking between her face down at her phone and back.

Clarissa, blushing, said, "I mean…I guess…I love Reggie, but I'm not sure how I'd react if he came up to me all googly-eyed, professing undying love when we met. Super awkward."

"Remember, different time," Loyd said, "Way before any women's rights and equality and it was all they knew. You were what you were, and no changing it, and you did *not* want to be an outcast. Less social media to tell you what you should think and more reliance on your own thoughts and feelings with the religious majority giving you a need to conform to society and its religious structure.”

“Your father and I dated for about a year before he finally proposed,” Laura said. “I knew from the first minute I saw him in the library reading ‘Harry Potter and the Sorcerer’s Stone’ while we were seniors in high school that we had a true match.”

“Gross,” Charlie said again.

“Ditto,” said Clarissa.

William laughed and said, “She came over, stared at me till I looked up, and then—”

“—She closed the book slowly and grinned at you, and you were smitten,” Clarissa and Charlie echoed together, then laughed.

“So, you’ve heard the story a few times?” asked William.

“Just a few times, but it’s okay,” Clarissa smiled and said, “It’s your meet-cute, but I feel like that was super rare. This guy doesn’t know anything about America or this girl or what he’s going do with his life, and he’s all like, ‘thou are so beautiful, and I wish to kiss thy face’ and stuff like that.”

William smiled and said, “Why don’t you guys go get ready for bed? Grandpa can continue when you are ready."

Clarissa and Charlie went to put on their pajamas as William, Laura, and Loyd took the mugs and dishes into the kitchen.

"How was the storm damage," Loyd asked them as he rinsed things off and put them into the dishwasher.

"It wasn't too bad, but I think the tail end of the storm will be worse since the first half loosened things. The store is fine, and most of the customers and regulars had cleared out before the storm hit, so we were able to beat most of it," replied William.

"I had put the sandbags around the doors, just in case, because I know that back alley floods," said Laura.

"Glad to hear and very glad you are both home, safe and sound," Loyd said. They returned to the living room, where the kids waited for him to continue the story.

"Please continue with the kissy-face scene, Grandpa," Charlie said and grinned.

"You bet," Loyd replied.

***

Sam finally looked away from Maria's face and took in the

106

surroundings. Noting the moon low in the sky in the distance, he knew he must leave her before folks would "talk" about them, meaning they would start disparaging Maria's reputation.

"I must leave ye, fair siren, yet I am drawn to ye like a moth to a torch," he said. "I would be with ye again, and I beg ye to think of me fondly after we part. If you have need of me before we meet again, leave a note in the apple tree closest to the gate on the side near The Tavern."

He helped her gather her things and then he handed her an apple blossom. "Something to remember me by when we are not together."

"Forsooth, thou must leave as I must away to my home before good folk know 'tis more than words we exchanged," she replied, giggling at the thought that they did do more. "I shall think of ye, and I doubt I shall need ye before we meet again, but I shall remember your words. I shall leave ye with a kiss and these words from "Romeo and Juliet," 'Good night, good night, parting is such sweet sorrow, that I shall say good night till it is morrow!'"

Sam and Maria each went their own way, him smiling and her

humming a tune that only she could hear. They would meet several more times over the following months as Sam settled into life in the New World.

However, another meeting and new beginning began that same year and shaped Sam's history—the building and launch of the ship *The Whydah Gally*.

PART TWO: A HERO'S JOURNEY

"The first object which saluted my eyes when

I arrived on the coast was the sea, and a slave-ship,

which was then riding at anchor, and waiting for its

cargo. These filled me with astonishment, which was

soon converted into terror, which I am yet at a loss

to describe, nor the then feelings of my mind."

— Olaudah Equiano, "The Interesting Narrative of the Life of Olaudah

Equiano or Gustavus Vassa the African", 1789

Chapter 7: The Trade of Slaves

Wellfleet, Cape Cod, America Present Day

Loyd knew the kids learned about some of the things he was about to tell them in school but wanted to ensure they had the foundational knowledge to understand the importance of *The Whydah Galley*.

"To understand why *The Whydah Gally* was a big deal, you need to understand the economy of the time and about The Triangular Trade.

"The New World opened many rich resources for European countries and brought wealth with it. The earlier explorers and the new colonists found they could grow things like corn, raise tobacco in nutrient-rich soils, and greatly raise the export business.

"The harvest of these items proved a severe lack of labor available to the population. The Europeans had brought indentured servants with them. Indentured servants were brought over in the early 1600s with the Jamestown settlement, but they were still not enough to provide the labor needed for the vast amounts of harvested crops.

"This led to the rise of the reprehensible practice of buying or stealing African people, including kids, from Africa. They were captured, intimidated, or sold by their own families who wanted to pay debts or curry favor. Whereas indentured servants signed contracts and knew what they were getting into, whereas the enslaved Africans did not and spent months at sea on a voyage to American colonies packed like sardines in a can and just as smelly in the environment."

"Again, with the history lesson, Grandpa!" said Charlie.

"Yeah, Grandpa, we get it, and we learned about it in school and all of that stuff, so what did any of that have to do with anything?" Clarissa asked.

"I'm getting there, don't you worry, but a ship, especially at that time, was considered almost human. Just like humans, they evolve and grow as their needs change, and we'll see that with this ship,"

Loyd said.

"*The Whydah Gally* was built for just one purpose: transport of human cargo and a capacity of six hundred slaves. With that in mind, she was large, three hundred tons, and could navigate the waters quickly as it had a shallower hull. Ships are normally called 'she' by those who sail, making them more human. She also had a large arsenal of weaponry to protect herself against enemy ships or pirates.

"The original spelling was "The Whidah Gally" or "The Whido," and it wasn't until the ship's bell was located by salvage archaeologist Barry Clifford and his team in 1984 that historians found they had been spelling it incorrectly. The bell says, "*The Whydah Gally.*" As a side note, Mr. Clifford has never sold any of the artifacts and wanted them available for anyone to see."

"How on earth do you even pronounce that?" Charlie asked, using his mother's phone to search the internet for it.

"The pronunciation of the port and the ship are the same; some believe the ship was named after the port. They both are pronounced "wih-duh" with a short "i" sound kind of like the word 'widow,'" Loyd told him, smiling, and then began the second part of the tale.

***

London, England 1715

Sir Humphry Morice commissioned the ship's building to provide faster transport for the enslaved people and goods so there could be more trips and increased profit. As he served in the House of Commons and as Director of the Bank of England, his income was more than adequate for his import/export business.

He is credited in history with funding one hundred and ten voyages and transporting over thirty thousand enslaved people to the New World. He was given the moniker "Prince of London Slave Merchants" and knew how to make any venture profitable so long as it involved his ships and his business.

On this note, he commissioned the ship to be built and enhance his coffers with the ability to journey more often through the Triangular Trade routes. More trips meant more money. More money meant he could continue to fund his extravagant lifestyle.

He chose a Dutch privateer named Lawrence Prince, a.k.a. Laurens Prins, to captain the vessel. Privateers were basically pirates who wanted to be able to pirate legally, so to speak. They usually held papers from private companies or monarchies to prove they were legal.

Captain Prince had already made a name for himself and his brutal methods of securing ports and cargo. Based out of Port Royal, Jamaica, he was not known for mercy and started a large portion of his career as part of a four-man joint effort to purchase a Spanish ship from an English naval officer, Commodore Christopher Myngs. After a failed attempt to raid the town of Mompos, they moved on to capturing a Spanish fort in Nicaragua and then the town known as Granada. Not to be confused with the island of Grenada in the Caribbean. It was rumored he sent the head of the Granadian priest in a basket with a bloodstained note stating he wanted seventy thousand pesos as ransom.

This last act was the one that got him into trouble with the Port Royal governor, Thomas Modyford. Accusations were brought to the governor that Captain Prince and his crew acted without letters of marque, which was what gave them amnesty as privateers against Spanish opposition. As an attempt to mollify the ones accusing Prince and others, he ordered Prince to join the naval crew of Captain Henry Morgan, a Welsh privateer, on his assault at Panama. Captain Morgan gave Prince third in command. Prince used his knowledge and tactics of close fighting to stage an ambush, routing the Spanish and ensuring Captain Morgan's victory.

After assisting Captain Morgan with the capture of Panama, Captain Prince retired to enjoy the spoils of his sailings at the age of eighty-five. Sir Humphry called Captain Prince out of retirement just to take command of the new ship, *The Whydah Gally*, which was built in 1715 in London. Its principal port for obtaining its slave cargo was Ouidah in Africa. The port's name is similar in pronunciation to the bird. The whydah is a species of finch with long tail feathers native to the African forests. Based on the previous history, Sir Humphry knew Captain Prince would be perfect for his ship, even though he was headed more for the grave at his age.

"A visitor for you, Sir Humphry," said a servant, bowing as he gave Captain Prince entry, then left quickly.

"Welcome, Captain. I hope the voyage was fair?" asked Sir Humphry.

"Aye, 'twas most pleasant and nary a swell," Captain Prince replied, bowing. "Me sea legs do keep me in good stead and able to manage after all me years aboard a ship. I feel me experience will be to ye're benefit, ye're Governorship."

Ignoring Captain Prince's butchering of his honorific, Sir Humphry told him, "'Tis good news, please, seat yourself hence, and we shall partake of my latest libations," Sir Humphry said, pouring a glass of rum for each of them. The bar was made from one solid teak tree cut down from the country of India.

After sitting in wingback chairs in front of the fireplace, Captain Prince's knees popping loudly as the captain took his seat, Sir Humphry gave Captain Prince the details of the ship and what he could expect in the journey. Captain Prince appeared in relatively good health even at his age, so Sir Morice did not worry about the captain not making good on his contract.

"It used to be that ships were licensed by the Royal African Company and due to give them 10 percent of the profits, but that ended with the Parliament rescinding their ability to be the sole funding source. My coffers will fund this ship and its voyages, so there should be more than enough money for your needs. It is my hope the trade will be sufficient for us to have plenty left over, if you understand my meaning," Sir Humphry took a drink then continued. "Have you looked upon the ship since you landed?"

"Aye, I did as soon as I could disembark. I believe she shall be splendid in her service, and I promise ye to keep ye're profit…safe." Captain Prince took a drink and saluted Sir Humphry with the glass with a smirk.

"Oh, aye, aye, I do hope that is the precise manner in which you shall undertake this endeavor," Sir Humphry said with a wink.

"I was unable to gaze much upon it as I wanted to ensure I attended to your summons quickly. There be still some fight left in this ole' sea dog. Can you tell me about it?" Captain Prince asked.

"Aye, good captain, I shall extol its virtues for you, and you can judge for yourself if anything is amiss," replied Sir Humphry.

"She is a big girl with a short bottom, so she will run through the waves like grease through a goose. She measured three hundred tons and can be either given full sail for the winds or rowed by the slaves you will have aboard for the shorter journeys. She has been timed at thirteen knots and has been built with a shallow hull so she shall not lumber around the water like other cargo vessels. She can hold around six hundred slaves, which is considerably more than my main fleet. I do not know if you noticed, but all my ships are named for my wife and daughters. This one was named similar to the port where I have obtained the most profit and the bird that inhabits the area.

"In addition, she'll carry a full complement of cannon, around eighteen at least, plus she possesses firearms and swords if you encounter any…resistance." Sir Humphry finished the description, watched Captain Prince's face as it showed admiration, and then closed back into the captain's usual visage.

"It sounds as if you have planned for all possibilities, and I shall keep the cargo away from pirates and other threats," Captain Prince stated.

"Nay, good captain, I care not as much for the human cargo as I do the cargo you bring back to me. I am sending you with guns, gunpowder, muskets, liquor, and cloth for their barter," Sir Humphry said.

"That will be sufficient, to me thinkin'. When do ye wish for me to begin this journey?"

"I believe a month from now as to give you time to learn the ship and its crew," he replied.

"It will be me honor to serve," Captain Prince stated, downed his drink, set the glass on the bar, then departed past bowing servants and others of whom he took no notice. His mind was already thinking of ways to use the ship to its best advantage and how to increase his own coffers.

Sir Humphry remained sitting where he was and ruminated on the small empire he had built and was hoping to add to with contributions from Captain Prince's voyages. He worried about a small contingent of businessmen from the port area of Bristol. It appeared they were slowly gaining traction with the local shipping industry and edging out the slave traders and had already cost him a small amount when they took the award of contracts previously sent to him.

His solution and downfall around 1731, after he left his post as governor and was once again made Director of the Bank of England, was to write bad checks. He amassed enough money in the space of a few months this way, estimated to be over three billion in today's money, according to historical documents. Of course, he was discovered and died later that year with gout listed as the cause, but some suspected he took poison to escape his debtors and fallen empire.

***

Loyd glanced over at his family and gauged their reactions to the purpose of the ship. A general sadness lay over the room like a blanket.

"Yes, it was originally a slave ship," Loyd confirmed. "However, *The Whydah Gally* will play a very important part in our hero's journey later on in the story, so it's important to know her history."

Loyd waited as everyone took a short break, and he closed his eyes, gathering his thoughts for this next part of the story. He wanted to ensure he didn't embellish too much, but it was a rough and, as they say now, not a "p.c." world. He knew they learned about most of this in school, but it was the general idea of things to just move through the curriculum. His late wife was a history teacher, so their children and grandchildren deeply understood historical events. They were not blinded towards the past, and how life "really was" back then.

Loyd stood and walked to the window, watching the winds

push over the pitch pines, making them bow to the wind's power. The thunder and lightning were picking up again as the eye had passed over, and now the storm renewed its fury. Turning, he saw everyone had returned and was waiting for more of the story, so he returned to his seat, noting someone had refilled his hot chocolate mug. He smiled at his daughter-in-law in thanks, and she smiled and nodded in return.

"Grandpa, I hope Sam burns it to the ocean floor. I hope the ship in the museum is just a replica," Charlie said, very concerned.

"No, my boy, he does not, but I think you'll find the actual tale more interesting," Loyd replied. "Plus, things are about to get even more interesting for Sam."

Chapter 8: Time For An Adventure

Provincetown, America 1715

Sam reflected upon the past few months of his life over the summer in America and felt it was a better life than he would have led back in England. He spent as much time as possible with the lovely Maria, away from prying eyes and notice of her parents. It disturbed him greatly to keep their love hidden, but Maria had told him her parents disapproved of their union before he could go before her father and seek blessing for a betrothal. They still hoped for Maria to match with someone they had chosen.

Sam knew he seemed poor compared to their wealth and the fact his family were not Puritans. He worked hard on his uncle's home and land to dig out a small portion of what he hoped would be his future home with Maria. His hope was to be someday able to have his own crops for export and be able to give Maria the life to which she was accustomed.

"How might I amass sufficient wealth to please my love's parents, Lily," he asked the cow pulling the wooden plow. She was stockier than the ones he tended growing up but suited the land here a lot better.

Lily the cow looked at him sideways as she chewed her cud and remained mute. Her job was to plow and provide milk. She could do both and still listen. She was a multi-tasker.

Sam jumped to the side as she provided manure to nourish the soil the old-fashioned way. Although it was almost the end of August and still quite warm, the second harvest was approaching, and winter supplies preparations were underway. Neighbors helped neighbors prepare their kitchen larders, smokehouses, and river troughs. The river troughs were dug out holes, basically, that food could be placed and kept cold as their form of refrigeration.

While Sam was seeking advice from the wise, multi-tasking bovine, his friend Paul came running through the field and waved to

Sam that he needed to speak with him. Sam waved him to come over, and Paul was nearly breathless, which meant he had run the entire way, also evidenced by the sweat pouring off him.

"Aye, my good friend, what doth ye know that has ye speeding so mightily this way," Sam asked, giving his friend time to catch his breath.

Paul took off his hat and fanned his face while using a handkerchief to mop at the sweat on his brow before replacing it on his head so as not to incite disapproval with the locals. His curly hair was limp and sweaty beneath it, and dark brown eyes finally looked up at Sam with something akin to a sparkle in them.

"Riches, my friend! Riches! I know ye have been seeking a way into the hearts of Maria's father and mother, and I have joyous news for ye!" Paul exclaimed. Lily stared at him as he yelled excitedly but continued her industrious work.

Sam's smile spread across his face, and he asked excitedly, "What mean ye? Where doth it lay?"

"'Tis not here, but down the coast and around the end of Florida near the Gulf of Mexico! Eleven Spanish ships carrying entire cargo hold full of gold and silver foundered in a hurricane on the thirty-first day of July, and the Spaniards are desperate to get them back," Paul managed to gasp out between breaths. "They are calling it a disaster, but I call it an opportunity!"

Paul straightened again after bending down twice in an effort to catch his breath. "The news given 'twas most ripe with details on the contents of those cargos, and methinks 'twill be the answer to thy money dilemma and a way to care for our families," he said with a smile. "Not for those reasons, but I could use the materials for new works of art for the people and merchants and add to me own income!"

Sam's pulse skipped a beat, and the world around him narrowed to nothing but Paul's smiling face. Sounds dull, and he could hear the heartbeat once it began pounding again in his chest. *This! This was a sign from God!*

"Ye must hurry and gather men of able body, and we must descend to the wreckage with swiftness 'ere we lose to the salvagers hired by the Spaniards," Paul encouraged Sam.

Sam's mind began spinning with details and logistics needed to begin the effort of salvaging a treasure thousands of nautical miles away. A lot of the menfolk here had sailing experience, so he did not fear lack of expertise barring them. It was the thought of leaving their families at the onset of winter when the weather was the harshest and unforgiving that would prove a barrier.

His excitement dimmed at that possibility as he would also be leaving Maria since she would have to stay behind. Women were not allowed upon ships unless they were passenger ships. A lot of sailors considered them bad luck and even went as far as to execute anyone smuggling a woman aboard.

Sam thought that line of thought was ignorant of the sailors and men in general. They must not know of Anne Bonny, of whom the sailors heard tales from sailing vessels bringing in goods. She, a woman of Irish descent no less, had been terrorizing the waters around the Caribbean for the past few years with her friend, Mary Read. Aye, her lover, Captain Jack Rackham, was also formidable, but she truly led their attacks.

Turning his attention back to his sweat-drenched friend, he brought up some of his concerns. "Aye, Paul, 'tis a fortuitous and miraculous occurrence! But, first, we must obtain a sailing vessel capable of hauling the treasure back here. Do ye know of such a thing?" Sam asked, trying to imagine the needed size for the tons of treasure he believed he would bring home.

"Of certain, I know of just the thing," Paul confirmed. "There is a man who still owes me for some very expensive pieces he commissioned from me, so I feel he will be able to part with a couple of pirogues to get us on our way. They will easily navigate the shallow waters of the Gulf of Mexico, and we will hug the coast on the way down as they are not quite made for sailing the deeper seas."

"Aye, those will work for us, and we'll need to quietly determine which men can be trusted to such a task. Let us ask Uncle Israel if he knows of any of his men who would be suitable for such an endeavor. Methinks the less that know, the better."

"Good thinking, and we can meet him at The Tavern as I am gut-foundered, for true!" With that, Paul turned and moved at a more sedate pace back towards town and food.

"Oh, Lily! My heart 'twill surely burst from such momentous tidings! I must away and hie to lovely Maria's side. Her parents must need to accept me upon my return with riches as Paul described," Sam said, petting Lily, knocking blow flies off her hide as he did so.

Lily bellowed a "moooooo" in agreement and excitedly kept chewing her cud but then resumed fertilizing the land and settled down content with her lot in life. She probably decided to let the odd human continue the rambling and dancing as she maintained a ladylike dignity.

Sam grabbed Lily's lead rope, led her into the barn area, cleaned and stowed the farming equipment, washed up as best he could in the pig trough next to the barn, and then hurried to set things in motion.

The apple orchard was in full bloom at the end of August, and it would not be long after juicy apples fell from the branches. It was the place of their first meeting and the one they continued to use as it provided privacy and was like a whole other world for them.

Sam had left Maria a message in an apple blossom on the fencing nearest The Tavern, which was their pre-determined method of requesting a meeting in the orchard. Sam waited, pacing, plans running rampant in his mind, and he could envision how things would fit together just as he did in his sailing days during the war.

***

It was not long before Maria came quickly down the trail leading into the orchard and to their favorite spot. She was smiling, and her face was aglow with anticipation of seeing Sam. He had seemed so odd the first time they met, but he had treated her with nothing but kindness and deference.

Before now, Sam and Maria had talked about marriage and their plans for when Sam could obtain her father's blessing. Sam remembered their conversation a month ago as they planned for their future. Closing his eyes, he pictured one of those times.

They even knew they wanted Reverend Mister Treat to marry them, and they would live on an island all to themselves. The reverend was the only one to turn a blind eye each time Sam smiled at Maria in public or Sam sought ways to touch her, like caressing her hair in passing.

"Just think of it, my love," Sam began, lightly touching her hand as they lay on a blanket after making love. "We shall post our banns in January and be wed in February, and ye shall be dressed in

129

the finest gown with apple blossom flowers surrounding us. All the townspeople will gather to see us joined in the eyes of God and give us their blessing as I shall be the richest man in the area by that time. This I swear!"

Maria, closing her eyes, could only see her father in her mind's eye as he swore, saying would find Sam and beat him bloody with a cane if Sam came near her again, let alone marry her.

"Sam, ye know my heart desires nothing more but I told my father about meeting you and how you have charmed me, and he has sworn ye will face his wrath rather than receive his blessing," she told him, tears streaming down her face. Rising, she leaned over him and put her palm over his cheek, and Sam felt the salt of her teardrops on his lips. "I will wait forever for ye, but it must be done in secret, and we must leave this town behind us to live as husband and wife. Somewhere we are unknown, where ye can amass a living, and I can provide ye a happy home."

Swallowing the lump that suddenly appeared in his throat, he blinked back his own tears at her words. For a moment, he felt like he was on top of the mountain, and now he felt like he was teetering on a precipice. Torn between his love for her and fear of her safety, he cleared his throat and told her, "Ye need not worry more, my love, and I thank ye for the news of thy father's temperament. It just means I must find my way to provide for ye faster than we planned."

Maria studied his face, closed her eyes, then opened them again with a small, sad smile. "We shall find our own island and I shall have ye all to myself and we shall live happily ever after as in the folk tales told around the campfires during solstice."

They had talked of small things since then, each parting tinged with a bit of sadness that he was determined to end and bring a smile back to his beloved's face and the news he was about to give her should do the task. He opened his eyes in time to see Maria approaching him.

"Maria, ye hast to hear the latest tidings given by Paul to me just this past moment!" Sam began after they embraced and sat upon a blanket she brought with her.

"Aye, and what hast ye so aflutter like a girl upon her first courting meeting?" Maria asked, eyes dancing with mirth.

"Upon the end of this past month, several ships of Spanish

build were caught in a hurricane and met the ocean floor with cargo holds full of gold and other riches," Sam explained excitedly.

"'Tis most glorious news, indeed!" she replied, kissing him. "But what hast that to do with ye?"

It was a short kiss, however, as Sam was too excited to stop his description of the treasures they might find if they made their way quickly to the location.

"Think of it, my love; I canst finally win your father's approval and gain your hand! He will not be able to deny us once I let hundreds of doubloons fall at his feet! I shall have a house built for you better than this, and we will be comfortable and happy."

"Oh, Sam, I am most happy now and will take ye whether we have a home of wealth or if we must carve out our own life from nature itself," she told him, though her voice held a small quiver.

Sam, caught up in his excitement, did not see the mirth slowly fade from Maria's eyes as she spoke.

When Sam finally noticed she was no longer smiling or responding joyously, and her words sounded hollow, he finally stopped talking and gave her a crooked smile. "Aye, 'tis most glorious news, but I hast made thy ears listen for too long. What ails ye, my love?"

Maria looked down at her hands, now folded in her lap, closed her eyes, took a deep breath, and let it out slowly. "I am excited about this news; however, there is more ye must know before thy journey."

Maria took Sam's hand and placed it upon her stomach, then gazed into his face and waited for his realization of what it would mean. Sam left his hand there, the smile slowly fading from his face, color leeching away, and then he met her eyes.

"Nay, say 'tis not true. 'Twould be a wonderous thing 'twere we married in the eyes of God and no doubt about it." His mouth opened and closed like a fish caught on land as he tried to think of what to say to her. "I am torn between love and fear for ye now, especially since I shall be leaving ye to face the wrath of the people. I know how ye will be treated, and it will not be kind. Is there anywhere else to go for ye, my heart?" Sam asked, knowing there was not, but now his heartbeat with fear for her and their unborn child.

Sam desperately sought answers in his mind as Maria shook her head negatively and murmured, she had no one and nowhere else to go. He could not take her with him; life was hard enough for a woman at sea, let alone one who was pregnant. Yet, he knew what she would possibly face when left behind. Unmarried women were ostracized enough, but those who had children out of wedlock were punished and incarcerated, most times.

Maria took his hand once again and held it while looking into Sam's eyes through tears. "I know thy mind, and ye must surely have plans whirling through like a child's dervish; however, ye must take care and return to me on swift wings," she said and placed a kiss upon his palm. Sam lifted his other hand and ran it over her hair, trying to give comfort and savoring every minute they had together. "Only then will we be able to celebrate this wondrous occurrence and a gift from God as validation of our love for each other."

"I vow ye this, then, that I will return as soon as I am able to gather enough riches for thy parents to look upon our match fondly and ensure our babe will be secure in life," he promised. "I know not how ye will fare, but know that I shall look upon the moon and blow a kiss, and it will reach ye."

"I shall look for that kiss when I see the moon, and I shall return it to ye," she agreed. "I will wait for ye to return to our home."

Sam held Maria for a moment as he thought of what was coming for her. A solution worked its way into his mind, and his heart immediately rejected it, but he knew he must give it a voice for Maria to decide for herself.

"My heart is aggrieved to leave ye in such circumstances, mayhap 'twould be best if ye did marry someone with prospects though 'twill surely rend my heart. I hope to return to ye in at least six months, but ye will most likely have the babe by then."

"Nay, my one and only love, I shall not take another to my side or my bed. Do not fear as ye do not yet leave me. I will participate in your hidden plans and help you with the necessary supplies. I beg ye to give me as much time as ye can spare before we are parted."

"Never fear, my golden princess, for ye are the greatest treasure I shall ever steal. The celestial bodies cannot break the bond between us, nor can the will of men. We are married in the eyes of God, though not in His house, which I shall ensure it happens upon my return."

He, once again, gifted her with an apple blossom.

They parted soon after, and Sam assured Maria there would still be time for each other before he departed; Maria volunteered ideas to help him with the plans.

***

"Just as I thought would happen," Clarissa stated sagely. "I know there wasn't much for birth control back then, but what, did they expect holy interference? Did she think she could claim it as a miracle like Jesus?" Clarissa huffed.

Loyd smiled at her and shook his head, saying, "Nope, I think they didn't think of that far at all. Remember, Sam believed he was going to get the blessing of Maria's father soon; they would be married, and all before Maria's pregnancy showed, but then reality set in as soon as the news of the pregnancy was given. They did have a sort of birth control then in the form of an early condom of sheep's bladder, but it was not widely available nor sought as families wanted to procreate as quickly as possible."

"I think they tempted fate too much for it not to bite them in the butt since they were probably 'together' all summer," Charlie laughed. "Seriously, it's like the worst century ever, especially if you wanna date someone.”

“Oh, there were worse centuries, my boy, but those are stories for another time,” Loyd replied. “For that time period, you didn’t get pregnant outside the bonds of matrimony, and you definitely did not get divorced even if Henry VIII ignored that tenant.”

“How did Maria think she would hide it?” Clarissa asked, perplexed. “I mean, even young, I’m sure she would have started showing fairly quickly. Did they have the ‘I swallowed a watermelon seed’ excuse back then?”

Everyone laughed, and Julia told her, “Nope, there were ‘wise women’ who could give special concoctions to prevent pregnancy, but that fell into the realm of ‘witch’ too often for girls to risk it. Punishment for pregnancy was bad, but it was even worse if you were suspected of killing a baby. Especially if you were thought to have killed it to hide an affair or premarital relations.”

“That bites,” Clarissa replied.

“Yea, verily,” William told her, mocking the speech of Sam’s century.

Loyd looked around at his family and said, “And now the real journey begins for both Sam and Maria," and settled back to continue the tale.

***

Maria sat by the fire in her home as her mother instructed the indentured servants to do their tasks and what would be expected of them the next day as night was approaching. She knew she should be paying attention so she would know how to run her own household someday; however, this twist of fate changed that course. She could not yet let her family know her condition. She ensured a small bowl sat under her bed as the babe caused her to vomit in the mornings and emptied it herself, hoping her parents or sisters did not espy it.

Maria only knew Sam about four months but felt God brought him to her from across the ocean as they were heartmates and fated to be together. This was the love expressed by Shakespeare and all the sonnets written by those who were far more expert on the subject than her, but she knew this was what it was. She was not prone to flights of fantasy, yet her heart lifted at the sight of him, and she could not help but dream of the future.

Maria laid a hand upon her stomach and wondered at the child that grew within. Soon, she would need to alter her dresses, so they hung without showing her growing belly in the coming months. She wondered how quickly she could get her father's blessing for marriage to Sam, and then her life would be perfect. She knew it was time to put away her childish things as the Bible said in book 1 Corinthians, which her father had read to them a few months ago.

Her book, *The Pilgrim's Progress* by John Bunyan, rested on her lap. It intrigued her as she followed the main character, Christian's journey, on his escape from The City of Destruction, hoping to find peace and contentment in the Celestial City. She understood the whole book was an allegory of Puritans on their faith journey promoting a life of righteousness and prosperity, but it irked her, as well, for the same reason. Bunyan wrote it as he was incarcerated for preaching to a group of more than five people outside a parish church without a license, which the Conventicle Act of 1593 prohibited. Though the main character's viewpoint was different, it upheld the Puritan rigidity and went against everything Maria wanted.

Standing, she went through her nightly ablutions, put on her night-rail attire, and prepared for bed. The house settled into a quiet murmur as servants finished their preparations for the next day and retreated to their own beds. As the days grew shorter, bedtimes became earlier to save on candles. There was not much to do when night descended, so many people, especially farmers, would go to bed and rise with the morning sun as the roosters crowded.

The servants had placed a bed warmer pan under her covers to warm it as the temperature at night had increased in the chill. She removed it and placed it back near the fire for the next night, then climbed into her straw mattress bed and closed her eyes. Her mind whirled with the day's revelations and Sam's plan to give them a prosperous start to their lives as a married couple.

I know not what he will do or what dangers he will face, but please watch over him, Heavenly Father. I commend his safety into your hands, and I know ye will bring him back to me 'ere his journey is made.

Feeling a sense of calmness envelop her, she fell deeper into sleep, dreaming of a child with black hair and piercing blue eyes like the father. Or, perhaps a girl to twine her father around her finger as she danced merrily through the apple orchard with her hair loose and flying behind her like laundry hanging on the line.

Chapter 9: Forming The Crew

Cape Cod, America 1715

Paul and Sam appeared before Sam's uncle, Israel, at his desk in his house. They would need a substantial amount for this salvage level to purchase a ship, rig it to their specifications, and crew it.

Sam paced nervously as Paul twisted his hat in his hands over and over in the front sitting area. After over a half-hour wait, Israel stood and stretched where he was located at a small desk and area built near one of the fireplaces for warmth and beckoned them over. Paul and Sam looked at each other and nodded in encouragement before walking over to sit in the chairs in front of the desk.

Israel Cole sat at his desk, which contained only a writing implement and parchment on top. His office area was very austere and imposing, like him. Sam knew him to be a just and fair man, but he felt a bit wary now.

"I have made time for you both on my schedule, and I hope it is for good cause," Israel began. "I need not remind ye, Sam, of the importance of my work though 'tis not in thy chosen path. Your help was invaluable on the last mission, but we must be able to do our errands in silence and with none the wiser."

"Aye, and I give thanks for all that ye do. My friend and I come to beg a boon of ye, if you are of a mind, as also a possible business venture for your… other types of work," Sam said, sitting in one of the bare wooden chairs while Paul took the other.

"I have no time for ye to waste upon ephemeral dreams. If that is why ye and thy like-minded friend hast approached my office, then depart ye may for mine ears will not listen to thy inevitable drivel. I know not of what 'other venture' you speak, and I was warned by your father should you choose to engage in mischievousness." Israel motioned towards the door and took one of the parchments from the side of his desk, dipped his quill pen into a small jar of ink, then began writing in dismissal of them.

Paul and Sam looked at each other, and Paul implored Sam with his eyes and face to give it another try. Clearing his throat that had suddenly closed and left his mouth as dry as the deserts he had heard the tale of as a youth, Sam broached the subject again.

"Uncle, I implore ye to consider again the gains from such a venture as presented," Sam said, leaning forward. "I know ye hast no need for riches such as rumored; however, ye surely wish to bolster the people and economy of this town. Ye would not engage in such clandestine activities if it were no truth."

Israel put his quill into the top of the ink pot and leaned back, crossing his arms over his considerable stomach girth. His eyes narrowed slightly as he regarded the two men in front of him. His nephew sought adventure and could not seem to accept the destiny laid before him. However, perhaps this would be a way to quench that fire when they returned weary and empty-handed, as he suspected would happen. He did not want to make it easy, though, so he stared at them a bit longer and wondered what type of meal was being prepared for him in the kitchen. Finally, he closed his eyes, shook his head, smiled ruefully, then stood and shook both their hands. Sam and Paul, already thinking it was no, were shocked at the change and smiled.

"I thank ye, Uncle! I will make ye proud!" Sam and Paul ran

out of the house as quickly as possible to begin their plans.

Israel stood watching them, then walked over to the coffers in

their hidden space and set aside the amount. He may be a fool, but the

thought of the sunken treasure was too good to pass up, and the town

could genuinely use the resources it would buy.

After the money was allocated, Israel decided it was time for

him to go out to check on the livestock among other things. Chuckling

to himself, he wondered how long it would take his errant nephew to

realize his folly, hopefully before too much of his money was spent.

He walked into the kitchen to inform his wife of their nephew's deal

and then left to find men suitable for the job.

Meanwhile, Sam and Paul met again at The Tavern and

discussed the logistics and supplies they would need to be successful.

They kept their voices low as they did not want to be judged by the

locals or want anyone to try and include them. This treasure salvage

would be for Sam and Paul to have better lives for their loved ones,

and they intended to use every bit of it for that purpose.

As Paul excitedly drew upon a piece of parchment and laid out plans, Sam's mind could not focus as he still could not grasp the news of Maria's pregnancy. Part of him was astounded and unbelievably happy to have something from their love bloom and grow. The other part of him felt like a lowly lecherous fool for putting her into this predicament, especially when he was about to depart for months.

Paul finally wound down as he noted Sam's gaze had become unfocused, and he stared at the table instead of at the parchment. Putting down his charcoal pencil, he sat down and turned to Sam to look at him.

"What ails ye, my friend? Are ye not excited about this adventure?"

Sam told Paul of Maria's pregnancy, and Paul clapped a hand on Sam's shoulder in commiseration. Paul also knew of the slander and ridicule Maria was going to face once she began to show.

"What will ye do, Sam? Thou art truly up a running body of water without a rowing apparatus. A hard life is ahead of fair Maria, and ye know not if she can stand the storm heading her way," Paul said, looking into his tankard. "I know when my wife, Elizabeth, was carrying, she still endured ridicule if her clothes were improper, if she chose to sit while doing her chores, and any other thing the hens out there could find fault with her. Maria will not have the luxury of marriage and a man to protect her from gossip and law. What will ye do?"

"I fear for her, Paul; I fear for her so much my heart will burst from it," Sam replied, looking into his tankard as if it held the answer.

"Is there no other place where she can go until the babe is safely delivered?"

"Nay, her family 'tis too prominent here for her to simply disappear." Sam looked around the room. "'Tis possible we shall return before she must face the stocks."

Paul emptied his tankard and went for more, then returned. "Let us look to other things to turn thy mind away from such drastic things."

Sam looked over his list and saw a few things they would need that he was unsure how to obtain. "Look, ye, at this list, my friend, and tell me if ye know where we might obtain these items."

"I have already tasked the dockmaster to let me know when a

couple of pirogues would suit our purpose and hold what is needed while also being fast with the wind. With the backing of my father and my own accounts, we should be able to buy, rig, and crew the ship within this month." Paul pointed a finger down at one item they added late."

They knew the Spaniards were employing their own divers to find the sunken treasures, so they would need something themselves to find it faster. They did not know if the waters there were shallow enough for their own divers to succeed or if deeper waters would need an apparatus designed for such a thing.

A voice sounded from behind them, close enough to have overheard their ship's needs. "Mayhap, I have just the thing, good fellows." The speaker turned and faced them. He was a plump-looking man with ruddy pallor to his skin and the look of someone who spent time in the sun, but he did not have the leathery skin of those exposed to the sun's rays for long periods of time.

"Me name 'tis Edmund Halley, and, as me name implies, I create things for the benefit of society!" Edmund paused a moment as if waiting for applause. "Nay, good men, you have truly stumbled upon the greatest event in your lives meeting me! Have ye heard of Halley's Comet?"

Sam and Paul stared at Edmund, turned away from him, and continued their conversation. Edmund merely moved his chair to the other side of the table, so he was again facing them. Sam and Paul paused, stared at him, then returned to their original position away from Edmund and his strange manner of speech.

Edmund moved his chair once again and then put his body between them with his arms on the table over their list. They finally focused on him, waiting for him to expound on why they should be so lucky and what a comet could be. Edmund turned his chair fully towards them and leaned in so as not to be overheard.

"Ye know, Halley's Comet, named after me? Because I am the one that discovered it was not three separate celestial events but one? Ye know, bright ball thing in the sky with a really cool tail trailing behind it?" Edmund huffed. "C'mon lads, work with me here. I know ye wish to embark on your journey secretly, so I shall strive for quiet in my explanation."

Edmund motioned them closer. "My good fellows, I have a

spectacular invention for you, and your quest sounds as if it would fit perfectly into your plans."

"What could a balmy and strange person such as you, with your odd speech, have for us?" Paul asked, raising an eyebrow.

"Me speech is but a product of a life lived with sea-faring folk, my good man. Ye do not have time to speak with 'thou arts' and 'away I hie to other places' in the sailing world," Edmund explained. "By the time ye are able to finish a sentence, ye will find yourself on a longboard with a splash-filled destination."

Edmund produced a parchment with an architectural drawing of a large barrel with a small window, three large rectangles hanging on the bottom, and an open floor. Sam and Paul were skeptical about how it would be used but encouraged Edmund to explain further.

"Behold, the diving bell! 'Tis a modern design on an ancient design as I have added a small window and better weights. This, my good fellows, is how your divers can maintain their breath while diving to the bottom of Davy Jones' locker!" Edmund gestured to the design on the table with a flourish.

The diving bell invented just a century before in the 1600s, was the most used apparatus, although still reliant on the diver's skills rather than mechanical tools. Basically, it was called a "bell" and was a wood barrel or a large kettle. It lowered over the ship's side and then slammed into the ocean to trap air as it descended. The divers would then refill when they ran out of breath by diving under it and up to the air space to breathe, then dive back out and resume their job.

Sam considered the drawing with much the same scrutiny as the old battle layouts from his days with The Scalawags and saw the idea take shape in his head. They could anchor closer to shore but outside the hidden shoals from Havana, and their divers could use this apparatus to gather treasure faster and more efficiently than if they used self-breathing methods. Paul's face remained skeptical.

"I am still skeptical," he informed Edmund. "How dost thou rig such a device on board a ship? Dost it shall not take up valuable cargo room?" Sam nodded, agreeing with the question.

Edmund pointed to the top of the diving bell, and it showed a round hole anchored into the top. "This is how it would be stored and lifted. See this? 'Tis a place to use a hook or rope and your sailing mechanisms already on board for storage. Merely anchor it up off the deck either inside or outside the deck and secure it with ropes; then ye shall have the room you need."

Sam and Paul turned from Edmund to discuss it. It sounded a bit far-fetched, but the mechanics of the thing were sound in their logic.

"How much does ye ask for such a thing? 'Tis surely a dear amount for this invention," Sam asked, bracing himself for the amount.

"Why, nothing, my good fellow!" Edmund exclaimed.

Sam looked at Paul. Paul looked at Sam and shrugged. Sam looked back at Edmund.

"Did I hear ye correctly? 'Tis freely given?" Sam asked, bewildered.

"Aye, the only catch is that ye let me journey with you to see the open seas and test it out for meself," Edmund replied.

Sam looked at Paul. Paul looked at Sam and nodded. Sam and Paul shook Edmund's hand, declared the deal done, and discussed the logistics of carrying it aboard a pirogue.

***

Loyd walked over and stoked up the fireplace so that the flames once again danced merrily in the hearth. He heard his loved ones talking softly behind him and re-joined them after assuring himself the fire was satiated with the wood he gave it.

"Finally, the story is getting better!" Charlie said enthusiastically, rubbing his hands together.

"I can't stop thinking about poor Maria," Clarissa said softly. "I mean, I get it, life was hard then, but, geez, I thought teenage pregnancy was frowned upon a few decades ago, but I guess I didn't realize how bad it was to have children out of wedlock back in the olden days."

"I guess it gives a whole new perspective on how far this country has come with women's lib and rights, huh?" asked Laura.

"No kidding," Clarissa agreed, then again looked down at her phone. "Still nothing, he's killing me; I swear I'm going to have an anxiety attack right here."

"I'm sure he's fine, my girl; just having to help out his family is the likely reason. They still live near the docks, right? I know they were an hour behind me pulling into port, so they may have been caught in the leading swells," Loyd told her.

"Yeah, I guess, but I wish he'd at least let me know," Clarissa said dejectedly.

***

Sam met with Maria later and informed her of the updates. She simply shook her head in humor and told him it would be good to see him in action and to say to her the details when he returned. He told her of the plans and how things were progressing.

She smiled sadly as Sam put his hand on her stomach and promised he would return to her a rich man so they could marry and live on the island they dreamed of. They talked of how they thought the child would be and whether it would be a son to carry on the name or if it would be a daughter full of beauty and fire like her mother. Maria steadfastly refused to bring up any daughter of hers to conform to standards, and both just hoped the baby was healthy.

"I shall return to ye on swift winds, my love," Sam told her as he sat on the ground with his back against the tree, and she lay on his shoulder.

Maria buried her head into the space between his shoulder and neck and breathed in the scent of him, committing it to memory to help her through the coming separation. She then looked up into his face, smiling.

"I admit to feelings of jealousy for ye to have such an adventure as this whilst I remain behind, twiddling my thumbs," she said, laughing.

"Nay, my love, 'tis of no moment, and it shall be a short parting when compared to our future together. I hope to return to you in six months' time with a ship so burdened with riches it lumbers into the port, and your family welcomes me with open arms." Sam ran a hand down Maria's hair and gently moved her to lay back on his shoulder while continuing to rub her hair.

"'Tis my fondest wish and dream, and I shall maintain a watch on the horizon with sharp eyes for thy return." Maria turned her head and kissed him gently. "I shall attend ye and assist in preparations, so send me what you need, and I shall endeavor to locate it." They continued talking softly until she finally said she had to return home. Standing, she handed him an apple blossom with a small grin. He sniffed it then placed it into his breast pocket.

Dread crawled down his spine for a moment as he thought of the tales he had heard from others about how women were treated in these colonies. Most of the time, married women were treated no better than livestock and were good only for keeping the home and breeding sons to help with farm tasks or business deals. Daughters were only good for making matches with other families to expand their land and add to the family's coffers.

There were other tales that circulated ever since the governor of Salem finally put a stop to the spreading wildfire known as witch-hunting in 1693. Women, even married, were said to be "in league with the devil" if they did anything out of the normal for their society. Your neighbor could be the most God-fearing woman and giving of herself to everyone, but all it took was one word to the wrong person to have that neighbor thrown in jail or beaten or, even worse, hanged.

With Maria's spirit and lack of reliance on the men of the town, Sam feared she would be a target. When the townspeople found she was with a child, that likelihood would grow and he would not be able to help. This meant he must hurry and fulfill his vow to her to get her away from here.

A feeling of anticipation and hope filled Sam as he watched her walk away, gliding between the trees. The timing of this must be the divine hand of God leading him toward the answer to all his problems. He could not wait to get his hands on the treasure!

Chapter 10: Hurry Up and Wait

Near the Florida Coast, the site of modern-day Cape Canaveral, 1715

Sam did not get his hands on the treasure or anyone who rushed to the wreckage site. At first, Britain, previously having declared the wreckage fair game and granting privateer status to those who sought it, reversed their decision after making peace with Spain. The Spanish had time to hire Native American Seminole sponge divers who knew the waters to recover most of the sunken treasure before Sam and other captains arrived on site. Sam and Paul made valiant attempts over the next month, but nothing had been left behind.

Other captains tried to quell their crews' rising tempers as they were becoming increasingly enraged by the lack of loot. One of those captains would be instrumental in Sam's future path.

Distantly, Sam and Paul could hear the waves crashing against the shore of the Florida coast near them as they surveyed the scene before them. Ships of several origins dotted the light blue and green waters in which swam turtles and flying fish that Sam had seen during his sailor days but were a new spectacle for Paul. Paul could not stop gazing down in the water at the acrobatics of one particularly bright-colored fish as Sam cursed softly under his breath. He slipped quickly back into his former life and spoke using the phrases and speech he learned at a young age among the salty naval crews.

"Blast these craven dogs! They scour the carcasses while we are left with nothing."

"Nay, Sam, 'tis just a turn of bad luck do cause this strife. We arrived as swiftly as possible, yet we could not compete with those already in these waters," Paul commiserated.

"Come, my friend, let us meet with the other captains on the ship anchored there to discuss our next steps. Take me for a fool if I return home empty-handed!" Sam gestured to Paul to give directions to the pilot to make for the port as he pulled his raven-black hair back into a queue with a piece of lace. He despised wigs and felt they had no place on the water.

Paul asked, "Do ye believe they will be willing to share in the spoils when they are also empty-handed?"

"Aye, methinks they know these waters better than we and would welcome more manpower."

Sam's ship pulled alongside *The Bersheba,* captained by Henry Jennings, a semi-retired privateer from Bermuda who also could not resist the news of the loot under the shallow waters. Once on board, they were escorted to the captain's quarters, which were rich in appointments and embodied a lifetime of wealth accumulated by force and put into the cabin's comfort.

Also in the captain's quarters was *The Bersheba's* crewman, Charles Vane, who would later become a pirate captain in his own right of *The Pearl* until his own crew would mutiny in 1718 in favor of his quartermaster, "Calico Jack" Rackham. "Calico Jack" would later add famous women pirates Anne Bonny and Mary Read to his crew. Charles was cruel and enjoyed inflicting as much pain as he could while disciplining the other crewman and favored the use of the cat-o-nine tails most of all.

Captain Benjamin Hornigold, who also sailed pirogues and a sloop named *The Happy Return*, stood off the side where he could see the map on the table before Captain Jennings. Captain Hornigold is recorded as one of the founding fathers of the Golden Age of Piracy and had Edward Teach, also known as Blackbeard later, as his first mate. History would record that Jennings, Bellamy, and Hornigold were the ones to create Nassau as a pirate haven. While talented as a pirate, Captain Hornigold had an odd moral compass that led him to avoid fights and captures of English ships and cargo. This would backfire on him later.

Sam and Paul stood in the background as the captains and crew members aired their grievances and frustrations. They all agreed action was needed to claim the vast amount of treasure recovered.

"Aye," began Captain Jennings, "according to me scouts, the Spanish dogs have built a stronghold fort off the coast there," he pointed to a map with the Florida coast outlined on it. "Me scouts believe 'tis here the devils have planted their gold and await rescue. Me plan be simple, mates, and it shall require your assistance in liberating them of their loot."

Captain Hornigold leaned in further and observed out loud in his crisp upper-crust style of speech, "Here is where we'll find dockage close enough to send out a raiding party." He pointed to an area near the stronghold. "I favor this plan; however, it will be mostly dredging through the God-forsaken swamps to gain access to it."

Standing near Jennings, Charles Vane maintained a stone face, yet his eyes seemed to take in everything including Sam and Paul, who lingered near the map nervously. Charles unnerved Sam, but Sam couldn't give a reason why he bothered him so much. In an effort to look away from Charles's face, he addressed the other captains.

"My friends, my ship and crew would stand ready however 'tis but small vessels comprised of fishermen and divers, not fighting men. We can help hold off any sea-faring Spanish cavalry attempting to rescue their land-bound treasure, but 'tis all we can do." Sam lifted his shoulders apologetically. "Your plan is sound, and your crews should be easy enough, and we can catch any that slip through."

Captain Jennings looked at Sam and Paul with disgust. "What do ye here, young pup, if not to take what the fates present? That treasure 'tis ours by right and by God, and we shall have it! We need not your puny crew of peasants, so you just sit back and watch how the grown-ups play."

Captain Hornigold, however, eyed Sam and Paul speculatively with a glint that gave Sam chills down his spine. Sam wondered if they would be sent over the railings without a rope. Captain Hornigold, however, merely nodded at him and then returned to planning as Sam and Paul made their way back to their ship and relayed the news and orders to the crew.

One of the crewmen looked at them aghast, "Why, 'tis surely a suicide mission! The Spanish cannons will make short work of them before they even reach the shore."

Sure enough, large blasts of cannons began as Captain Jennings and Captain Hornigold started their assault. Smaller rowboats made their way to the shallows, where they deposited several men who proceeded to the mainland.

The soldiers on the mainland were ill-equipped for such tactics, and soon, Captain Jennings was sailing away with as much treasure as they could carry. Sam heard him shout across their bows, "Aye, my lad, 'twas an easy haul and at least 120,000 pieces of eight! Once again, I have found my calling, and bid ye join me as I once again go on account! Privateering was never this profitable!"

Sam and Paul looked at each other, knowing that "to go on account" meant to turn pirate. "What say ye, Paul? We've come away with naught but our sunburned skin and salty hair. 'Tis not how I foresaw our homecoming."

Paul lowered his head and closed his eyes, wondering how his father, gone these past few years, would approve of a son who turned to piracy. "Me father had all but disowned me before his death, anyways, so it probably would only confirm his suspicions of me. I hope he looks down from Heaven someday and finds me worthy. Mayhap this is the way? I can ill afford to return to my family with nothing to show but the blisters on my hands. Elizabeth will not condone such a thing and would truly leave me, taking the children and moving back to her parents' house."

Sam and Paul turned towards the assembled crew below, who had overheard Captain Jennings and were waiting for their answer.

Sam saw a piece of black cloth laying near the bulkhead and grabbed it along with the paint used for the mast poles. Looking over at the other two ships, he quickly sketched out a skull with two arm bones crossing it in an "x" and then held it up for all the crew to see.

"My friends, what say ye? Do ye wish to return to your homes, in debt from this venture with nothing gained except a future of hard toil to repay this folly? Or do ye wish to join with these others and make our own way?

"This flag represents not death, but resurrection. Never again will you be slaves of the wealthy. From this day, we are new men. Free men!" Sam held the flag higher, and the crew cheered.

Almost as one voice, Sam and Paul heard "ayes" and celebration of hope they had found a better purpose and would not have to face ridicule and shame at home. Rum that had been stored for celebrating the sunken treasure's recovery was brought out for this occasion instead. Sam and Paul raised their tankards and said, "My fellows, let us celebrate this new venture! Welcome to the pirate brotherhood!" The rest of the day consisted of instruction and plans with Sam and Paul, full of hope for their new adventure.

Paul looked at Sam over his tankard and noted, "Methinks we shall need better vessels to keep up with the ships we chase."

Sam smiled and said, "Well, my good fellow, 'tis our first goal then, aye? We shall find ourselves a new ship out there," he gestured towards the open sea.

Paul laughed and held out a telescope and two pistols, handing them to Sam. "Presents to bring good fortune to our endeavors!"

"Where did you get these, my friend?" asked Sam.

"'Twas the damnedest thing, I noticed them among the items in Captain Jennings's cabin and were set apart from the other things looking all lonely. I hate for anything to be lonely, so I am giving them a new home."

"Truly, you are benevolent, Paul," Sam chuckled, slapping a hand on Paul's shoulder. He put the pistols into his sash, hefted the telescope, and then peered through it, looking for his destiny.

***

Maria walked along the coast, wondering how Sam fared on his journey. She was beginning to show and spent most of her time now letting out her garments away from prying eyes, but she knew she could not keep her secret much longer. The whispers began to circulate, and she could not even walk to the market without heads turning her way and leaning together to share the latest rumors. She began keeping vigil at the beach even though she knew it was very early in Sam's journey. She felt closer to him as she gazed at the waves breaking along the coastline. A few months ago, when they were still available, Maria threw apple blossoms into the ocean as an offering to for Sam's safety. She tried to preserve some to last through the winter.

As she sat there, she felt the first real flutter inside. At first, she merely thought it was something she had eaten earlier that was causing stomach distress; however, the flutter came again. With wide eyes, she patted down her dress and placed her hands on her stomach. The fluttering became a little more pronounced, and she gasped and smiled. She knew it was the baby quickening to life.

"Oh child, ye shall be so loved and already are by me," she began. "Ye shall most certainly be a boy with hair black as night in winter and eyes like the sky. Your father will show ye all the ways to be a man, and we shall all live happily on the island of our dreams whence your father returns to us."

A brief shadow moved across her thoughts as she thought back to the way some of the townspeople reacted towards her the last time she went to the market. The whispers were faint but some of the words reached her ears. "Witch" being the most prominent of them. She knew her daily walks in the woods instead of chores brought out the vindictive spite of other women in town. She felt it was due more to jealousy than suspicion, however. It seemed everyone found ways of taking offense and blaming the devil for everything be it spoiled milk or rain that swept away entire fields.

The day passed, and the sun sank lower on the horizon until Maria knew she needed to head home. She packed up her belongings and, with a spring in her step, took a path she knew well. She dreamed of the future she would have once Sam returned.

***

"Wow," said Charlie, "so he became a pirate?"

"That he did, my boy and his crew had voted unanimously to join him," Loyd confirmed.

Clarissa looked down at her phone, sighed, and then asked, "Did he let Maria know, somehow, the change of plans?"

"Nope, how could he? There were not a lot of mail carriers

168

back then, and it was months between communications, most times years. Makes you appreciate the ability to text someone now, huh?"

"Well," Clarissa began, "when they answer you, yes."

"Grandpa, what were 'pieces of eight,'" asked Charlie.

"Well, back then, coin was the king of the money, and paper money was not very well used as it could be damaged too easily. It was also common for the Spanish people to cut the coins into eight pieces or 'bits' and use those like pennies today as pieces of a dollar, although figuratively and not literally. So, the Spanish silver coin was about a dollar and could be cut into eight bits called 'reales.' Make sense?"

"I guess," Charlie agreed, "but what did Sam know of pirating?"

"You'll have to remember he was a sailor for many years, and I'm sure he had his own run-ins with pirates while with the navy. His crew, though, needed training, and what better way than to start capturing ships and loot while under another captain's supervision?" Loyd asked.

"So, Sam and Paul's education begins on all the pirate things and ways. There was even a code pirates followed created by Captain "Black Bart" Bartholomew Roberts, and all who sought to become pirates had to sign them. Here, I have a framed copy of them from the book written by Daniel Defoe, who is famous for *Robinson Crusoe*, under the pen name Captain Charles Johnsson in *A General History of the Robberies & Murders of the Most Notorious Pyrates*. However, his work is disputed as accurate, so take it all as a rough translation. Just remember, the spelling then is not like today's spelling of things, so you may have to sound out some of the words."

The Ship's Articles

I. Every man has a Vote in Affairs of the Moment; has equal Title to the fresh Provisions, or strong Liquors, at any Time seized, and use them at pleasure unless a Scarcity make it necessary for the good of all, to vote a Retrenchment.

II. Every man to be called fairly in turn, by List, on Board of Prizes, because (over and above their proper Share,) they were on these Occasions allowed a Shift of Cloaths; But if they defrauded the Company to the Value of a Dollar, in Plate, Jewels, or Money, Marooning is the punishment. If the

Robbery was only between one another, they content themselves with slitting the Ears and Nose of him that was Guilty, and set him on Shore, not in an uninhabited Place, but somewhere, where he was sure to encounter Hardships.

III. No Person to Game at Cards or Dice for Money.

IV. The Lights and Candles to be put out at eight o'Clock at Night: If any of the Crew, after that Hour, still remain inclined for Drinking, they are to do it on the open Deck.

V. To keep their Piece, Pistols, and Cutlash clean, and fit for Service.

VI. No Boy or Woman to be allowed among you. If any Man were found seducing any of the latter Sex, and carried her to Sea, disguised, he is to suffer Death.

VII. To Desert the Ship, or their Quarters in Battle, is punished by Death, or Marooning.

VIII. No striking one another on Board, but every Man's Quarrels to be ended on Shore, at Sword and Pistol.

IX. No Man to talk of breaking up their Way of Living, till each has shared a 1000 l. If in order to this, any Man should lose a

Limb, or become a Crippled in their Service, he was to have 800 Dollars, out of the publick Stock, and for lesser Hurts, proportionately.

X. The Captain and Quarter-Master to receive two Shares of a Prize; the Master, Boatswain, and Gunner, one share and a half, and other Officers, one and a Quarter.

XI. The Musicians to have Rest on the Sabbath Day, but the other six Days and Nights; none without special Favour.

***

"So, they weren't really all that lawless, were they?" asked Clarissa. "And, seriously, death if you bring a woman on board? Crazy!"

"No, they had a pirate code of sorts, but that didn't stop the bad ones from being bad. They were just sneakier about it." Loyd gestured to the framed words. "Many believed women were bad luck and incapable of the hard life."

Clarissa laughed, "I guess Anne and Mary proved that wrong!"

"Yes, but their stories didn't have happy endings," Loyd said. "But let's move on because I can tell Charlie is ready for all of the action!"

Chapter 11: The Mooning

Bahai Honda, Florida Keys 1716

Sam always felt the sea at night was a beautiful setting. The sounds of the waves moved in time to the shifting ships in the docks. It was almost as if he were wrapped in a Stygian blanket and far from spying eyes. Paul joined him on the quarterdeck, and they stared out over the dark horizon lit only by the stars as the moon was in its new phase.

"Do ye think we'll find something on the morrow?" asked Paul.

"Aye, I feel it in me bones; tomorrow will bring us our first capture and more loot than we can carry!"

Sam stood a few more minutes, then went to the captain's

cabin to make final preparations. Paul followed him, grinning. Once inside, Sam stared down at the table that held a nautical map he had purchased from a captain on a nearby ship. He did not know if it was accurate, but it had so far been reliable. There was a small lump underneath. Looking under it, he spied another pistol. Sam gave a questioning look to Paul, who was still grinning.

"There I was, minding my own affairs, when this little one jumped into me hands from nowhere at our last shore leave! Naturally, I could not leave such an orphan and am simply giving it a new home."

Sam shook his head and let it join the two in his sash. Paul stood a while longer and then went back below decks to his sleeping berth.

Twice now, they had attempted to capture smaller ships, employing scare tactics to compensate for their small size. They would brandish their cutlasses and guns and then yell obscenities about the other sailors' questionable parentage and diminutive reproductive parts. All they succeeded in capturing was a basket of fruit thrown at them from the latest attempt. Paul had actually caught it, grabbed an apple from it, and stood eating it in front of the enemy crew. He had thanked them for the bounty of fruit and then turned, dropped his trousers, and mooned the entire crew. Laughing, the rest of Sam's crew followed suit, except for Sam, until almost the entire ship was mooning the enemy ship.

Sam considered that one a victory as the sailors on the other ship laughed so hard that some of them fell into the water. Sam and his crew had then left the area to regroup here in Cuban waters. They had succeeded in raiding Portobello, Panama, in the Caribbean and gained some much-needed supplies and a decent sloop.

However, they would need more than exposed anatomy tomorrow, and he set about planning their next attack. He made ready for bed but had not lain there an hour before he heard some shouting outside his window on the docks.

"Oy! Random ship that scurvy dog, Samuel Bellamy, could not even name properly," the voice yelled in a slurring tone. "Ye get ye're mangy arse down here, young pup!"

Paul entered Sam's cabin, walked to the window, looked down, and smiled. "Ye are not going to believe it."

Sam joined Paul at the window while he finished dressing. Down below, he saw the outline of Captain Jennings. Sam and Paul exited the cabin, instructed the night watch, then disembarked.

"Avast ye, took ye long enough, little pups," Captain Jennings said, waving his tankard around. "Have ye not partaken of the delights of this little island?" He turned and began walking towards a small tavern, and they followed.

Inside, the smells of multiple unwashed bodies assailed them, and Paul coughed into his sleeve. The odor mingled with the smell of liquor and tobacco smoke, creating a nauseating haze. Women wearing little to cover themselves maneuvered between tables and groping hands to fill tankards of ale. Some found themselves pulled down onto laps, but, experienced as they were, they knew how to laugh, flirt, and disengage to escape.

After finding seats at a table in the corner, Captain Jennings ordered rounds for them and then turned to business. "I hear the tale of a ship 'baring a full moon' complement aboard," he began. "Do ye know of such a thing?"

Sam smiled into his tankard as Paul looked everywhere but at the captain.

"Aye, 'tis as I thought. You need proper instruction, lads, or you shall join Davy Jones in the deep." Captain Jennings let out a tremendous belch that had Paul nodding appreciatively. "'ear me now, aye? Ye shall join me on my next voyage and learn how to pirate properly."

Sam felt his eyes widen at the prospect. *Finally, they might capture a ship worthy of the chase!* He felt wary, however, as he had witnessed Captain Jennings' brutality with his own eyes. He wasn't sure if he could join such a man, but he knew pirating was a blood-thirsty business. Looking at Paul, he saw the same misgivings in his eyes.

"Aye, we'll join ye on your next chase, but I cannot promise ye after that," Sam said.

Captain Jennings nodded and then offered up his tankard in a toast. "To the next adventure!" They clanked their tankards together, spilling some of the rum, and saluted.

***

"Oh, ye hast done it now, my girl," Maria's mother lamented, having come in on Maria while she was vomiting into the basin. "I feared this 'twould happen with some feckless man turning your head with fancies."

Maria's pale face peered at her over the basin and then down as she resumed expelling her stomach contents. She had refused to divulge the name of the father, although she was certain her mother knew his identity. This would not stop the local townspeople from speculating and, possibly, attributing it to the devil in some way once her condition was known.

"Come, ye need to break your fast and get something into thy belly," her mother stated, handing her a cloth to wipe her mouth and face.

"Aye, mother, 'tis a child of love, and we shall be married upon his return with none the wiser," Maria told her.

"Nay, ye are already too far along for the old gossips here not to be able to count the months and know 'twas conceived far before the nuptials."

Maria emptied the basin out the window and returned it to under her bed. Her mother sat bawling into her apron and then wringing her hands. Maria rolled her eyes, as teenagers have done since time began, and sat beside her.

"Mother, I beg ye, do not tell Father until the last possible moment. I hope Sam will return by the next moon and have enough money to provide for us to your satisfaction." Maria hugged her mother, who continued the cycle of bawling and handwringing. Maria winced, realizing she had revealed Sam as the father.

"I knew it was that lackabout farmer! However, I fear your father knows, my dove, and is waiting to see if ye carry it to term. He knows that babes do not often survive in the womb, and he has no wish to see harm come to his daughter. However, do not mistake his patience for forgiveness; he will see justice done even to his child. Ye must surely pay a fine, but I doubt ye will receive lashings since he has influence in this town."

At this time, children out of wedlock were to be avoided, although it was hard without birth control. There are many tales of men who seduce young women with promises of marriage only to leave the girls to face the consequences once the men have gifted them with their bodies.

"I beg ye, reconsider the offer of Goodman Carver. He is a good God-fearing man and would provide for ye. If the banns are posted, and hurry is made, then ye can say the child is his. I believe he will take the child for his own and raise it."

Maria had thought about the dowry offered by Goodman James Carver; it was appropriate, and he would provide for her and the baby. Her heart, however, would always belong to Sam, and she could not bear the thought of giving it to another man or letting someone else touch her body.

"Nay, Mother, I cannot live a lie and 'twould be a lie being wed to Goodman Carver, not to mention the boredom he and the rest of the men in this town offer."

"Methinks ye wish too much for adventure, and ye now pay the consequences, for I do not foresee thy lover returning anytime soon."

"Mayhap, Mother, but I beg ye to let it alone for another month, and we shall see if my fondest wish is granted."

Maria's mother left, and Maria knew, at that moment, that Sam would not make it back in time to save her from ridicule and hardship. She began planning her escape and knew precisely where she would go.

The dunes of the coast were where she could build a hut and keep a watchful eye out for her beloved's return. It would be the perfect place for her to hide her advancing pregnancy and be the first to greet the ship when it made port as it would sail right past her.

Not wasting a moment, she packed what she could in her rucksack, grabbed bread and cheese from the cupboard, and stuffed *The Pilgrim's Progress* inside as well. A knock sounded on her door as she cinched it closed.

"Maria," a voice called softly, and Maria recognized her childhood nanny and friend, Gladys.

"Aye, Gladys, come in," she said near the door.

"Here ye go, milady, a bit of tea to help ye get to sleep," Gladys told her loudly as she closed the door, peering around it to ensure no one was nearby.

Once inside, Gladys handed Maria the tea but then admonished her once she noted Maria's rucksack and supplies. Lowering her voice, Gladys told her, "Nay, milady, ye will not survive out in the wilds, especially with winter approaching. I do not believe thy father will treat ye so harshly as you imagine."

"Aye, Gladys, 'twill be exactly as I fear. Ye heard my mother and her words. They shall not be able to stave off curiosity and the law for long once I am discovered." Turning, Maria picked up her items and reached for her cloak. "Please, do not betray this confidence, for you are my dearest and truest friend."

"No worries, my little dandelion-head, I shall not betray ye, but ye must also take care. Where shall ye go?"

"I know of a place among the dunes on a beach near the coastal edge of Justice Doane's land. He never goes out there, and it is well hidden."

"Then I shall help ye and bring ye supplies and news when I can get away."

Maria hugged Gladys, glad to have an ally. Looking outside her room and ensuring no one was around, Maria slipped out and escaped the home and farm she had known her entire life to start her own adventure.

***

"Holy crap! Seriously, though, what was the big deal? She was pregnant and, according to history, she's not the first one to do that without marriage." Clarissa's face was the epitome of an indignant teenager.

"Oh, yes, she was not the first, but you must remember her parents' times and standing in the community. Only about twenty-five years had passed since the Salem Witch Trials, and that shadow still covered their memories. Humans can be cruel." Loyd moved over and stoked up the fire again. "It wouldn't take much for someone to point at her and say, 'That's the devil's spawn,' or some such thing, and then her life would be over."

"Oh man, I can't imagine getting out of this house now, and I'm sixteen, as well. It had to have been even scarier for her at that time and before indoor plumbing and heating. I can't imagine how cold living out on the dunes with the winds sweeping through there could get. I can't imagine those were lesser way back then," Clarissa told everyone.

Laura hugged her and told her, "We couldn't imagine you doing such a thing, either! I can't even imagine a mother who would force their child into such decisions, but I'm also not a Puritan or stodgy old lady with no rights and living at my husband's bidding."

"Now, let's find out how Sam did at pirating!" Loyd said, changing the subject. Sitting near the fireplace, he once again tells the story of Sam's education by Captain Jennings.

Chapter 12: *The Sainte Marie*

Off the coast of Cuba, 1716

"See that ship on the horizon, lads?" Using the telescope, Captain Jennings pointed out the water's shape. "That shall be ye're prize today, and we'll see how you do with it."

"I wish to join ye, *por favor*," said a voice on the deck.

The voice belonged to a young man, around sixteen, with skin the color of dark tobacco, eyes like onyx set in a strong face, and a stature barely reaching Sam's height but lithe in form.

"Aye, lads, this is John Julian; he's a Miskito Indian from inland here in Central America," Jennings said, introducing them. "He's young, but he be the best damn pilot ye could get for these waters!"

"We welcome ye, John, and glad to have ye to help," Sam said, shaking John's hand.

Sam, Paul, and John returned to the ship and crew for planning. The ship Jennings had pointed out was smaller but would work for their initiation.

Once aboard Sam's ship, he introduced the crew to John Julian, and then Paul shouted orders in preparation for the capture of the ship that had moved closer to the coast.

Sam looked through the telescope and mentally plotted the best course to intercept his prey. Smiling to himself, he felt something being pressed into his palm. Paul smiled as Sam saw Paul had placed a pistol in his hand.

"What do ye with this?" he asked.

Paul smiled and said, "Well, 'tis like this. I noted it stuck amongst some other small arms on Jenning's ship, but the space looked cramped, and it was unable to breathe properly. You know how I hate for things to be cramped and unable to breathe," he said to Sam.

Sam shook his head, laughing, as he put the pistols into the band of the sash around his waist to join the previous one Paul gave him.

The sails went up, and the wind caught them, propelling them forward to the sound of cheers from Jenning's ship in encouragement. Sam, grinning, stood at the bow, imagining how they must look to the poor ship that was about to be captured.

"Close on, aim cannon to starboard, heave to, lads!" Paul was in his element as he snapped out directions like a seasoned mariner.

At the helm, John Julian showed no emotion as he maneuvered the ship following Paul's direction. Only a few times did John correct Paul or give his own advice. He seemed ill at ease doing so as if he had not been heeded in the past. Once he saw Paul and Sam were listening to him, his voice grew stronger as he contributed to the instructions.

"One shot across their bow to help them decorate their underwear, me lads," shouted Sam.

A cannon fired, and a ball flew close to the ship but did not make it all the way. It splashed into the waters just shy of the ship's hull. A very embarrassed crewman shouted his apologies to Sam as he tried to retake aim.

"Nay, 'tis hopefully enough for them to notice us. Now, to arms, lads, and cry out as loud as you can and wave your swords."

As Sam's ship pulled near the other ship, he noted the main sails were down, and they were waiting for them. *He could not believe his luck! This could not possibly be this easy.* They boarded and found all the men waiting on the deck, including the captain. Putting on his sternest face, Sam walked up to the captain and made his demands, which the captain quickly capitulated. Soon, Sam and his crew were looting the ship.

"Will ye take our ship, pirate? Will ye at least let us put down our small canoes and make our way to the mainland?" asked the captain of the captured ship.

Looking thoughtful, Sam looked at Paul who nodded and told the captain, "Not for me, this ship, for what I seek shall be grander and faster than this little scull. Ye may keep your ship, but your loot belongs to us."

Sam left Paul to oversee the looting and, as Sam's quartermaster, equal distribution of the goods once they were back on their own ship. Just as Sam saw Jenning's ship sailing up behind him, he heard shouts from its decks and saw the main sails fly up, and it took off like a shot by Sam's vessel.

Running to his bow, Sam took out the telescope and spied a ship in the distance, much larger than the one he had just looted. Focusing on the ship's nameplate, he saw it was *The Sainte Marie.*

Jennings shouted to Sam, "Ye earned your status with that little canoe; now earn your manhood with this one! 'Tis full of gold, and I want it in one piece for 'tis a spectacular build!"

Having stowed all their stolen goods, Sam's crew jumped back to their positions to raise the sails and get underway after Jennings. This time, as they approached the ship, however, it began firing cannons back at them.

"This dog has a loud bark, it seems," said Paul.

"Aye let's see if it has the teeth to back it up," shouted Sam in reply.

Jennings's ship pulled up on the port side as John Julian moved Sam's ship along the starboard, both keeping out of firing distance of the ship of prey. Knowing Jennings did not want to hit the ship and damage it in any way, Sam went over the options in his head. Finally, he looked up to see his crow's nest and the man leaning out.

"Do ye think you can set a grappling hook in their mast?" he asked the man. Masts could be easily repaired.

"Oh, aye, captain, that I can! 'Tis easier than casting out lobster cages!" the man said, readying his grappling hook.

Sam's ship moved closer and finally within range, so the man in the crow's nest let fly, and it crashed through the main sail and embedded in the mast pole. The sudden jerking of Sam's ship against the other ship brought it to a halt and almost over on its side. Sam grinned at the confusion breaking out on the French ship's decks as they tried to determine how they were stopped.

The captain stepped out and sighted through his telescope to see Sam and Jennings alongside him. With a look of defeat, he ordered his men to stand down and prepare for boarding. He also muttered about animals in French, so Sam figured it was just an affectation of the French men to curse so oddly.

Sam, Paul, Jennings, and Charles Vane boarded from their respective sides and met with the captain. Jennings immediately grabbed the front of the captain's uniform and demanded to know the gold's location. The captain denied it and did not give any indication where the gold was hidden, ending with spitting a wad of tobacco juice in Captain Jennings's face.

Jennings wiped his face with his scarf, then addressed Sam and Paul, saying, "Ye lads tend to the others while me crew questions these lads."

Sam felt uneasy about the look in Jennings' eyes but, as a new man in the fold, still wanted to impress him and did as he was told. Soon, Sam could hear the splash of bodies hitting the water and boats being launched. Jennings came up to the quarterdeck where Sam and Paul stood, wiping his hands and sword on his sash.

Sam felt his face pale and asked in almost a whisper, "What did you do, Captain?"

Jennings smiled and said, "The good captain and some of his crew have decided to abandon ship."

Sam cringed but had to ask, "All of them?"

Jennings looked out over the water and then back to Sam. "Nay, lad, some of them were stubborn, so they can tell their secrets to the fishes now."

Sam closed his eyes, silently sending up prayers for those who were only upholding the honor of their new ruler, King Louis XV, and the country of France, no matter who was in charge. It was known King Louis XIV ruled for seventy-two years and only passed that same year. According to stories Sam heard in various ports, the new king was beloved but useless when it came to matters of state.

Others of *The Sainte Marie's* French crew were press-ganged into service under Jennings if they had a needed skill. None of them protested when faced with the consequences of refusal.

Once they were back in dock, both ships emptied of cargo and re-packed for the next voyage. Captain Jennings took Sam aside, put an arm around him, and turned him towards the open waters.

"There, aye, there ye see it. 'Tis a wide-open field for us to take what be ours and damn those who try to stop us!" Jennings turned Sam towards the docks where men were readying another ship. "Those are our stallions, and they shall take us to our glory. They shall be the chariots on which we ride to fame and fortune. If ye stay with me, lad, ye shall reap the benefits and learn ye a thing or two about pirating."

Sam couldn't get the image of men being pushed overboard or

swords slicing open their bellies as they begged for their lives. Men with families depended on them and only wanted a chance to improve themselves. Knowing he could not betray the thoughts on his face, he schooled his countenance in stone and nodded as if acquiescing to Jennings' statements.

Later, Sam and Paul sat in the tavern while others of their crews talked about the capture of the French ship and of the torture the men endured under Jennings' "questioning." Some thought it was duly given, while many others whispered cruelty but not loud enough to be heard by Jennings's crew. Paul sat, nursing his ale, staring at the table, and lost in thought. Sam's mind raced with his thoughts of the day, and he began questioning his choice to turn pirate.

A hand thumped down a tankard at their table, and John Julian joined them. He looked around the room and leaned in closer to Sam and Paul.

"This room…*muy enojada*…very angry," John said, furtively stealing glances at the gathered men. "Captain Jennings is an exacting leader with no tolerance for things such as mercy and benevolence."

Sam's crew was clearly on one side of the room, with

Jennings' crew on the other, glaring at each other. A few sat in between, so Sam didn't know where those loyalties lay. Today had been eye-opening for many of his crew and probably just another day for the other crew. Paul chuckled softly, then looked over at Jennings, who had two young women on his lap who had a stern look about them, saying they had been used poorly most of their lives.

"He sits as a king in his court with the fawning courtiers doting on him and him enjoying his own riches and self-appreciation," Paul said, shaking his head. "'Tis a murderer and no doubt on that, my friend. I do not wish to follow those footsteps as they can only lead to the gallows with a stretched neck."

Sam nodded, concurring with that statement, but he didn't know how to extricate them without more bloodshed. Suddenly, a thought occurred to him as he remembered The Scalawags of his youth and their plans. A slow smile spread across his face as he leaned over the table to the two men and said, "I have a plan. Are ye with me?"

The two men smiled and softly said, "Aye," as Sam told them of his plan.

***

Sea birds called shrilly across the sands as winter gave way to spring. Maria sat on a small stool outside the small hut she had built with her hands near Marconi Beach. It was not very sturdy, but she had made her own home with added branches and pieces of driftwood over time. She had survived the long winter with Gladys's help, who gave her supplies, rumors, and news whenever she snuck into town to meet with her.

Today was her next meeting with Gladys, and Maria waited as the sun moved lower on the horizon so darkness could help hide her. As always, she looked out to the horizon, hoping to see sails that belonged to Sam, but six months had come and gone with no sighting. Maria sighed and placed a hand on her enlarged belly, knowing her time was growing closer as she estimated herself to be six months along.

Gathering her bags with items she had knitted for Gladys to hand out to others, she slowly approached the town's stable. The sound of the horses would cover any sounds or conversations she had with Gladys, and she always brought an apple for them, so they looked forward to her visits.

Gladys waited in the shadows and stepped out only when she saw Maria and hugged her. "Oh, my child, look at ye! 'Tis been a month since I could see ye last, and ye look ragged, child," she said.

Maria hugged her and gave her the bag with the knitting. "What news hast ye, Gladys?"

Gladys placed the bag on the ground and turned to Maria, wringing her arthritic hands despite the pain. "Ye have been outed, girl, and thy father hast paid the fine for ye. The elders still call for the name of the father of thy babe."

"They can call and scream for all I care," Maria said obstinately. "'Tis my secret to keep and none of their concern. They will know rightly enough when my love returns to claim me and our child."

Gladys looked around fretfully and said, "Thy name is also being slandered; they call ye a witch!"

Maria's eyes widened as she remembered the witch hysteria that had engulfed the colonies not too long before she was born. It was a very severe accusation and came with a death sentence. She sighed, closed her eyes, and shook her head.

"'Tis not of a moment's thought, dear Gladys, my reputation was golden, and I doubt even my carefree abandon towards life will shade their belief in my innocence. My father would not put up with such tales."

"Oh, my love, my darling girl, thy name has become but dust under their feet with the news you have lost your maidenhead to a drifter of no name and now carry his bastard beneath your apron." Gladys stifled a sob as she hugged Maria once more.

Maria still firmly believed she would not be punished but now had an inkling of how deeply she was in trouble. However, now she was alerted to be wary. A small cramping pain settled low in her stomach, and she gasped.

"What is happening, child?" asked Gladys, placing her hands on Maria's shoulders.

The pain lessened and then disappeared. Maria patted Gladys's hands and assured her, "Nought, Gladys, 'twas just a gas twinge, naught more and already passed."

Gladys, more knowledgeable in such things, cautioned Maria, "That pain is but the beginning, my child, and ye are soon to see your babe if that continues. I shall come to ye when I can and help ye bring your babe into this world."

Maria nodded, took the bags of foodstuffs and supplies Gladys gave her, and made her way back to her hut on the beach. Over the next month, the baby would drop lower in her stomach, and she knew her time was nearing. She hoped Gladys could make her way quickly when the time came as she did not trust any of the midwives.

***

The wind outside Loyd's home had calmed a little so that the whole house wasn't shaking anymore. The clock's ticking gave way to soft bongs, indicating it was ten o'clock and most of the storm had passed.

Clarissa looked at Charlie, then back at Loyd, saying, "I have a bad feeling, and I don't know if it's for Sam or Maria."

William looked at his daughter, smiling, "Young kids always think they know how the world runs, and they will be the exception, most times."

"Did you seriously just say 'kids these days,' Dad?" Clarissa asked.

William laughed, saying, "Well, kids, *those* days and today."

Laura smacked him on the shoulder.

"Carry on, Dad," William said, rubbing his shoulder and smiling at Laura.

Clarissa picked up her phone, sighed, and put it down again. "Yep, keep going, Grandpa, and take my mind off my boyfriend's lack of communication."

"Sam had a grand plan, and it would prove to be a major turning point in his career as a pirate," Loyd told them.

Chapter 13: An Old Gag and a New Life

Still off the coast of Cuba, 1716

Water slapped against the hull of *The Sainte Marie* as she stood in her berth at the dock. Snores and gastric emissions could be heard over the bells on ship decks, which rang in time with each wave's movement in a lulling and sleepy motion.

Figures dressed in dark clothes and weapons wrapped and covered to hide and muffle them, stalked towards the French ship's gangway and deck. Motioning with hand signals, one of the figures beckoned the others into the vacant captain's quarters since Jennings was still holding court in the tavern even this late at night. He had decreed the ship would be his flagship now and had not yet started the process of moving his belongings over.

Unbeknownst to Jennings, belongings had been snuck over in various trunks and bags, just not his. As the figures moved silently across the deck, some split off to go down the ladder to the decks below, where the crew had their sleeping areas. One of them, the one giving the commands, slipped up to the helm area along with a shorter shadow figure.

The figure in the lead to the decks below hailed the men in their sleeping berths softly, barely a whisper. The crew, who were sitting up and pretending to snore, smiled and nodded. The ones emitting the gastric emissions let more rip, which was no problem after ale and the lousy food at the tavern.

Waving a hand in front of his face, the lead person below indicated for them to make ready the ship. The commanding figure on the top deck motioned to the more petite man beside him to take the ship's wheel. Other black-cloaked men moved along the sides of the decks, removing ropes and slowly drawing up the anchor in time with the bells and other night noises to cover up the sound.

The sun began to break over the horizon, illuminating the ship as it was pushed away from the dock and drifted towards the bay opening. Someone on shore finally noticed the movements and shook off their hangover long enough to raise the alarm.

Captain Jennings and most of his crew stumbled from the tavern in time to see the ship making its way for the open waters. He began shouting for his crew to load up his ship and give chase. His men tried to get underway; however, the sailors found as the ship started moving that the ropes were all knotted, and the anchor had been drawn up and wrapped around the tavern building.

Loud creaking and groaning were heard as the building moved, pulled by the anchor rope. Several islanders ran outside and attempted to hold it up, but Jennings' ship was more robust, and soon, the tavern crashed down and was pulled into the bay.

Looking out over the water to *The Sainte Marie*, Captain Jennings saw men waving at him from the deck and shouting. It took a few seconds for the sound to travel, but eventually, he heard them.

"We thank ye for your hospitality and the gift of this lovely ship!" Sam and Paul waved from the forecastle as the ship pulled away and out to sea.

Silently, Sam chuckled, remembering how Jib had pulled

almost this same feat of pulling a prize from under the enemy's noses. Some of Jennings' crew had joined them, and Paul got everyone squared away in duties and sleeping arrangements.

Sam looked at his old crew and the new additions with pride. He was in awe that so many wanted to join his crew, and many colors and cultures were represented before him. His men knew no prejudice against color or nationality. He waited until they were out in open waters before calling the men to gather on the deck.

Pirates from all walks of life gathered below and stared up at Sam, with Paul looking on from beside him.

Paul spoke to Sam quietly, saying, "I took the liberty of mixing the old crew with the new, and there were some who requested to have…the same berth," he said wryly.

Sam nodded and smiled since he was a believer in "live and let live" in this world. It mattered not to him who bunked with whom on his ship as long as the work was done. His new crew wore items denoting their culture and creeds, and all were accepted. Piracy was harsh and cruel, most times, but they were truly the first people to show belief in equality and for every voice to be heard. Sam queried his new crew and asked if they were willing to join him and find the riches they deserved.

"Are ye ready for adventure, lads?"

The crew cheered, and yells of "aye" were heard across the entire ship. Smiling faces peered up at Sam, finally gaining the freedom they wanted when they first signed on as pirates.

"Do ye stand with me, men?" Sam yelled the question.

"Aye" was heard again and was like a wave around the entire ship, gaining momentum and passion as it went until finally it was back to Sam.

"This ship is grand, but I know in me bones there 'tis one out there for us that would bring even a king to his knees," Sam said with conviction.

More cheers followed his announcement, and Paul bellowed orders to put up sails and find their next conquest. The next thing Sam knew, a compass was sitting on his stool near the helm. He looked around and happened to see Paul's grin as the man moved away, still calling out orders. Sam just shook his head figuring it had been lonely or cramped somewhere. He added it to the four pistols and telescope he already had in his sash and moved to the railing. The weight of the items in his sash was somewhat comforting.

Just as the sails snapped open and the ship began to move, a cry from the crow's nest sounded. "Ship, ahoy, to the starboard and off the east!"

Sam and Paul both looked through the telescope, and then Sam grinned.

"Stand down, men; we know that old sea dog!" Sam gestured to John Julian to move them into a position for the ship to intercept them.

Soon, the other ship pulled alongside them with the name *The Happy Return* emblazoned across the back. Sam couldn't believe his luck happening across Captain Hornigold now of all times.

"Ahoy, *the Sainte Marie*, prepare for boarding!" cried a sailor on the approaching ship.

Soon, Captain Hornigold came across Edward Teach following close behind. They shook hands with Sam and Paul, and Sam led them to the captain's quarters. Hornigold did not seem surprised to find Sam as the captain of the ship.

Staring at Edward, Paul finally asked, "What happened to the beard, Edward?"

Edward, smiling, said, "'Tis how I scare the enemy, my friend. I light the ends of my beard afire, and they believe the very devil comes for them!"

Paul shook his head and moved slightly away from Edward, trying to be subtle.

"I shall not mince words, and it was fate to meet ye here, Sam, but I thought you had tied your mast to Jennings?" Hornigold asked.

"Nay, Captain, I but sought instruction, and he was more brutal than I wanted," Sam answered.

"Aye, he has a heavy hand in his dealings with captured ships and crew and his man Charles Vane is worse than him, so it gladdens me to see ye do not take the same stance," Hornigold said. "I want to offer to have ye join me as we seek out Spanish gold and fame for our deeds."

Sam and Paul conferred and agreed to his request.

"Excellent, we will make our way to Tortuga, a small island that is…hospitable…to our kind," Hornigold instructed.

Later, after drinking about each other's health and swapping news, Hornigold and Teach returned to their own ship. Sam gave orders for *The Sainte Marie* to follow *The Happy Return* to their new home dock.

***

Two months had passed since Maria last saw Gladys, and the pains began to come more often and closer together. Fearing her old nanny had been found out, she felt she needed to make her way home. She could not do this herself, and she sought her mother's comfort and help. She hoped enough time had passed that she would be able to be welcomed home and at least given somewhere warm and dry to sleep, even if she were sent to her room with no one to talk to her.

As she trudged through the sand and over the dunes then through the snow towards town, the moon lit her way. Torches lit up the area and flickered around the town square, and she attempted to hide from the lights as best she could. It was difficult as she lost flexibility and stealth as her girth expanded, and now she was no better than a clumsy cow in the field.

Soon, she passed near the fences, indicating she was close to town, but a voice rang out asking, "Who goes there?" Silently cursing her ungainly speed, she froze as she tried to think of a plan.

Maria tried to keep silent and continue on her way, but a pain caught her unawares, and she gasped loudly. Dogs barked, and soon, men came out of their homes to see what was causing the ruckus. Maria felt despair as she knew she would not make it to her home in time. Looking around wildly, trying to find anywhere to offer her shelter, she spied the barn belonging to John Knowles outside the town and away from the men giving chase.

Waddling wildly, she kept to the shadows and made it into the barn, breathing heavily and feeling as if she needed to squat and bear down as the pains began in earnest and were not letting up. She moved into the darkest corner she could find with the cows eyeing her balefully as they stood chewing their cud. They were not like that rebel, Lily, and knew how to perform one job at a time.

Laying out her cloak, she sat upon it and tried to even her breathing. The barking dogs and men moved away further off down the road towards Eastham. One of the men stopped a short way from the barn, talking to the others.

"I spied hair of gold that could only be that witch living on the beach," he said. "We still have not made the nurse talk, so a few more days in the stocks should loosen her tongue."

Maria gasped softly. Gladys *had* been caught; now, there was no doubt. Maria's heart swelled as she understood Gladys was not giving way to her secrets and sought, even now, to protect her. She also understood there would be no protection or help at home.

She thought frantically of what to do now. The barn offered some protection, but the air was still chilled, and she had no birthing supplies, nor could she make a fire. A pain ripped through her, taking away the last of her coherent thoughts. Nausea rose swiftly, and she put a hand over her mouth to try and keep her food down.

When the feeling passed, she looked around and saw bales of hay near the corner. Pulling some loose, she created a bed as best she could and then hovered over it as she felt her time nearing.

The need to bare down and push was overwhelming, so Maria continued to squat as she had seen servants do when they gave birth. Her hips felt as if they were splitting apart as she continued to bare down with each pain and pressure.

She rested when she could between pains and stood to walk around when she was able, thinking it would help move the baby down. Finally, after a few hours, the need to deliver was too strong to ignore, and the baby was crowning, and she could stifle her screams no longer. Wrenching sobs and screams accompanied her pushing and the baby's head crowning. She could reach down and feel it and gave silent thanks the babe was not turned the wrong way or had a cord around its neck.

Pushing a few more times helped the baby get its head and shoulders out, and then she caught the baby as best she could to lay it gently upon the ground on her blanket and covered the babe as best she could. A bit later, as she sat back against a hay bale, the door to the barn opened, and light from torches flooded the area. Outlined in the light was none other than John Knowles, who had heard the screams and came running thinking one of his cows was in trouble.

Maria, sitting in blood and weary, could only stare up at him as he towered over her. He bent, moved the blanket away from the baby, and jumped back, pointing an accusatory finger at her.

"Murder, murder most foul, ye witch!" He yelled and then ran out to get the other men.

In her weary state, Maria didn't comprehend his words immediately, and it was with a lunge that she picked up the baby once she understood what he had yelled. Her baby, a precious baby boy, was stillborn. Her mind fogged, and her breaths came quickly as the import of her unmoving child's body slammed into her. No, she thought, no, not our babe. She promptly struck the baby's back and attempted to start breathing. She stuck her finger down its throat but found no obstruction. However, nothing she did was to any avail as the baby's blue pallor did not brighten, nor did the eyes open. No breath passed his lips, and she realized she had never heard the birthing cry that babies give when they join the world.

Sobs wracked Maria as she cradled the child, unbelieving what had happened. She slapped at the hands that suddenly appeared around her as they attempted to take the baby from her.

"Leave go, witch, ye shall not have this babe for your infernal rites!" a man said.

"Nay, nay, nay, 'tis not what it seems! I have birthed him, and he was gone before I could hold him!" Maria cried.

"Ye are a witch, and so shall ye be named. Ye murdered thy babe to cover the sin ye committed in its conception," the man accused. "Ye shall be tried and hanged as soon as possible, evil one." He grabbed the blanket with its lifeless occupant and strode out.

Women came in and helped her expel the afterbirth; then, they dragged her to the cells in the constable's office. She was given a basin of cold water and a rag to wipe herself with and clean up as best she could. Maria felt numb and did not register anything happening. Their child, the child conceived with such love, was gone. She could not think past the next minute, let alone how she would tell Sam.

Feelings of anger rose in her. If he had not left, this would not have happened! She imagined he was off having the adventure of a lifetime while she was here, enduring such abuse and ridicule and now having lost their child.

No, that is not right; sailing life could not be any easier. He only left to give us a better life. Maria thought her brain played tricks on her and knew it was not Sam's fault that any of this happened. If only she had begged him to stay but could no longer keep him from leaving than she could become a proper young lady.

Sitting on the stone bench, her back against the wall, she closed her eyes and tried to sleep, knowing she would need her strength in the days to come. Her last thought was of a tiny cherubic face with his eyes closed, so perfect and only hers for a short time. She prayed for God to watch over his little soul.

***

"Okay, if anyone else gets pregnant in your story, I'm leaving. This is awful!" Clarissa lamented.

Laura smiled sadly, "It was a hard life, and Maria had it harder than most."

"Some stories say she gave birth to a live baby, but then it choked on a piece of hay or froze in the cold while she went out to get food," Loyd said. "I prefer the tale that he was stillborn and didn't have to suffer."

"Please tell me this gets less depressing; can we go back to the ship stuff?" asked Charlie. "Sam's got a good ship now, right?"

Loyd settled back and continued his tale. "He has a good ship now, and he's under Hornigold's tutelage, so things are definitely looking up for him, and he has no idea of the tragedy that occurred with his child, which is sad."

Chapter 14: *The Marianne*

Island of Tortuga, 1716

Sam, Paul, and many of the crew gathered around the pirate's haven, listening to stories from old sea dogs as well as the banter of crewmates as they tried to one-up each other in their heroics. Women were plentiful and did not want any strings attached, which suited the men as they didn't want to tie any strings themselves. Sam declined the advances of several, as did Paul, who still had a family waiting for him back home.

The air was ripe with bawdy laughter, swirling pipe and cigar smoke, and dingy furnishings, but Sam still felt welcome. Hornigold kept his word and introduced many of his crew once they arrived on the island by small canoes while their ships anchored further out to sea.

Hornigold's ship was big and fast, boasting musicians and many skilled artisans to keep it alive and afloat. Some of the men introduced to Sam would later be part of his crew: Richard Caverly (Rhode Island), Peter Cornelius Hoof (Swedish-born), John Fletcher, and Jeremiah Higgins.

Those men and Sam's crew melded together quickly, and Hornigold's men volunteered to crew with Sam's men to teach them the ropes, so to speak. It was the start of a very cohesive arrangement. Edward Teach was learning to lead on his own and would soon be leading his own crew.

After celebrating till night had long-held reign, the two crews went to their separate ships to sleep and prepare for the next day.

Dawn came with a blazing sun as the heat settled early in that part of the hemisphere in late May 1716. The crews of both ships got underway, and soon, they were all headed northwest toward Cuba.

A few days out, a sloop was spotted that Hornigold recognized as carrying valuable cargo, and he signaled for both ships to come to a stop as the other ship approached. Hornigold, standing near the quarterdeck railing, shouted across to Sam.

"Heave to, lads! There is a worthy opponent and of French origin!" Hornigold gestured to the ship off their starboard side.

Paul started the relay of orders to ready their ship for possible battle, and Sam instructed John Julian to turn *The Sainte Marie* to follow *The Happy Return*. Shouts were heard from the enemy ship when the enemy crew spied them, and Sam could see the cannon doors opening on the sloop.

She was a beauty, and her name was *The Marianne*. Sam liked her lines, and he saw that she was built for speed and could be a great asset in chasing down other ships. In addition to a central mast and two smaller ones, it had gaff rigging between the boom and the topmast. This design enabled it to capture the wind from more directions than the typical ship build.

Cannon fired at *The Happy Return,* which was turning to place their cannon range within limits. Soon, they answered the sloop's cannon volley with their own, and theirs managed to hit part of the sloop's deck.

"Easy now, lads," yelled Hornigold. "She's a beauty; we want to keep her as together as possible!"

The battle was over as soon as *The Marianne* spotted *The Sainte Marie* coming from behind *The Happy Return*. They were outmatched and surrounded, and they knew it. The white flag soon rose, and Hornigold accepted, yelling for his boarding crew.

On board *The Marianne*, the captain gathered his crew, and they awaited their verdicts. Captain Hornigold walked among them, finding out what skills they had to see if there were any needed aboard *The Happy Return*. After divvying up the goods, Hornigold gave the crew the same offer many pirates made to their captives: join or leave. Some crew chose to stay with Hornigold, and Hornigold let the captain and any who decided to leave to take one of the small sailing boats. Hornigold took over command of *The Marianne,* thus beginning Sam's real introduction to piracy. He let the captain and crew of *The Marianne* take one of his pirogues and leave.

The Happy Return, *The Sainte Marie*, and *The Marianne* formed a flotilla of ships that moved along the Cuban seas in concert. Sam added Hendrick Quintor and John Brown to his crew, both of African-American descent, and he believed he had a genuinely phenomenal crew and could take on anything. However, his heart still ached for his Maria, and he constantly checked the cargo to see when he believed he would have enough to return home. It was never enough, though, and he continued to search for his prize ship. The one that would be large enough to burst with all the treasure he would capture. He wondered how she had fared and knew the babe had to be born by now. He spent the rest of the day imagining the baby and the homecoming he would receive, with Maria and her family welcoming him with open arms.

Paul walked up to stand with him, putting an arm across Sam's shoulders. "Ye should rejoice, my friend! Look ye at the haul!" Paul pointed out the various cargo stacks around the ship. "This is a remarkable ship; she'll race the wind!"

Sam agreed this ship was going to be perfect for harnessing the wind and chasing down other ships. He nodded and shook off his melancholy mood. This was a time for celebrating!

Hornigold hailed them and said they were moving on to the Cape of Corrientes and the ships that traveled through there that needed relieving of their goods.

Soon, they were chasing ships through the cape and Isle of Pines areas, adding to their crews and cargo holds. Sam learned more about the art of pirating, and Paul grew more confident in his supervision of the crew and their duties over the next month.

One day, off the coast of Cuba, Hornigold alerted Sam to a sail on the horizon. A Jolly Roger, the name given to a pirate flag, with an outline of a skeleton splayed out on the field of black, snapped in the winds.

"Ye shall like this one, I wager. 'Tis La Buse 'The Buzzard' himself, Olivier Lavasseur!" Hornigold snapped his telescope closed and beckoned to his bosun to get ready for boarding. The ship, *The Postillion,* pulled closer to Hornigold's ship.

Sam looked at the ship that pulled up and shouted for his men to do the same. Paul approached him, and Sam asked if Paul had heard of the man. Sam spied Olivier through his telescope and noted a patch covering one eye and a swagger to his step as he walked along the rail.

"Oh, aye, I know of him, and he was usually in the company of John Taylor, who got his start under the pirate Edward England. According to my knowledge, the Buzzard was born in Calais to wealth and attended the best schools, landing a naval officer billet."

Sam thought a moment, then remembered where he knew the name. "Aye, I remember his name from the Spanish War! I think I heard he turned privateer, but apparently, he decided piracy more to his liking?"

"So, it would seem! Let's go meet the man!" Paul shouted as he headed for the boarding planks.

After getting settled into Captain Hornigold's quarters, the men were introduced to The Buzzard, an average-looking man with a scar that went from his forehead to his cheek and sported an eye patch over that eye. La Buse noted their scrutiny and addressed them.

"*Oui*, I lost my eye to a rogue that imagined himself my better during the War. He took my eye, and I took out his liver with my sword!" La Buse said, chuckling.

Hornigold gestured towards La Buse's ship and inquired how it went for the pirate.

"Very well, very well, indeed. Privateering was not for me, too boring, too…*pas stimulant*…not exciting, *non*?" La Buse said, "I desire for the adventure, the possibilities."

"You are welcome to join us, La Buse," said Hornigold. "We sail for richer waters."

He passed a tankard over to La Buse. They lifted their tankards for a toast as Hornigold said, "To the pirate brotherhood!"

If only they had known how short that brotherhood would last.

***

Maria was taken to the town center, where a whipping post had been newly installed. She had no trial, no chance to give her side of her story, no pity, and no public spectacle. She was already judged and found guilty in the eyes of the town. Her father was quick, she laughed deprecatingly to herself. She had underestimated how her freedom and carefree attitude was viewed by others.

Shivering, cold, numb with grief, and her face streaked with tears, she was tied facing the post. On her walk over, she had glimpsed many faces she had known since birth. They once adored her, and now they spit at her and gestured towards her with their thumbs holding down their middle and pinkie fingers and pointing their other two fingers in a ward against witches.

Her dress was ripped in the back as Justice Joseph Doane,

believing he was doing God's work, wanted to ensure the whip had enough room to taste flesh. Plus, he was angry to know she had been living on his land. Maria looked toward her right and saw poor Gladys in the stocks, shivering and suffering from the weather and starvation. Despite those things, Gladys nodded to Maria in apology and support.

Beloved Maria, fallen so far in the eyes of the town and now suspected of witchcraft, was already weak from childbirth and loss was a pitiful creature at that moment. Some in the crowd murmured about the act's rightness and whether she could be redeemed and saved from this punishment. There were whispers asking for lenience and for Maria to confess and repent.

Others like Goodman Carver, who once willingly offered to wed Maria, now looked at her with disgust and self-righteous indignation. Their eyes were blazing with the light of those who felt they were right.

Maria's parents stood to her left, her mother clutching to her father with wracking sobs and her father staring at her stoically. Always a hard man, but there was a slight tremor to his hands as he watched his daughter, whom he had helped deliver to the gallows, stand in full view of the town with her back bared and grief shaking her body.

The city elders came together and discussed if this was the appropriate punishment, but decided the lesson needed to be taught to all in the town, not just to Maria. Judge Doane carried out the punishment swiftly and efficiently, and Maria cried out with each lash until she passed out.

The jailors roused her and led her to her cell, laid her on her stomach on the straw pallet on the ground with only her ragged dress as a blanket, and left her fate to the mercy of God. She eventually woke up and used the water in a bucket provided to rinse her face and take stock of her situation.

Sitting in her cell, ill with fever and constantly shaking with cold, Maria silently vowed that when she saw Sam, she would welcome him with open arms…and then brain him with a skillet for leaving. Pulling the scraps of the dress she was wearing when arrested around her, she shivered and gazed at the wall with scratches indicating days upon it from previous prisoners. She still felt as if she had been in a haze for the past few days, which did not seem real—her time as a prisoner only made her more desirable, according to some historians. The events gave her a very fragile look inspiring the thoughts of men to ride gallantly to her rescue. Her jailor, Thomas, would check on her and try to bring her bread and watered-down gruel, but she barely touched it, only taking enough to keep her alive. Maria's stare of remorse and grief stoked up his desire to protect, and surely he could prove her no witch under his firm hand.

One evening, with the dark lit only by the torch on the wall that flickered and danced, making shadows on the wall, he delivered a small bowl to her with a spoon. Standing in the shadowed corner, Maria trod softly on her bare feet and slipped out and through the jail door into the night.

Maria ran, stumbling in the dark but determined to make it to the coast. Branches slapped her in the face, and she felt stings from various plant life and snow on the bottom of her feet. In the distance, she could hear the waves breaking on the shore and knew she was close. Finding her second wind, she put on speed and felt the sand flying behind her. Reaching the coast, however, no lights were spotted, no rescuer in the form of her love; no one was there. Voices carried behind her, and lights from torches lit their way.

Exhausted, feeling her hopes dashed, she sank to her knees in the dunes. The men captured her quickly and returned her to the cell, where she fell into a surreal dream of imagining Sam rushing to her rescue from the dingy cell and carrying her away. She did not even think about how she would tell him of the loss of their child. These dreams were only for happy thoughts.

***

"I think if I could choose a pirate name, it wouldn't be a buzzard," Charlie said, rolling his eyes. "Mine would be something cool. I'd be Crazy Eyes Charlie or something."

"You'd be Booger Snot McGee," Clarissa laughed.

Charlie looked up at Loyd and asked, "Seriously, though, how many guns does a guy need?"

Loyd chuckled and said, "as many as he can carry."

The news anchors continued their coverage of the storm and stated that it was moving out of the area and dissipating, so outlying areas needed to worry about flooding, but most of the wind had decreased in speed. Their on-scene reporter was breaking in over the newscast.

"And this just in, Great Pond is flooding over Cahoon Hollow Road, and it appears some of the roadway is eroding under the water. Please do not attempt to cross the water; you don't know how deep it is, and we want our community safe! Now, back to the studio for more storm coverage!"

Clarissa's face paled, and she looked at Loyd and said, "That's the way Reggie goes home! What if he got washed away?"

Loyd's face creased, but he knew the flooding was minor and understood Clarissa's reaction. "I'm sure he's fine; he's a smart young man. I'll continue the story, and you just keep an eye on your phone. However, let's check in and see what *The Whydah Gally* is doing as all of this is going on in the fall of 1716."

Chapter 15: Different Types of Escape

The Bahamas, Caribbean Sea 1716

The Whydah Gally cut through the pristine blue Caribbean waters as flying fish and dolphins sailed in and out of the wake. Her journey had been through rough seas, but she made it completely intact with her human cargo of about five hundred enslaved people. Some men would look at her fondly and call her "The Paradise Bird of the Golden Coast" after one of the birds that inhabited the region for which it was named.

Captain Prince surveyed the horizon from his stance at the bow, constantly vigilant after his experiences during his privateering years in the Spanish Main. He was aware that this area was rife with piracy and was only on his second voyage on this beautiful ship.

The Whydah Gally, so far, performed admirably with a full cargo below and all of the various humans and weaponry, not slowing her one knot. Her sails were full mast at the moment; however, they would make landfall soon to…unload. His lips curled as he thought of the disgust some of the crew showed when they learned they were on a slave ship. They could be disgusted all they want, he thought, until they saw the profit gained by the slave auctions.

His voyage began out of London from the English Channel into the Atlantic and then down the African coastline. He had made many stops to fill the holds, including places like Gambia, Nigeria, and Gabon. He almost felt terrible knowing the enslaved people on board from the first stop had the most misery as it took him at least two months to sail between all the ports before setting out towards the Caribbean.

They had quieted down, at least, and only moans could be heard now and again when one of the crew dribbled a ladle over their lips and tossed breadcrumbs to them like birds. Shackled as they were, moving was difficult, so they spent most of their time in one spot. Some of them were injured from the branding irons imprinting their slavery status onto their flesh. Those wounds would bleed and become infected.

Well, he thought, it's not like they were going to have a life of fun and adventure. He had acquired some through trade for gold, which the natives had no use for but were more than happy to mine the metal dust for the ship traders. Others were captured and kidnapped from villages to weaken them and let attacking enemies be victorious. The women were the most prized, especially if they were of childbearing age since they could create more enslaved people. However, that also made them rarer as villages needed them, so primarily males comprised the holds. Captain Prince thought that practice was disgusting, but he knew it happened often when the enslavers or plantation owners wanted to "sample something exotic," so to speak.

The crew took buckets full of seawater and sloshed them across the decks and slave holds daily to try and inhibit disease and dysentery. Captain Prince still didn't take chances and kept topside going only top deck or stayed in the captain's quarters.

His quartermaster, his second in command basically,

approached him to alert him to the trouble below.

"There is a slave that insists on speaking with you. He says he has information you could use, though I doubt it. I believe he is just looking for an excuse to come topside. I've heard rumblings these past few weeks from the 'cargo' in the hold," he said.

"Aye, I'll see him, though I doubt him he shall be informative, and as you say, he shall simply want to breathe fresh air," Captain Prince replied.

The male slave, about twenty-five years old, was brought before Captain Prince shackled and scarred. The man kept his head down all the way from below decks to a few feet in front of Captain Prince.

The quartermaster, pushing the man towards Captain Prince, told him, "Here is the young buck who states he has the knowledge for you, although I doubt me he even speaks the King's English."

Captain Prince waited for the man to speak. Minutes passed, and the man did nothing. Eventually, as if by some signal, the man looked up and spit into Captain Prince's face, smiling. The spit was mixed with bile and blood, and the hope might have been to incur some type of disease on him.

Quickly thinking, the bosun splashed water on the Captain's face, and the Captain wiped it with a handkerchief he gave to the bosun to burn.

"Ye have a solid pair of bollocks on ye to attempt such a thing," he told the man.

The tired and dirty man, still smiling, just continued to stare, squinting in the bright sunlight. The quartermaster shoved him down to his knees and held him down in that position.

"What shall we do with this bloody cur, Captain?" the quartermaster asked.

The Captain sized up the kneeling man and told the quartermaster, "Ye know what to do for such infractions. Ensure he is seen by others who may want to try their hand at mutiny and uprising."

Later that afternoon, the birds circled the ship and dove about one side of the hull. On that side was a rope holding the man now bruised and bloodied by the neck, dead, swaying with the waves and slamming against the hull where portholes allowed the other enslaved people to see him. Captain Prince had no more problems.

***

Somehow, the haze in Maria's mind finally lifted one day, and plans began to swirl. Looking at the various stonework and mortar around them, she noticed some of it had gouging and deep grooves. The next time they delivered her gruel, she kept the spoon and hoped they did not see its disappearance.

Working silently between guard shifts, she pried loose one of the bars at the bottom, then timed her rocking it back and forth to the nearby church carillon bell. It was slow going, but she finally managed to make an opening for her to crawl through. Losing the baby and not eating thinned her down significantly, and it was no problem for her to squeeze through in the night after everyone had gone to bed.

Dogs barked in the distance as she crept along and down to the end of the town when a voice called to her softly from the back of one of the buildings. Creeping along the side, she met the voice, and it was her dear Gladys!

"Child, ye must not go to the shore, for they know the path ye will take," Gladys warned.

Maria gasped, shocked she did not account for that, then asked,

"Will ye give me away, Gladys?"

"Nay, child, nay. Ye are like the child of my heart, and ne'er would I give ye to those men," Gladys told her. "Especially after they imprisoned me!"

"I must hie to the coast, but how? It has been longer than the six months he promised, and he must be on his way back by now," Maria lamented.

"Here, take this with ye," Gladys said, handing her a clock and basket with food and other clothes.

Maria hugged her and started towards a barn she knew of near the coast but would do for hiding until she could make her way to the shore without being spotted. It definitely was not John Knowles's barn. She ran up the ladder quickly, changed her clothes, and buried the basket beneath a pile of hay. She had barely heaped a mound of hay for her bed when she heard dogs barking outside the barn wall.

No, she thought *they could not have found her so quickly.* She bent over so she resembled another mound of hay. The noses of dogs never lie, though, and soon, the men were inside the barn and found her.

Once more, she was returned to the cell in the Eastham jail. She kicked her pallet and groaned loudly. Why couldn't they just let her go? She was hurting no one, and she was *not* a witch! This time, she wasted no time in escaping a third time. She waited until the jailor arrived with her gruel, then picked up the bucket and slammed it upside his head, knocking him down.

Once she ran outside, she ran as quickly as possible until her lungs burned with the need for air, and a cramp began in her side. Still, she ran; still, it was not enough. She was captured. Again.

This is ridiculous, she thought. *Why could they not just let her live in peace, for she had paid a high price already with her child's life?* Her body had still not recovered enough from the past week's activity, and she fell into a deep sleep.

Soon, a noise sounded down the stone hallway leading to the cells. A rhythmic *tap tap tap* in time with someone walking reached Maria in her dreams. Slowly, she woke as the sound came closer.

A man dressed in white tights, beige breeches, and red brocade vest over a silk shirt came into her view. He carried a wooden cane crafted from teak wood, tipped with a golden handle in the form of a crane, and wore a black with a gold-lace tri-corn hat.

Rising from her pallet, Maria approached the door of her cell as he approached. Stopping, he tapped his can along the door frame, and one of the bars sounded hollow when he banged against it. Dust fell, and he hit it again and then smiled when a *crack* sounded.

Laughing, he addressed her and said, "M'dear, these men could not find their heads with both hands tied behind their backs!" He hit the bar again, in time with his last word, and it cracked fully to the side.

Maria had no idea what he spoke but was grateful he appeared to want to help her. He applied pressure using his cane as a crowbar to another of the poles and wrenched it free of its mounting.

"Kind sir, do ye not fear for the sheriff to hear the noises?" Maria asked.

"Nay, m'dear, the sheriff be sorely in need of a tonic as he has caused himself a great pain in the head region, probably caused by the falling of a rock from up high," he chuckled. "Silly of him to be walking with no purpose other than to swagger like a right git under me balcony."

He pried off the bars and assisted Maria in slipping through, and they were out the door quickly. Looking around, Maria noted no one was watching, and a small crowd was around the local boarding house. She guessed that was where the "git" had earned a headache.

The man tipped his hat towards her and said, "I knew ye're lover from a previous…employment…and I know what it is to love someone enough to change ye'er ways. Waste not this opportunity, m'dear, and hie ye'erself to ye're abode on the shore."

"What name can I apply to my savior, good sir?" She inquired.

"Me name is Edward, Edward Low, but ye can address me as Ned," he replied, striding off in the opposite direction after handing her a blanket basket outside the jailhouse door.

Maria ran as fast as she could and vowed she would not return. A search was launched but over quickly as the townfolk had tired of her constant escapes, and it was decided to let her live away from the town with only her witchy powers to keep her company.

***

"I can't believe slave ships were a thing and thank God they finally left Maria alone!" Clarissa complained.

"So, was it a devil or this 'Ned Low' guy?" asked Charlie.

"No one knows for certain, and stories say it was the devil, and he made quite a deal with her in exchange for her soul. He offered her a contract, which she signed in blood, it was said, and she gained actual witch powers. We all know that was pure baloney," Loyd told them.

"I can't believe how much nonsense was believed in back then. I mean, seriously, c'mon people do better," Clarissa grumped and then sat back against the couch.

"I'm a firm believer there are things outside our realm of 'normal,' but you have to remember, there weren't a lot of science innovations for these colonists at the time, so their religion was their world, and it was rigorous.

"Think about Shakespeare's quote, 'There are more things in heaven and earth, Horatio, than are dreamt of in your philosophy,' which means even The Bard knew that there was more to faith than what could be seen," Loyd informed them.

"What do you believe, Grandpa? Do you believe in witches and devil deals and all that?" asked Charlie.

"I do, my boy, I do. There is just too much of this world that cannot be explained any other way," he answered. "Now, where were we? Ah, yes, let's get back to Sam!"

Chapter 16: The Youngest Pirate in History

Between Cuba and Hispaniola, in the Late Fall of 1716

Sam, Paul, La Buse, and Captain Hornigold stood at the captain's table as they looked over their maps. Edward Teach moved around the ship as quartermaster, ensuring everything was being done as it should, or else the culprit would face his wrath.

"Gentleman, we have captured quite a few ships and turned a profit so far. Let's continue upon this course and see what other fish may land in our net, so to speak. Agreed?" Hornigold asked.

Sam, studying the map, didn't hear the shouting outside the port windows at first, but then all the men turned and raced out the door.

"What's ahoy?" Hornigold shouted.

"Sail ahoy starboard, captain! She is a full sail and making way for the Cuban mainland!" The shipmate hollered back.

Teach gave swift orders for all three ships to follow them, taking the flagship position. Sails unfurled and snapped, catching the wind and launching the ships with a lurch to follow. La Buse shouted orders in a mix of English and French to his ship's quartermaster and bosun as Sam and Paul did likewise. Paul was able to get back aboard *The Marianne* to assist the crew.

Seaspray drenched the deck as the ships raced, and the ship's colors could be made. In the crow's nest, the shipmate yelled back down at the deck.

"Oy, Captain! It be an English ship and riding heavy in the water so she be ladened with loot, for sure!" He said with a smile stretching across his face.

Hornigold sighed heavily and closed his eyes. Rubbing a hand over his face, he called back to the helm, "All stop, helmsman! Release the sails!"

Everyone looked at each other in bewilderment. What? He can't possibly mean that. Hornigold yelled again for all the ships to stop the pursuit. La Buse looked at Hornigold askance, then issued the directives to his ship. Sam and Paul, flabbergasted, followed suit but did not understand the sudden turn of attitude.

"Gentleman, please return with me to the captain's quarters; there will be no chase today," then Hornigold turned and walked towards the cabin.

Murmuring from the crew reached Sam's ears, and they all seemed disgusted. Mutiny was not expected, but it was also not rare, and sudden decisions to keep from looting an obviously fat pigeon like that ship would not sit well.

In the cabin, Hornigold poured himself a rum and gestured towards Sam, Paul, and La Buse asking if they would also like some. All three took the offer, and then Hornigold turned to them and took a deep breath.

"Gentleman, no matter what path I follow now, I shall always be in service to my country even if it does not feel kindly towards me, most times. With this, I have vowed never to attack a ship from England. The ship that was spotted belongs to my country, and I shall not reap benefit from the holds that might be used for my family and families of others back home." So saying, Hornigold threw back the shot of rum and reached for the bottle to refill it.

"*Monsieur*, I believe you are making a grave mistake, for that bounty could fill our holds, and we could use it to finance our own families," an exasperated La Buse told him.

Hornigold closed his eyes, seemingly gathering strength again, then looked up at La Buse. "Aye, it may seem that way, but how could ye be certain unless you let it ride." Swirling the rum in his glass, he addressed Sam and Paul, "Ye may also think me diseased of the mind, but I am hale and hearty and follow my heart on such things."

Sam had no words as it never occurred to him to let any rich fish through the net they wove. Paul was shaking his head and murmuring about "sun-fried brains." Sam had to agree, but he wasn't sure he could voice such a thing since he was new to this life.

"Aye, and ye have been called the Prince of Pirates, or according to some, the Robin Hood of Pirates," Hornigold told him, shaking his head and chuckling. "Ye have good faith, and I know ye have yet to shed blood in your conquests, but I ask ye to consider the moral fiber of your being. Could ye not have loyalty to a country that birthed you?"

Sam had no time to reply as there was a banging sound on the heavy oak door, making it shake in the frame. Shouts from outside could be heard through the door. The men filed out with Hornigold in the lead and found all the ship's crew gathered on the mid-deck area and hanging from the rigging.

Teach approached them and said in a low voice to them, "I tried to explain ye're reasons, captain, but their blood is hot for the chase, and there ain't no reasonin' with them."

"It's okay, my friend; I knew it would happen one day. I just didn't think it would be so soon," he told him, patting Teach on the shoulder.

Hornigold's bosun stepped up in front of them, wringing his scarf around and around in his hands. "Captain, we have decided that was a damn foolhardy stunt ye just did and cost us a lot of loot which we ain't gonna be havin'," he told them. "We've put it to the vote, as per the articles, and have voted ye out as captain effective forthwith."

Hornigold looked around the crew and at Teach. "Do ye agree with this, Teach?"

Teach shook his head and replied, "Nay, I do not always agree with ye, and I don't really agree with this love for England, but I'll stand by ye, damn their eyes."

Hornigold addressed the crew, "If that is how ye all feel, then I cannot argue per the articles, but may God judge ye for I cannot."

Many of the crew made signs of the cross and put up their hands in an effort to ward off the evil eye, forming their hands into horns by extending their pinky and forefingers and bending their thumbs and two middle fingers back into the palm.

"It is decided, then, so who will join me, and what would you have done with me?"

"To be honest, sir, for ye are no longer captain, I shall not address ye. We also put that to the vote and have decided young Bellamy there will do for it," the bosun replied.

"I shall stand with ye," said Teach to Hornigold.

Some of the other hands on the deck agreed to follow Hornigold and left to gather their meager belongings. Hornigold turned to a shocked Sam, shaking his hand and that of La Buse.

"This is where I submit myself to ye, Captain Bellamy. What

would you have me do?"

Sam thought a minute and then turned to the crew, asking them, "I greatly respect Captain Hornigold and those of his crew, so any who wish to stay, ye may," he said, turning to Hornigold. "Captain, ye may take *The Sainte Marie,* for she's been a good ship, and I wish ye Godspeed!"

"If it's all the same to ye, Captain Bellamy, I shall remain with you, *oui*?" said La Buse. "I feel these waters will yield a great bounty."

The next few hours comprised of men moving Captain Hornigold's belongings and those of the crew following him over to *The Sainte Marie*, and soon, Sam was captaining *The Marianne*. He also gained more crew: Simon Van Vorst, Thomas Baker (a tailor), James Ferguson (a surgeon), Edward Moon (ex-privateer), Joseph Rivers (a veteran pirate himself), and William Osbourne (gunner's mate). La Buse and his *Postillion* rode the waves beside him. Several captured sloops and pirogues followed as they formed their new flotilla, headed for richer waters around Hispaniola, and made their home port at Saint Croix.

"You collect ships more than a tavern wench collects the pox," said La Buse to Sam.

Sam laughed and stated, "'tis my fondest wish, my friend, that I get the best out there!" La Buse clapped him on the back and then made his way across the gangway connecting the two ships.

The waters danced around them as they sailed, and the sun showed brightly above them as they approached the end of this new year. And he closed his eyes, envisioning his return to Maria with his flotilla and goods stored on all the ships. A cold wind blew across his neck and made him shiver. His heart stuttered at the ill omen, but he brushed it off as the last gasps of winter in this warm climate.

The ships were unlatched, and then all the ships began floating south, where they would turn back towards St. Croix. Before they had sailed long, shouting could be heard, and Sam tried to locate the source.

A ship sat as if adrift in the distance, yet all hands appeared to be scrambling. La Buse looked over at Sam, and Sam shrugged, and by tacit agreement, they turned their heading in that direction.

As they sailed closer, the figures were more apparent, and Sam could see some type of kerfluffle near the helm. The shouting became increasingly louder, and Sam started to make out the words. Apparently, there was some type of mutiny occurring! Sam yelled his discovery to La Buse, and they decided to take advantage of the situation as the ship looked intact and sea-worthy.

None of the crew put up a fight as Sam and La Buse pulled up beside them. They were starting the boarding operations, but the other ship's captain climbed down into a dingy with a few of his men and made his way swiftly to *The Marianne*.

"I see ye are here to plunder me, lads, but, as you can see, we have a bit of a situation happening," the captain said. "My name is Abijah Savage, and I am the captain of *The Bonetta*. I beg ye to clear off 'afore the harpy on board knows what is happening."

"Harpy? Ye have such a mythical creature on board?" asked Sam.

"Oh, aye, if you saw or heard, her ye would know what I speak is true."

Just at that moment, a loud shrieking came across the waters, and Captain Savage literally put his hands to his ears. "Weeks upon weeks of that. I implore you to turn now before you are caught in its web."

Sam saw Paul shaking his head and miming capturing the ship and then tossing imaginary bags of loot around. La Buse was just bewildered and was smoking harder on his pipe with the increasing pitch of each shriek.

Sam started to ask what aid they could give when the source of the shrieks made its way toward the railing closest to his ship.

Lo and behold, a *woman* approached the ship's side to continue her hysterics. None of Sam's men could speak as they weren't sure they were seeing what they were seeing. She seemed to glide across the decks, and many of the crew of *The Bonetta* moved their feet or arms away from her as if fearing she carried a plague. Sam noted many of the crew looked hard-put and miserable.

"Ach, now, she's found ye out, and you are well and truly caught in this snare, my fine fellows. Please join me aboard and pray to whatever gods ye have that you come out unscathed." With that, Captain Savage returned to his ship.

La Buse looked at Sam and told him he was on his own and La Buse would assist from afar. He told Sam that he would await him in

St. Croix to disperse the loot and arrange the cargo and crew among the flotillas. Sam gave orders to grapple onto *The Bonetta* and then went to stand in front of the tiny woman and her verbal firing squad.

"We do not need your aid, pirate, and I suggest you hie yourself hence from this deck and these waters, for I will not be deterred from my destination." The woman was petite, perhaps no more than five foot four, and barely approached Paul's waist. Her straw-colored hair was pulled back into a severe bun, and her stark black dress was fitted to her from the top of her neck down past the tops of her boots, and every part of her was covered, which had to be uncomfortable in the heat of this area.

Captain Savage looked on with weary resignation, something else Sam could not reasonably interpret. It almost looked like…relief. The tiny woman continued her harangue, but Sam tuned her out as he looked around the ship and noted the crew were slowly moving away from the small whirlwind. Finally, she poked a finger into Sam's chest and again caught his attention.

"I am a widow and God-fearing woman, you miscreants, making my way from Jamaica to Antigua, and we are making slow enough progress as it was. I am due in a few weeks to our new posting that my late husband's captain gave us."

Captain Savage finally spoke and said, "ye see, we were not making enough haste for the young lady here, and she was…informing us thusly…when you arrived."

Sam felt for the poor captain as he knew this could not have been an easy voyage. First, the fact they allowed a woman on board a cargo ship was rare, but apparently, they let her boss them around, as well.

"M'lady, I assure ye that I do not wish ye harm; however, the good captain here has assured us we can make use of this ship and its cargo however we see fit. I am not accustomed to receiving orders from a woman, and ye are a passenger here till we decide your direction."

As Sam turned, that finger of steel once again embedded itself into his coat. He could almost feel it aim for his heart.

"I shan't be part of such barbaric practice, and you, foul spawn, will take your men and leave us."

"Believe me, m'lady, and our greatest wish is to dispense this capture with all haste and speed you on your way. We will give you all the courtesy ye are due as we make port nearby." Sam turned before the whirlwind could attack him with her word-filled claws, and Captain Savage agreed very quickly to follow the flotilla into their home port in St. Croix.

Lodging was found and instructions given to the lady and the rest of the crew, and soon, everyone was arranged where they should be. However, while the lady walked down the gangplank to the docks, she was joined by a small boy of around ten. He was swaggering down the gangplank as two crewmen followed, carrying all sorts and sizes of baggage and staggering under their weight. Neither the woman nor the boy gave them any aid, and Sam's eyes followed them as they made their way to their lodgings.

Captain Savage awaited Sam in his quarters and wiped his forehead with a handkerchief before accepting the tankard Sam offered.

"Ye have no idea of the storm you stopped with that one," he said, pointing in the woman's direction.

"What is the story with that?" asked Sam.

"She is the widow of a British naval captain who ran operations from Jamaica exporting sugar cane to their country. He was killed in some uprising from the slaves, which was quickly put down, but not before he took a bullet to his head. I still think he jumped in the path of that bullet after meeting that woman."

Sam could not disagree and merely nodded.

"The boy, he is no better and her only child that she dotes on and caters to his every whim. He has climbed everywhere aboard my ship and caused barrels to fall into the waters along with several goods intended for English Harbor in Antigua. He thirsts to know everything no matter how much of an inconvenience, though I find him to be more malleable than his mother, and I believe he merely needs a strong hand to guide him."

Sam informed Captain Savage that, while not a prisoner, he would still need to stay within the confines of the camp or on board the ships. Captain Savage, relieved to turn over custody of the woman to Sam, was all too happy to take his leave.

During the course of two weeks, Sam and La Buse divided up the cargo and goods between themselves, their crews, and the flotilla.

The capture of *The Bonetta* did not keep Sam and La Buse from pursuing other ships, and they managed to take more ships and crew still as Captain Savage waited in port. Captain Savage felt a begrudging admiration of the young pirate.

Whether Captain Savage agreed with his semi-incarceration or if he felt resentment is a matter of difference in history. Some say he was very taken with Sam and his ethics; others say that once he was released he continued to Antigua, where he complained to the governor, who informed the British leadership. In the latter explanation, an ambush was planned for Sam, but they only managed to capture five ships and crews of the Irish pirate Walter Kennedy.

Either way, Sam gave his same offer to join his crew to the men of *The Bonetta*. Some chose to join, and then a voice pierced the men's cacophony.

"No! No, you shall *not*! Come back here, young man!"

The boy, John King, made his way to Sam's side and spoke loudly and proudly, saying, "I will join ye, and ye're crew, captain!"

Sam did not know whether to smile or frown at the statement, although the boy's mother was definitely making a spectacle.

"No, no, no! Ye are meant for greater things than this rabid and diseased lot!" the mother cried out as men restrained her somewhat carefully.

Sam held out his hands in silence as he looked down at the boy. The whelp had his hands on his hips in a stubborn stance and waited for Sam to make the offer to him. Before he could answer, though, John King turned to his mother.

"Mother! You have said I am a man, so I shall be this way, I shall make my mark upon the world! Fear not, continue your way to Antigua and leave off your caterwauling, or I shall run you through with a sword myself!"

The woman's cry ended abruptly, only to have her jaw fall open. Men looked everywhere but at her. Sam wanted to join the men in the crow's nest but knew he had to let the boy fight his own battle.

She regained her composure enough to weep copiously and wrenched free her arms to run over and envelop the boy. He struggled against her but finally still and rolled his eyes at Sam. Sam turned away, choking on laughter, so he did not let the mother see him.

"Now, I shall be safe in the instruction of these men, and I shall write you often, but I am joining this crew!"

Finally accepting his words, the mother stood, crossed her arms under her breasts, harrumphed, and then walked slowly and stately back to the cabin aboard *The Bonetta,* where her things were once again stored.

Captain Savage grasped his forearms with Sam, and Sam informed him he could keep command of *The Bonetta* and wished him fair winds. Sam also offered the captain a bottle of rum to ease the trip for him since he still had to carry the "harpy" to their destination.

It was late afternoon when shouts were heard on *The Marianne,* that a large galley was spotted. Rows of oar windows were seen but were not being used, so Sam was not sure they had the oars or the crew to power the vessel through the shallower waters. The lines on it were sleek and made to be carried by winds with great speed. Sam looked through his telescope, trying to make out the name on the back of the ship. La Buse, on his ship, did the same and then whooped with delight.

"Mon ami! 'Tis *The Sultana*! Let's away after that fat pigeon!" La Buse shouted across the water and yelled at his men to prepare.

Sam could tell *The Sultana* would be leagues more advanced in build for pursuit and knew he had to have her. He smiled and shouted to Paul to prepare for battle.

Shouts from both ships echoed as cannons were wheeled into place and cutlasses and pistols readied.

"Remember, ye wretches, let not anything hit that ship as I want it!" Crewman cheered as rigging was pulled, and the mainsails and mizzenmasts were raised.

The Sultana lived up to her reputation as the sails rose out of the decks quickly to blow full and wide, confirming Sam's suspicions there were no oarsmen on board to assist. Seaspray leaped up from the hulls of all the ships as they gained speed, and *The Postillion* and *The Marianne* were soon almost neck and neck with *The Sultana*.

The captain on board *The Sultana* was seen on the stern barking orders and gesturing wildly to some of the crew members. It was overtaken within the hour despite reaching speeds faster than most ships. Grappling hooks from *The Postillion* and *The Marianne* were thrown and latched onto *The Sultana's* railings, and soon boarding parties made their way onboard. Sam and La Buse moved through quickly, securing crew and goods.

As the day neared its end, Sam told La Buse he wanted *The Sultana,* and La Buse agreed. Paul was given command of *The Marianne*. Later, they would plan their subsequent conquests over tankards of ale in St. Croix, and Sam decided the waters here were prime and full of worthy prey. *The Sultana* was converted to a full galley, more storage capability was added, and the new crewman powered the oars and took the title of Sam's flagship.

The flotilla of *The Sultana*, *The Marianne*, La Buse's *Postillion*, and many other smaller ships were now a force to be reckoned with in those waters.

***

"Let me tell ye the tale of the Sea Witch of Billingsgate area," said a scarred and weathered old man seated by the fireplace at The Tavern. Cold winds and moaning woods always heralded the winter that was taking hold in the New England area as they began to droop with ice. "Heed me, or else ye take ye're fate into ye're own hands."

Several patrons of the tavern turned towards the man as he was known as a sailor of great renown and not known to lie or tell falsehoods. Young sailors sought his wisdom before their maiden voyage and swore his advice saved their lives.

Settling back in the chair kept specifically for him, he waited for his ale to be refilled and his pipe lit before he continued. As if sensing something important was about to happen, the noise level in the tavern dropped until all you could hear was the occasional cough or scrape of a chair.

"It is said, there be nothn' like a woman scorned. Ye have all heard of the young Maria Hallett and her conviction by Goodman Justice Doane not too long past. 'Twas the devil himself that released her from her cell, and ye shall hear no other talk of that in this place 'fore he appears. Ev'ryone does know that if ye speak his name, then Ole' Scratch will appear and take ye're soul.

"'Tis thought Goody Hallett was given a pair of red-heeled shoes and now has an old scraggly cat and a goat with black on it and with one eye as familiars who aid her. T'other eye of the goat 'tis of glass, and she can see through it as if it were her own eye casting over the dunes for unlikely sailors. The shoes 'twere a gift from 'Ole Nick himself and gives her powers that be beyond reckoning in exchange for the souls of the unwary.

"Goody Hallett was once the town's prize; a girl of such beauty, men would come from around in order to woo and pursue her and her family's money. Aye, 'twas true till her innocence was taken by a sea-farin' scoundrel and a spawn of Satan put in her belly 'ere he left her. Now, she is said to haunt the dunes off the coast and use wiles and deception to lure in the sailors akin to mooncussers baiting ships with their false light. Beware the false light, and do ye not stop for anything along that route," he finished and closed his eyes, hoping his words landed.

No one said anything, and then someone tried to laugh, only to be quickly prodded in the stomach by his mate sitting at the table. Most in that tavern had heard the tales of Goody Hallett, who was condemned to a cell yet managed to escape easily under the watchful eye of the town sheriff.

Suddenly, a man stood, looking over the crowd, and addressed them. "I believe ye, old one, as I have encountered the witch," he told them. Murmurs accompanied his words as the men around him parted to let him have the floor to speak.

"Me name be Captain Sylvanus Rich; ye may know my father, who has been sailing these parts for many years." Several men nodded.

"Just a fortnight ago, I had to rescue him, his crew, and his ship from the clutches of the witch of whom you now speak and describe. Such a tale as he did give to me when I finally reached him. He said that he had made his way to the coast in search of something other than the ship's hardtack and rum. His intention was to purchase some milk from a local farm or tavern where he could thicken his stew.

"On his way through the dunes headed towards Eastham, though, he came upon an old crone who had some to spare. 'Oh, he thought, now I need not go all the way to town,' he gave her coin and returned to his ship. This is where the tale gets muddled, and I still scarce believe it meself, even seeing things as I have in my years on the seas.

"He told me he dreamt of naught but a beautiful lass in red-heeled shoes who bade him carry her wherever she wished and used him till his spirit was broken and his will gone from him. He spouted nonsense about a whale where she lived that could wreck ships and blow fire from its spout like a geyser." Captain Rich paused to take a drink from his tankard before continuing the story.

"His hallucinations continued for a few days until his mind cleared of the witch's spell, and his soul returned to him. I shudder to think what may have happened had I not come upon his ship on my return to Boston's harbor." Captain Rich looked around the room and then sat back at his table.

The men in the tavern made the sign of the evil eye or crossed themselves and then bent back to their conversations. No one took heed of the cloaked figure in the back corner carrying a bag and small cask that left soon after.

Stepping outside into the night, Maria pulled down the hood of her cloak and looked at the bottoms of her boots, which were a rust-brown color from some of the dunes and their contents. Chuckling, she returned to the shore after getting more foodstuffs from Gladys behind the tavern.

The tale of the older man had drawn her inside as it was not the first she had heard of her alleged witchy powers and how the animals she had found were actually her familiars. Some days, she could believe the cat was something from the devil with the way he hissed and swiped at her, but then he turned loving and wanted to be held other times. The old goat had wandered in and was injured, but Maria had nursed it back to health.

Still laughing softly, she continued her walk back to her home on the dunes, thinking about both men's stories. And this, she thought, was why people should not eat the wild mushrooms that grew in the woods. All the locals knew of their hallucinogenic properties, and all she had done for the man's father was assist him back to his ship when he had shown up begging for her aid while vomiting from one end, expelling acrid waste from the other, and delirious. She imagined the son had not wanted anyone to know the real reason for his father's mental stress, and it was always easier to blame things on a witch.

News had finally reached her of Sam's exploits in the Caribbean, and now she despaired riches had seduced him and would never return. A tiny ember of resentment glowed softly in her, but she still longed for the day when she would see his sail from her home on the dunes, and he would return to her.

***

"You aren't serious, Grandpa." Charlie looked at Loyd's

askance as he held onto the ship again. He had been mimicking the movements of Sam's ships as Loyd told the story. "A wicked witch?"

Clarissa gave a small snort and shook her head. "This just keeps getting better and better. How the heck did people survive to now with all these stupid ideas."

"It wasn't until the 1960s and 1970s that Wiccan practices became more widely accepted," William told his kids. "Regardless of your thoughts, it wasn't *that* long ago."

Laura smirked and hid her grin behind a slight cough. Loyd could only chuckle and agree with them.

"Is Wiccan…witchcraft?" Charlie asked.

"No, kid, Wiccan is more earth-based and…ummm…crunchy, I guess you would call it." William went to the bookcase, retrieved a book, and brought it back to show the kids. "See, this is a book by a famous Egyptologist, Margaret Murphy, who first talked about 'witch-cults' in her book, "The Witch-Cult in Western Europe," she wrote in 1921, as being benevolent and helpful to man instead of the wicked witches you are thinking of from past stories. So, more hippy-dippy than cackly-wacky."

"Regardless, the fear was truly rampant, and neighbor was afraid of neighbor everywhere you turned in the 17th and 18th centuries. Even children weren't immune to being accused. Although, kids can sometimes be little terrors, so not surprising," Loyd laughed.

"Hey, I resent that remark!" Charlie stood and swooshed an imaginary sword through the air. "I am to be feared and the master of my own seas!"

"Actually, there was a tale of a young boy, about ten or eleven, that was the oldest recorded pirate," Loyd informed him. "Probably young John King."

"Get on with the tale, ye scurvy doggie," Charlie told Loyd, gesturing with his sword for Loyd to resume his spot, and then Charlie did the same.

"Watch how ye talk to ye're betters, or ye'll walk the plank!"

"That actually happened?" Clarissa asked him.

"No, not really, but the keelhauling thing was real."

"What's that?" Both kids were attentive now.

Pulling out his phone, Loyd looked up a website and asked the kids if they could handle some graphic violence. They nodded, although Laura looked a bit concerned as she knew what they were going to see. Loyd showed the kids a video made by the makeup artists of a popular pirate drama detailing the 'keelhauling' practice.

"They basically tied the guy's hand and feet so he couldn't swim and then tied a rope that was strung from the yardarm of the bow, and then that rope was run under the ship until it came up the stern in the back where men stood to pull it. The man, with his hands tied and his feet tied, was then attached to the rope and usually had some kind of weight attached like a cannonball to his feet to keep him from floating up and to make it easier to drag him."

"Wait," Clarissa said, her face turning pale and then a shade of green, "wait. Just, wait, ummm, wait. They didn't do what I think they are gonna do?"

Loyd let the video play, and it showed a stunt double being pulled from the front of the ship, underneath the water under the hull, then to the back, scraping barnacles along the way, and being pulled up out of the water at the back of the ship. The sailor was bloody and gashed from the sharp barnacles and barely alive, if alive at all.

Clarissa drew a shaky breath, and Charlie moved closer to his parents.

Loyd shut off the video, replacing his phone in his pocket. "There were tales of some captains who were so cruel that had it done to a man more than once. Luckily, Sam wasn't that type of captain."

"Thank God for that, at least," Clarissa grumped.

Loyd settled back in the chair and told them, "Let's catch up with Sam, La Buse, and the flotilla and see where they've gotten to at this point."

"Dude collects boats like some girls collect shoes. We've had the love, and I guess leaving Maria was the loss? Now, let's get to the loot!" Charlie said excitedly but stayed near his parents.

"Yes, well, we are getting there! Let's go back to St. Croix and see what's happening after how Sam recruited the youngest pirate ever recorded!"

Chapter 17: The Chase Begins

In the Caribbean, South of St. Croix December 1716-January 1717

Sam and La Buse made their way around the waters near Cuba and Hispaniola, searching for prey. Many ships would fall to them, but one of the important ones would be *The Saint Michael*.

Sam's policy, and that of most of the pirates of those days, was to offer captured ships and the crews an opportunity to join the crew, or they could be released to find another ship or make their way home. One of the caveats of that offer being that those same men did not possess a skill needed aboard the ship that was victorious in the capture.

Thomas Davis, a carpenter, looked at his captors with disgust and hate. He had only served aboard *The Saint Michael* a few months and enjoyed the freedom he had among the crew and the ease of his life. Now, he could see it all crashing down upon him as Sam and Paul made their way down the line of sailors, asking each one their job on the ship and their wish. By now, several had heard of Black Sam Bellamy and his benevolent way of piracy.

Sam reached Thomas and asked him the same two questions. Thomas stared straight ahead and did not answer. Sam looked at Paul, who shrugged, and then Sam repeated the question. Thomas again stared into the distance while his mind raced as his options. Finally realizing his fate was in the hands of the man before him, he turned his head, and Sam almost flinched from the fire in the man's eyes.

"I be the ship's carpenter, and I have no wish to join ye're crew. Cast me off with the others and let me go," Thomas said spitefully.

Sam, taken aback at the vitriol in the man's voice, asked Paul, "Do we have one of those?"

"Nay, my good captain, though methinks this one does not wish to join our merry crew and reap the spoils," Paul replied.

"Well, do we usually keelhaul or abuse our men?" Sam asked.

"Nay, we do not, nor do we falsely split the loot among the men."

"Why do ye think this man dost not wish to join our crew, ay?" a perplexed Sam asked Paul. Looking back at Thomas, he asked, "do ye believe ye shall find ill service aboard my ship, crewman?"

Thomas shuddered at the hidden steel in Sam's words but felt he could give no ground. "Aye, I believe ye to be no better than the others that prey upon these waters no matter what tales are told of ye."

"Paul, have ye been spreadin' tales of evil deeds?"

"Nay, Black Sam, not to my knowledge," Paul said, hiding a smirk.

"Then 'twas some young lass of yours, crewmate, that I dishonored?"

Thomas narrowed his eyes and said, "Nay, but ye are not known to be soft-handed in ye're treatment of all the captured crews."

Sam thought for a moment, then realized what Thomas spoke. "Ah, I see. Ye think about my treatment of slaver ships, I reckon."

Sam turned to the rest of the ship and shouted to be heard. "Ye have heard that some of my prey are not allowed to go upon their merry way, singing tra-la-la and avasting their mateys. I shall not permit a ship full of humans in misery to be let off lightly. We are all one brotherhood, no matter ye skin color or godly belief. If ye feel differently, then I pray ye to turn your yellow-hide toward yon canoes and make ye're way off my new ship."

Some of the men grumbled and filed towards the rope ladder off the side of the ship near them. However, Thomas was not deterred in his belief and stood fast, as well as his crewmate, Thomas South, as Sam gave the vote to his crew per the Articles. The crew, however, knew Thomas Davis and Thomas Baker did not want to join so they decided to make life hard for them and press them into service.

"I shall enjoin ye to stay; however, 'twill only be temporary until we find another obliging ship's carpenter; however, per the Articles, I must give my crew a chance to vote. What say ye, lads, do we convince Mr. Davis and Mr. South here that we insist upon their services or let them join the others in the boat that is quickly moving away?"

Sam's crew had heard Thomas Davis in his assertions of Sam's depravity and his unwillingness to join them. And, so, they voted that

Thomas Davis would join them, and thus was he and Thomas South press-ganged into joining.

Sam and La Buse continued their conquests once the crew and goods were divided amongst the flotilla ship.

Soon, Sam and La Buse sailed on with the addition of the crew that had been left without ships, thanks to the ambush from the British navy. During a brief stop at Blanquilla, La Buse informed Sam it was time for them to part ways.

Sam started to protest but also felt there were other waters to explore, and he offered La Buse a tankard for a good parting. La Buse accepted, so they and their crews spent a short time celebrating on their ships as they all wanted clear heads for sailing the next morning.

Later that evening, Sam and Paul met and decided it might be time to head northward towards the Windward Passage as Sam felt richer waters would be had there. They discussed their current roster of ships and loot and men from just about every walk of life.

A month later, in February 1717, a ship was spied in the waters of the Bahamas. Sam did not yet know it, but his greatest prey was soon to run before him, and he would make history.

***

"Captain, we are now fully loaded, the crew has been mustered, and we are ready to depart, Sir!" The quartermaster of *The Whydah Gally* reported on their itinerary. Captain Lawrence Prince was well pleased with the goods they received in exchange for the slaves sold on this plantation island in the Bahamas.

The Whydah Gally's hulls were filled to the brim with items they received in trade for the enslaved people who had survived the crossing. More sugar and rum filled the holds in addition to bags of gold, gold dust, and silver. These items joined the elephant tusks, gold jewelry, Jesuit medicine bark, and other items Captain Prince would be bringing back to their home port and Sir Morice Humphry.

His old bones longed to be done with this venture and return to his warm island and even warmer mistresses waiting for him. He may be well past his prime and lurching towards his final sailing on his beloved seas but he still enjoyed having women at his bidding.

Turning, he addressed the crew waiting on the decks below him. "Men, this ship has served us faithfully, and it is now time to return home. Prepare the sails, and let's make our way! Bosun!

Prepare for departure!"

Crew members scrambled like ants in a disturbed ant hill, and soon, they were back in the open waters of the Bahamas. Prince licked his finger and lifted it to the wind, then closed his eyes, feeling the direction of the airflow, and found it favorable.

In all his years of sailing, he knew that it was bad luck to believe a journey would be easy, and he would not start now. Though they had good luck on the crossing over, despite the incident with the enslaved person, he was going to remain vigilant with a weathered eye on the horizon. He surveyed all the waters close and far away and told the lookout to keep alert.

Little did he know that he was about to meet his destiny. A small speck on the horizon caught his eye. He turned to return to his cabin and –

***

"–Yes! Yes, finally! Go get him, Sam!" Charlie yelled, interrupting Loyd as Charlie jumped up from his seat and fist pumped in the air over and over. "Finally! That bad dude is gonna get it! I just

275

know it!”

Loyd smiled and said, “Yes, he’s definitely in Sam’s crosshairs now, though Captain Prince doesn’t quite know it yet.”

Clarissa’s phone rang, and the sound clip of the priest in The Princess Bride during Prince Humperdink and Buttercup’s wedding, quoting the lines where he says, “Wuv, twue wuv…” played and Clarissa excitedly clicked the “answer” button. The call was fairly short, but Clarissa’s face paled, and her breathing shortened.

“That was Reggie’s mom! They found his truck near the area where the flooding was happening, and search crews are out! Why would he get out of his truck? He knows better!” Clarissa covered her face with her hands and ran for her room.

“I’ll go see to her, guys, and let you know,” Laura told them.

After a few minutes, Laura and Clarissa returned, and Loyd could see Clarissa’s tear-stained face as she tried to gain composure.

“Now, we come to the good part,” Loyd said, smiling and resuming his tale to distract them.

PART THREE: A HERO'S END

"Yes, I do heartily repent. I repent I had not done more mischief; and that we did not cut the throats of them that took us, and I am extremely sorry that you aren't hanged as well as we."

— Anonymous Pirate when asked on the gallows if he repented

"My bounty is as boundless as the sea,

My love as deep. The more I give to ye,

The more I have, for both are infinite."

— William Shakespeare, "Much Ado About Nothing", 1599

Chapter 18: Capture of a Lifetime

Waters off The Bahamas, February 1717

Sam broke his fast and then joined John Julian at the helm towards the stern of the ship. Rainbows formed where the spray hit the hull and parted before them as the flotilla sailed. When he woke up this morning, he had an odd feeling and could not fathom what it could be about. Looking off to his starboard side, he spotted *The Marianne* and the other ships trailing behind it as they set a course north to the Windward Passage.

In his mind, he kept replaying Maria and the way she has seen him off on his journey. If he closed his eyes, he could still hear her words reaching him on the wind as he sailed out.

I shall wait for ye, Samuel Bellamy, till time ends and the worlds become dust. Keep me in your heart.

His chest clinched, and he remembered a pang of regret as he watched her figure become smaller on the horizon, and thoughts of treasure immediately took regret's place. He felt so many threads pulling him in different ways now. He could easily return now and claim her and his child. But, there was always one more ship he could take to ensure he had riches enough to suit Maria's father.

Sam thought of Paul and how his family had also seen him off at the docks but his wife had only shaken her head sadly and herded the children towards a waiting carriage. Paul's marriage was not a joyous one but Sam believed it was more than that Paul's work kept him away from home often. Many of the city of Boston's wealthy needed his jeweler's skills for their baubles. To them, that sailing probably was no different than other leave-takings by Paul.

Sam couldn't believe it had been a year and a half since he last held his beloved and hoped she was well and would not be too angry with his choices. He would probably leave out a lot of the adventures but he could not wait to share them with her. Maybe he would tell his child, and future children, of how their father was a great mariner who made his fortune with great feats of valor and courage.

A slight breeze played with the sails, making them snap and wave in tandem with the gusts, bringing him out of his reverie. Sam looked over to Paul and they saluted each other from their respective places, but Sam was still uneasy and felt his soul shake slightly as he looked over the waters. Distantly, specks became ships of differing sizes but none that appealed greatly to him.

"John, bring us around to let the wind be at our backs and bring her to line with the others," Sam told his helmsman. He had a strong feeling pulling him that way and wanted to see it play out.

"Aye, c'pn," he replied, spinning the wheel slightly to follow orders.

As they sailed on, Sam caught a whiff of the stench that followed slaver ships. His upper lip curled as he covered his nose. He despised them and would not let one suffer to remain in these waters.

"Bring to bear, head towards that green cloud following that one ship, and give chase, John, but do not gain on it swiftly. Let us see what ill it bears to smell like the ass-end of a horse."

Sam had his bosun signal over to *The Marianne* to let Paul

know his plans, and even from Sam's position he saw that Paul grinned broadly. So informed, they would work together to hem in this rank fish, but Sam wanted to find out if it was full of human cargo or if it was sailing home. Sam's quartermaster, Richard Nolan, who had replaced Paul, got to work handing out detailed instructions.

As they moved closer to the other ship's view, Sam could see the nameplate: *The Whydah Gally*. The name did not strike any memory, so he thought she must be new. Despite the smell, the wood still held its gleam, and the sails were white and crisp, confirming his deduction.

A new ship full of riches! This must be a sign from God!

Sam's heart pounded as he realized the meaning of his thoughts and he felt even more strongly this ship was meant to be his. First, however, he had to catch her.

The ship did not change course and kept its distance. Sam told John Julian to hold steady and follow it a little until they could get an idea of its size. For two hours they sedately followed behind the stench-ridden beauty as she flowed through the water effortlessly.

Watching her move made Sam covet her even more.

Finally, though, Sam could hear shouting from its decks and knew they had been spotted. He waited to see if they would figure out they were being chased or simply in the same ship lane before he took action.

The Whydah Gally's main sail, already billowing with the wind, was soon joined by the foremast and mizzenmast sails whizzing up their masts and opening to catch more air. Confirming Sam's suspicion they knew they were being chased, Sam grinned and jumped up down and ran to the forecastle near the bow to get a better look then turned to his crew.

"Well, nothing for it but to get 'er! Avast ye lazy mutts, get to work, and let us gain this odiferous prize!"

Looking over, Sam saw Paul had noticed the change in *The Whydah Gally's* speed, and they all also raised their sails to begin the chase.

Sam called out to Thomas Baker and told him to spread their flag and let them know who their new captain by the end of the day would be. Thomas did so, and he would later tell someone that "they spread a large black flag, with death's head and bones across, and gave chase to Captain Prince under the same colors."

The Whydah Gally had three masts and soon, they were blooming with the sails and rigging extending and billowing out to catch the wind. In fact, it was speeding up quickly instead of lumbering into a run, which told Sam she did not have a hull full of people and was going to be a lively chase.

"More sail, boys, this is going to be a wild ride!" Sam shouted down and then ran to the bow to watch *The Whydah Gally* and her course better.

Even with all of their sails unfurled and their shallow draft, *The Marianne* began lagging behind, and *The Sultana* kept pace with *The Whydah Gally*. Sam's admiration for the enemy ship grew, and he knew in his heart and soul this was it. This was his greatest desire, and she was truly showing him what she could do as if begging for him to claim and possess her.

The Whydah Gally shifted with the wind coming in from

behind to propel it even faster forward as it gave a hard turn and pulled even further away. Looking through his telescope, Sam could make out the captain strutting around on the deck, bellowing orders, and then looking back at *The Sultana* grinning.

Sam could not believe his eyes. There, through his telescope, was none other than Captain Lawrence Prince. Or, as older sailors called him, Laurens Prins. Sam thought the old sea captain had met his end years ago, but apparently, some dark god kept the maniacal old sailor around. Knowing *The Whydah Gally* was in the hands of someone who could not appreciate her like he only served to stoke his desire for her.

"By God, I must have her," Sam said reverently to John Julian.

"*Sí*, captain, she is fast and may be too fast for us, I fear!"

Waves broke along *The Sultana's* bow as she cut through them, attempting to catch up to *The Whydah Gally*. It became a cat-and-mouse game of *The Sultana* drawing closer, but then *The Whydah Gally* would jump ahead. The chase continued into the evening hours and *The Whydah Gally* pulled so far ahead they were a small black dot and then disappeared altogether.

"Damn and blast!" shouted Sam. "We almost had them! She must be a remarkable specimen of modern technology, and I *will* have her!"

The crew members, weary and feeling the bitter taste of loss, began slowing operations. Sam felt the ship lose the wind, and his greed overcame him. Signaling over to Paul, he let Paul know they would leave off for now and make way for a nearby island tavern. Sam regretfully shook his head and hoped Captain Prince enjoyed his brief respite.

An hour later, Paul and Sam were in a small, packed tavern where Paul stood over Sam's map and discussed possible routes *The Whydah Gally* might take to get away from them based on the direction they were heading.

"I know that captain, and he definitely has experience in these waters and eluding pursuit. I glimpsed him briefly when we were almost in spitting distance, and he knew what he was about."

"What think ye we should do, Sam? It's a plump pigeon

waiting for us, and even these ships and their speeds could not keep up." Paul gestured to the map. "They could be anywhere."

Sam surveyed the topography and then started to smile. "Here," he said, pointing a finger near Long Key in the Bahamas, "here is where she'll try and go and hope to get back to their home course. The waters will be like butter for her there."

Sam and Paul parted, and each went to sleep with their own dreams of victory.

***

Captain Prince stood in his quarters, surveying the sea as the wake of ship trailed out below his windows. Today had been a close one for the ship chasing them was built for speed unlike his which was made for cargo.

Wiping a hand over the stubble on his face, he took a drink from his flask of rum and walked over to his berth, unbuttoning his captain's coat as he walked. It was not often he felt his years weigh on him, but today taught him he still had a few tricks up his sleeve however he was unsure how much longer they would work until someone sent him to the deep fathoms below.

Sitting on his berth, he looked around his cabin and looked at the treasures he had accumulated on this trip that would add to his cache back home. At some point there comes a time when the ship must dock one last time and he felt this trip would be his last.

Thinking back on all the tales of other ships and their encounters with pirates combining with his experience as one himself long ago, he did not expect leniency nor quarter given, especially at his age. He was too old to be press-ganged into service or of any use, really. The thought was a sobering one so he took another drink to bring back the haze to cloud his mind.

Aye, he knew what would happen once they were caught. He did not see red coloring the jolly roger that had bloomed up on the main mast indicating only death awaited the captured crew, but it might have been a trick. Sighing, rubbing his hand over his face once again, he made his decision of what to do if he was captured. With no recourse or hope to survive, he would forfeit this beautiful ship and treasures so he could live out what few years he had left in comfort.

Once, he would have found such thoughts cowardly and against his very code however age has a way of dulling the edge of heroism. He would, however, give them a chase worthy of the greatest of tales.

***

Sam and his fleet sped through the waters. Three days of the chase and little to show for it except frustration and grumbling from his crew. All the men scrambled around each day, getting the ships moving quickly to the areas where Sam tracked *The Whydah Gally*. The dolphins ran up beside them as if joining the chase off and on as if finding it all entertaining.

However, in a very anti-climactic fashion, they once again found *The Whydah Gally* in a few hours on the third day, precisely as Sam had guessed, and it had not yet laid on speed. Sam looked incredulously through is telescope, wondering if his eyes were deceiving him. It had to be a trick.

"Ship ahoy and heel too! Let's go get 'er, boys!" Sam cried out.

Onboard *The Whydah Gally*, Captain Prince spotted them

bearing down on them, cursed softly under his breath as he prepared

himself for what he would do, and then called out orders. His men

deserved to think they were still evading the enemy.

"Mangy mutts closing in on us again as if we were scraps

behind the butcher's shop! Get us underway, helmsman! Bosun, move

your crew!" Captain Prince raised his telescope once more, spying

Sam and Paul's ships closing in.

"Captain, she's gaining fast! She must have tossed some

weight to keep up with this girl!" said the helmsman. "Methinks she

will actually catch up to us!"

"I do not want you to think, helmsman, just do."

"Aye, captain, aye," the helmsman responded with a sigh.

Captain Prince ground his teeth as he saw *The Sultana* and *The

Marianne* with their flotilla closing in behind them, wondering how

they would treat him. As his ship flew on the waves, the other ships

gained on them, and soon, it was apparent *The Whydah Gally* would

lose, so Captain Prince ordered the men to bring the ship to a full stop and prepare for boarding.

It was time to meet his fate. Captain Prince placed his hat on his head and made way down to the quarterdeck.

Sam could not believe his eyes and blinked at them rapidly to see if what he was seeing was what he was seeing. Were they about to overtake *The Whydah Gally*? Not one to deny fate bearing gifts, he gave orders to prepare for capture and boarding of the prize vessel. He looked over, and Paul was laughing at him and shrugging.

"Load cannon and prepare to fire!" Sam called out as his men hopped to do his bidding. Soon, they drew close enough, and Sam gave orders to fire across the bow but not hit the ship.

Captain Prince flinched as the cannonballs splashed near them and knew the chase was over. In his decades of experience, it was no secret that surrender played out better than resistance in his and the crew's dispositions.

Once *The Sultana* and *The Marianne* came broadside with *The Whydah Gally*, Captain Prince had all his crew above decks and ready for their judgment. Never one to cower, he stood proudly and in full uniform before Sam and Paul as they boarded.

He addressed them, saying, "Gentleman, I am Captain Lawrence Prince of *The Whydah Gally* from England under the auspice of Sir Morice Humphry. We will submit to you and only ask for fair disposition."

Sam was astounded but gladly accepted the surrender, introduced himself, and began ordering his crew to take the usual gain and to give Captain Prince's men the same offer they provided all they conquered to join them. This had to be one of the quickest surrenders in naval history.

"Ye were not hard to find, Captain, as we only followed the trail of misery and shite to gain on ye," Sam told him.

"We have delivered our cargo and were on the way back to England, Captain Bellamy, when you encountered us."

"Well, ye shall not be taking any more of the slaves from their homes and journeying them across wide oceans, you twat-faced gorilla. I claim this ship for me own but never say I am not a fair man. I will let ye have *The Sultana,* and ye will never find a better ship.

Well, except for this one, and it is now mine!" Sam walked away.

Captain Prince smirked sadly and then he and his crew began the move over to *The Sultana*. His crew mumbled and grumbled but none knew it was the captain's plan the whole time.

"Captain Bellamy, ye gotta see this below!" yelled Paul from the decks below on *The Whydah Gally*.

Making his way down below, Sam could not believe his eyes as he took in the bounty that was arranged before him like manna from heaven. He wiped a hand over his eyes and then almost used that hand to shield his eyes as the rays of the waters outside the port windows glinted off the gold, silver, jewelry, tusks, and enough riches to surely secure the approval of Maria's parents.

After it was all said and done, Sam and Paul left Captain Prince and decided to truly try out *The Whydah Gally's* capabilities back south near Haiti in the Bahamas. Once they made sure she was truly the best ship out there, Sam would return to Maria.

***

"Hahahahah, oh my God! 'Twat-faced gorilla??'" Charlie

chortled as he laughed so hard he fell out of his chair.

Loyd grinned and said, "Yeah, I thought it best to clean up the language for telling this tale. Ye need not hear how they actually cursed back then."

"Time for that guy to go home and not leave his 'beloved' waiting to hear from him anymore, unlike *some* people," Clarissa said flatly.

Laura sadly shook her head when Loyd glanced at her and decided to leave her be for now.

"Okay, now he's headed back down to familiar waters just for a bit, right? Then he'll go home, and angels will sing, and the heavens will bless them?" Charlie asked naively.

"Ah, my dear summer child, if only life were like that, but let's see what happened next," Loyd replied.

Chapter 19: Time to Go Home

Waters off Haiti then North towards Rhode Island, March-April 1717

During the voyage back towards Haiti, *The Whydah Gally* proved her worth and then some as they captured more ships to fill her more significant hold. Sam decided it was time to head back towards New England, and so they turned to leave the Haitian waters, but not before capturing a sloop. *The Tanner Frigate*, out of Haiti with Captain Beer, was one of the ones most detailed during this time.

Sam and his men had a set system of capture, loot, and democracy they followed with each ship, and it was no different here. However, sometimes, democracy did not work in Sam's favor. Later, Captain Johnsson, a.k.a. Daniel Defoe, would detail pirate democracy in his book.

By this time, Sam's flotilla consisted of dozens of ships, and his crew voted to send *The Tanner Frigate* to the deep while Sam wanted to let the captain keep it. Sam was out-voted, and it angered him, as evidenced by the speech he gave Captain Beer later when the captain questioned why Sam let his crew make decisions that should be his and his alone to make.

"I am sorry they won't let you have your sloop again, for I scorn to do anyone mischief when it is not to my advantage; damn the sloop, we must sink her, and she might be of use to you. Though you are a sneaking puppy, and so are all those who will submit to be governed by laws which rich men have made for their own security; for the cowardly whelps have not the courage otherwise to defend what they get by knavery; but damn ye altogether: damn them for a pack of crafty rascals, and you, who serve them, for a parcel of hen-hearted numbskulls. They vilify us, the scoundrels do, when there is only this difference: they rob the poor under the cover of law, forsooth, and we plunder the rich under the protection of our own courage. Had you not better make then one of us than sneak after these villains for employment?"

Captain Beer replied, "Not in my good conscience can I break the laws of God and man."

"You are a devilish conscience rascal! I am a free prince, and I have as much authority to make war on the whole world as he who has a hundred sail of ships at sea and an army of 100,000 men in the field, and this my conscience tells me! But there is no arguing with such sniveling puppies, who allow superiors to kick them about deck with pleasure."

After scuttling *The Tanner Frigate* down then moved Captain Beer and his men to *The Marianne* for incarceration to keep them from alerting authorities, Sam took his flotilla back north towards home. John Shuan, a Frenchman and a member of Beer's crew, joined Sam on his ship. They encountered no blockades nor attempts to overtake them, so they felt it would be an easy ride home. Sam continued his run of pursuit and plunder, and each time, the crew had a vote in the disposition of the captured crew and ships.

By April 26, 1717, Sam had enough and turned for home. Paul met with him and informed Sam he would be returning to his own home near Rhode Island to see his wife and children instead of pulling into port with Sam but would sail with him up to that point.

"I understand your desire, Paul, and I also long to hold my sweet Maria in my arms again!" Sam told him.

"Aye, it has been a grand adventure, but methinks there is a time for every season as is in the Bible," Paul replied. "What will ye do, man, with all of this cargo, though?"

Sam chuckled and gazed out over the ocean waters and let his eyes close for a few seconds, then open again. "I am unsure if my wandering will be at an end, but I shall leave that up to fate and my soon-to-be-wife and a child I long to meet. As for the cargo, I imagine my uncle will have a way to disperse it through his means."

"Have ye thought often about the child?"

"Aye, almost every waking moment. I have worried about Maria's health and safety as I know it could not have been easy for her, and I was not able to get word to her or her to me in return."

Paul clasped Sam's shoulder, looked him in the eye, and said, "ye know it will be a rascal alike enough to be your twin, and ye shall be of constant worry as he will surely be like his father."

Sam laughed, clasped forearms with Paul, and then they hugged and parted. Paul made his way over to *The Marianne*, and he and his crew sailed further east and then north.

Soon, they captured a ship named *The Mary Anne*, holding a very rare prize of Madeira wine. Barrels of it were stored in the below decks, and the captain's cabin had several bottles of the expensive vintage. Captain Crumpstey was not very obliging in their excitement and gave way under vehement objections.

Sam had parted with the other ships except *The Anne,* that had formed his fleet as they captured them, except *The Mary Anne* was different. Who knew that the names of "Mary" and "Anne" or some variation would be on the nameplate of so many ships? *The Mary Anne* was such a beautiful "snow" type of ship, plus the treasure of liquid in its holds had spoken to Sam's greed and knew it would fetch a fair price. He believed that his men would be joyous at the find and the return trip would be uneventful.

How very wrong he would be on that thought.

"Dude, he better be headed back to Maria, or I'm going to start screaming," Clarissa pronounced.

"He just said Sam was going to head back. Sheesh, simmer down," Charlie replied to her.

"I'm just sayin', is all. I mean…seriously, quit being a child and take responsibility for once," Clarissa said with a small amount of venom. "Isn't he like twenty-seven and still gallivanting around even though he's old?"

"Ouch," said William.

"Wow, I feel seen and no longer have the will to live anymore," Laura chastised her daughter.

Charlie hid his mouth behind his hand and shouted, "Doh! Now you've done it. I would like to request her share of Christmas presents this year."

Clarissa scoffed and pinned her brother with a glare. "You are going to be keelhauled real soon, buddy, if you keep it up."

"So," Charlie said, changing the subject. "Has Maria been walking the beach this entire time while she wasn't conjuring devils and making people sick from bad milk?"

"She has been doing knitting because not everyone hated her and she had to eat, but her main focus was on the beach every day, watching for Sam."

"I know the feeling," Clarissa told them as she glanced down at her phone.

"You probably do, and now just imagine being this worried for a year-and-a-half," Loyd told her. "Well, it's time to get Sam home and finish up our tale."

"Wait, Grandpa, you said that in a foreshadowing and creepy way," Charlie told him.

"Did I? Hmmm."

***

Sam heard raucous laughter filter through his cabin door. Walking out, he saw some of the crew opening crates of the Madeira wine onboard *The Mary Anne* and pouring liberally. John Brown, who

Sam believed had more liquor in his blood than the actual red

substance, was loudly telling men to take part and handing them

tankards but only filling them slightly full, keeping the rest for his own

cup.

"What is the occasion, men?" Sam asked after he joined them

on board, accepting a tankard.

Sam saw Thomas Baker among those bending elbows to throw

back the rich drink. He raised his tankard and addressed Sam, and all

the men gathered around the deck. He knew that the men had all been

talking of their plans for their shares of the vast loot they had acquired.

"For those who graciously gifted us their prizes, for those who

enabled us to have fine ships to carry them, and for those who did not

get out of our way fast enough and lost all but their pants!" So saying,

he quaffed down the wine, and everyone cheered and did the same.

Sam laughed and turned to sit on a barrel as he sipped his wine

and watched his men. He saw John King holding a tankard with both

hands, and Sam turned to glare at John Brown.

"What?" John Brown asked, "his is watered down; it won't hurt him none."

Overhearing that statement, John King huffed, poured out the contents of his tankard, then reached over and took John Brown's when he wasn't looking. Sam laughed and then sent John King a wink. Who was he to be the child's father? Sam surmised the hangover the next day would be punishment enough.

The crewmen imbibed, some making their way below decks to be out of prying eyes so they could imbibe to their heart's content, and soon the air felt celebratory, and among the men was a playwright who was busy recreating a play called "The Royal Pyrate."

The play consisted of an actor, Jack Spincks, playing Alexander the Great, who was interrogating a captive pirate. Crew members watched, shouting encouragement, and then gave anatomically impossible suggestions for torture at times, which caused even more laughter.

A pivotal point in the play was reached as the actor playing Alexander pronounced, "know'st thou that Death attends thy might crimes, and thou shall'st hang tomorrow morn betimes." The actor then pronounced the limbs would be cut off and various other added atrocities.

Suddenly, some of the crew burst up from below, carrying their cutlasses and tossing grenades. Sam stood for a moment in shock and then tried to restore order.

"Men, what means this? What is the cause of your anger?" Sam cried out as he attempted to tackle one of the men.

"We ain't gonna let no white-livered tyrant be takin' one of our own, captain!" the man pronounced as he swung his cutlass and removed the actor's arm.

Another man yelled out that his knee was surely broken. Sam could not believe what was happening and finally realized that the drink-addled men did not know about the play and had only come up in time to see what they thought was someone taking their ship hostage and about to execute one of their shipmates.

Needless to say, Sam forbade the play from ever having a second showing. He sincerely hoped this would end bad luck and then set off to determine the damage to *The Mary Anne's* decks. After a brief discussion with the bosun and Thomas Davis, the carpenter, it was decided she would make the trip without having to stop for repairs, but only if the weather held. They had forgotten the changeable nature of New England's weather.

Chapter 20: So Close and Yet So Far

Off the coast of Cape Cod, April 26-27, 1717

As night fell and the crew left for their various bunks, some of them decided to stay aboard *The Mary Anne* to sleep off their overindulgence, but Sam, John Julian, Thomas Davis, John King, and a few others chose to go back aboard *The Whydah Gally*. John Brown, Hendrick Quintor, Thomas South, Peter Cornelius Hoof, John Shuan, Thomas Baker, and Simon Van Vorst remained aboard *The Anne* and *The Mary Anne*.

The morning breeze on the 27th began to kick up, and as the day wore on, a fog lifted from the waves as they plowed through them. By late afternoon, it became so dense that Sam required *The Whydah Gally, The Mary Anne,* and *The Anne* to put up lanterns so they could see each other. Even with those precautions, *The Mary Anne* fell further back and could barely see *The Whydah Gally*. He ordered both ships to take down their tack and sails to allow the ships to slow, ready their oars, and ascertain if the fog was a prelude to a storm or if it was just a passing weather front.

Soon, he heard voices cutting through the fog and realized another ship was out with them as it made its own way toward the port. Sensing a possible guide through the reef-and-sand-bar-laden area, he hoped the ship would lend a hand.

"Sing out, ahoy!" he called.

"Ahoy, 'tis *The Fisher*!" a voice called back.

Soon, a small snow came into view, and the captain stood near the rail. The ships stayed far enough apart to ensure the safety of their hulls. The men were busy taking down their sails and preparing to put in oars.

"I am Captain Bellamy, and we are headed into port. Do ye have knowledge of these waters? I was only here for a brief while before and not able to study the nautical events."

The captain stared at Sam for a minute, looking at him, *The Whydah Gally* and *The Mary Anne* trailing behind and *The Anne* further behind. It took him no longer to figure out exactly what business Sam was about. "Me name is Robert Ingolls, captain of *The Fisher* and bound for the Cape, aye, what of it?"

Sam exuberantly pronounced, "Great! As ye can see, me holds be full, and I can offer ye, and ye're crew a share if you aid us in navigating the reefs."

Captain Ingolls stared again at Sam as if another head had sprung from Sam's shoulders. "What?"

"Congratulations, Captain Ingolls, ye are about to be very rich!" Sam yelled and then ordered both ships' crews to follow *The Fisher*.

Captain Ingolls, aghast at the way Sam had commandeered his vessel, took a few moments and then slowly smiled. "Oh, aye, we'll get ye in there, won't we boys?" His previous run-ins with pirates had taught him to trust none of them, and deduced his own ship would be taken and added to the "riches" of which Sam spoke.

Turning, the captain called out to his men to prepare for making his way to the docks nearby as four of Sam's crew made their way over to take over *The Fisher*.

Sam knew if the weather had been clear, he would have been able to see the coastline, which had to be only about five hundred feet away from their position. He wondered if Maria would hear of their arrival and meet him at the docks or if he would need to find her and their child.

The fog boiled in like steam off a pot; soon, only specks of light could be seen. Sam ordered John Julian to follow as close as possible to *The Fisher* but 'ware the reefs. The captain of *The Fisher*, though, softly instructed the helmsman to douse their lantern and to pull the rudder to the east and fall behind the ships instead of in front, although no one knew anyone's position in the stillness of the foggy atmosphere. The four crewmen aboard attempted to correct the heading but soon could not see *The Whydah Gally.*

The wind began to blow in earnest, and soon, rain pelted them as thunder crashed and lightning slashed the sky. Feeling confident and determined, Sam challenged the weather and called out insults to it. There was no damn way he was going to wait any longer now that the coast was so near. The storm could rage, and he would still get to his love.

All of his pain and plunder led to his goal of presenting it all to Maria and her family and living off of the wealth for the rest of their lives. Maybe they would return to one of the islands he had found in his travels. Thoughts of warm breezes flowing over them had him smiling as he yelled out toward the sky and told God, "Not today, my Lord, for I have much to live for!"

The veteran crewman, those who had weathered many a storm during their careers, felt the change in pressure and knew what it foretold. They muttered under their breath which was also punctuated by curses as they began the mighty battle against the force of nature itself.

"Nor'easter, captain! 'Twill be a nor'easter sure enough!" one shouted.

Sam barely heard the words, but his ego would not let him acknowledge them. The waves picked up and tossed the ships around like toy boats in a swollen river. The wind grasped the masts and made them moan and creak as the wood tried to bend to accommodate it.

The Anne was further behind *The Mary Anne* and ran neck and neck with *The Fisher* by the time they entered the reefs. The winds continued to rise as cold air from Canada mixed with the warming waters of the Atlantic, creating a storm stew of such ferocity that it had been seen only rarely.

Swells doused the decks of the already damaged *The Mary Anne,* and she began taking on water quickly. Richard Nolan tried to keep *The Whydah Gally* in sight, but it was proving impossible, and soon, he concerned himself with just holding everything together. The next thing he knew, the ship abruptly and unevenly jerked to a halt as they ran aground. The masts were groaning and bending unnaturally, and finally, Thomas Baker grabbed an axe and chopped the rope to the main mast to mitigate any more damage. But, for the moment, they were dead in the water, and Richard Nolan desperately prayed with the other men that they would not also fit that description soon.

The Anne and *The Fisher*, further behind, kept away from the reefs but also took on damage. Sam looked back and could not see any of his ships or crew in the mists spread out from the ferocity of the waves and knew their lives were in God's hands now. At that moment, the weight of that burden fell on his shoulders and he prayed the men were safe. These men, some of them having joined involuntarily, placed their very souls in his safekeeping, and he was going to uphold his end of the bargain. This knowledge, more than anything else, spurred him into action.

He ordered the sails tacked up and everything secured as much as possible. Men wrapped themselves with ropes and rigging to avoid being swept overboard as gigantic waves crested over the decks. Sam gave silent thanks that at least Paul was spared this disaster.

The wind's howl and the ferocious screams of Sam's men drowned out the snapping of timbers, but Sam could not be blind to the horrors he beheld. *The Whydah Gally*, her graceful form tossed about like a leaf in a storm drain, groaned and wept salty tears as her masts snapped as if no more than kindling. Men cried out as splinters flew and drove them to desperately evacuate over the ship's sides ahead of the falling masts. Those masts, clinging to the ship by ropes and rigging, dragged in the water behind the ship as a canoe's oars amid riptides. They pulled the ship harder off course and away, not that Sam had much of a course to speak of any longer.

Sam could not see beyond his the deck of his vessel through a veil of mist, such was the storm's black fervor. His desperate attempt to toss sea anchors to slow the ship and even more desperate attempts to toss his primary anchor affixed to the bow were fruitless, though they relieved his vessel of some small weight.

Sam knew his mind was clouded in delirium of terror and denial, but if he could not force his vessel to take the waves bow first, they would be destroyed by the primal forces of the ocean and nature. Unfortunately for Sam, he would never have the chance to face the storm head-on. *The Whydah Gally* shook like a bronco released from its corral, sending men off their feet and many overboard. With great horror, Sam realized precisely why she bucked and growled.

"The reefs! The reefs!" he shouted, desperate to be heard above the cacophony of wind and screams but no one could hear his cries as his men tried to avoid their own fates. The reefs *The Whydah Gally* had been tossed against ripped through her hull, tearing great rents that sang the death knell for her. Battered against them, *The Whydah Gally* was ripped open along her belly like a sharp blade upon a shark. Sam's heart broke with every groan and tremor, and he knew in his heart of hearts that the abandonment of his ship was his only way to survive.

He shouted and prayed to God but to no avail, as no one could hear him, and it appeared even God had abandoned him. The wind grew fiercer; men crossed themselves and prayed to whatever deity in which they believed, and none of it helped. Most of the men attempted to jump overboard, only to be crushed and drowned as the mighty ship rolled. The prisoners held below had long ago gone silent as waters flooded the holds. Off in the distance, *The Mary Anne*, foundered on a sand bar, also struggled. The crew of *The Anne* and *The Whydah Gally's* crewman on *The Fisher* all watched it happen in horror as they heard the screams above the wind.

Captain Ingolls and the rest of his crew aboard *The Fisher* could only stare in disbelief and guilt-ridden despair as they watched the epic struggle before them, knowing it was partly their fault for their deception in leading the ships toward the reefs. The force of nature pitted against the force of man's will.

Sam, determined to meet his fate with courage, rode the ship over, scrambling to find purchase on the slick hull only to find air as his hands slipped off the side. For a moment, he was weightless and flying, and then he felt his back pop when it hit the water. It was just a momentary twinge, however, as the ship was still capsizing, and Sam did not want to join the ones already under it. Try as he would, though, he could not get out of the pull of the water as it sluiced under the huge ship's hull like a great river wash. He tried to keep his head above water, but the currents and debris hitting him made it impossible. He managed to get one last large breath in before he was rolled under and tangled in rigging. His chest felt as if it would explode as he desperately clawed at the ropes binding him, but soon, his limbs slowed, and darkness claimed his vision as he knew no more.

According to later sources, one hundred and thirty men and sixteen prisoners between *The Whydah Gally* and *The Mary Anne* left this world. The storm finally abated, and the ships left behind took stock of survivors. The four men who had boarded *The Fisher*, including Richard Nolan, made their way over to *The Anne*. All of them bowed their heads and sent up prayers of thanksgiving for themselves and the souls of those lost. The captain of *The Fisher* wasted no time getting away.

Richard Nolan, tears silently falling down his face, made a sign of the cross in the air and said parts of the last rights given to those who have died. "…may the Lord in His love and mercy help you with the grace of the Holy Spirit. May the Lord who frees you from sin save you and raise you up." As he finished, he heard others repeat the words softly, and then he took a vote among the crew. It was decided they could no longer wait without being arrested, and they took off on *The Anne*, making their way further north, hoping to meet up with Paul on *The Marianne*.

The sun began setting against a red glow, heralding the passing of the storm and –

***

"—no, no, NO, no," interrupted Clarissa. "Nope, just gonna nope right outta this one. That's not how it ends, is it? It can't! It just can't! What the heck???"

Loyd stopped and saw tears falling silently down Clarissa's face, and Charlie's eyes glistened.

"I'm afraid so," he sighed. "The story doesn't end there, though. Are you okay to continue?"

Clarissa nodded, sniffling and wiping her face, and Charlie looked down at his lap and gestured for Loyd to continue. With his arm around Laura's shoulders, William touched Charlie's arm and

315

then smoothed a hand down Clarissa's hair in comfort.

***

The beaches were teeming with locals who knew the loot shipwrecks would give up, and they were out in droves to claim their share. It was not that they were evil or bad people. They just never had a lot of this bit of treasure sent to them, which was enough to help them through hard winters or when illness struck. Some of their hearts, though, were hardened enough to chop off the fingers and ears of dead men in order to get the jewelry from the water-swollen limbs.

Maria, holding her lantern high, held up the bottom of her skirt as she trod between the men. She knew, somehow, that Sam was somehow involved in this. She had watched and then barricaded herself in her hut against the storm. She could have sworn she had heard Sam's voice, challenging God and cursing hysterically, but that was probably a trick of the wind. She believed she would feel it in her heart if Sam died.

Each wave brought more loot and more bodies, and Maria looked for the faces of Sam and Paul among them. As the hours wore on, however, her hope began to wane. She had waited so long, and

God could not be this cruel to have him reach her only to perish so close to the coastline where she could see the ship lights and watch the events and foundering occur.

She picked through every item and body she could find to find Sam or some clue if he had been aboard. She also picked up a few items she knew would fetch her money as she was practical. Various coins, dishes, jewelry such as bracelets and necklaces were tossed onto the beach, and yet she could not find her love. She moved further and further down the shore and away from the other people.

Maria saw outlines of figures wading in from the waters and ran over to see if her Sam was one of them. Hendrick Quintor, Peter Cornelius Foot, Thomas South, John Shuan, John Brown, Thomas Baker, and Simon Van Vorst stumbled up to the beach and collapsed. Marie did not know them but knew they would have news of Sam.

Bending down, she asked the closest one to her, Thomas Baker, if he knew of Sam or Paul's location.

"Nay," he rasped, his throat swollen and scratchy from the seawater. "He was our captain, milady, Captain Sam Bellamy, but he was known as Black Sam Bellamy to us. His second mate, Paulsgrave, was not here as he wanted to go see his family, and I pray he met a kinder fate at his destination."

Marie could not believe it. Not only did her Sam come back to her, but he came as a captain of his own fleet of ships loaded with cargo and loot. And Paul would surely have survived if he had made port before the storm. With renewed hope, she asked if Sam was among them.

"Nay, milady, he was aboard *The Whydah Gally*, his flagship ye see yon keeled over, and I fear if you do not see him here, then he has gone to game dice with Davy Jones."

Maria paled and looked out over the water and back up and down the beach. She knew then, she knew all the way to her bones, Sam was no longer among the living. The men knew if they were caught, they would be arrested for piracy and had no wish to swing, so the group moved silently further in. Maria continued her search and vowed to continue until her breath left her body.

Further down the shoreline, out of sight of everyone, two men struggled to gain purchase on the sand and swiftly moving water. Coughing, they helped each other stumble their way up onto the dunes and then laid on their backs to catch their breath.

"Are ye okay, lad?" asked Thomas Davis.

"Aye," John Julian replied as he coughed.

"Damn that man, I never wanted to join his crew," Thomas said while spitting out sand.

"Oh, aye, we knew that which is why ye were made to stay," John said, then laughed and told Thomas, "ye could have left had ye but done ye're job, but ye had to vent your spleen to all who could hear, *es verdad*. It is the truth."

Thinking only of finding shelter for the night, they walked towards town, keeping to the shadows, and soon came upon a house set apart and out of earshot of the townsfolk. Thomas and Julian did their best with whatever they had to look like fishermen caught in the storm and marooned on the coast.

Samuel Harding had laid down only an hour before when the storm had finally moved away. He heard tentative knocking at his door, and his wife rolled to look at him. Donning his clothes quickly, he saw his son going to open the door. "Careful now, my son, ye know not who 'tis at this ungodly hour."

The boy opened the door, revealing Thomas and John standing outside looking bedraggled and very wet. However, Samuel kept his hold on his gun as he wanted to make sure the two men were not ruffians in disguise.

Samuel used the gun to point inside, indicating the men had entered. Thomas and Julian moved inside, and the boy shut the door but not before slipping out quietly. Samuel noted his son's departure and nodded to his wife, who understood the boy was going for the sheriff. None of them were fooled by the men's appearance so soon after a storm, looking like the whole ocean was in their clothes.

"Kind sir, we've coin to pay if ye can put us up for the rest of the night, and then we shall leave 'ere after the brief respite," Thomas told Samuel.

"Oh, aye, I imagine ye will, though ye dress like something our cat would drag in from the docks," Samuel said, lowering his gun and asking them to sit at the table.

Being observant, John had noted the boy leaving and knew what was going to happen. He attempted to get Thomas to leave with him, but Thomas only thought of the warmth of the fireplace, and his mind was still in trauma from the events that had occurred.

Seeing that Thomas would not budge, John looked at the couple and told them, "I have family nearby, so I shall not be stayin' here, but I thank ye for ye're kindness." So saying, John slipped and almost disappeared into the night with his swarthy skin melting into the shadows.

Thomas moved to stand by the fire and warm himself as the wife took out a trencher and filled it with the stew that simmered constantly over the hearth. Once seated at the small table, Thomas dug into it with gusto.

Soon after that, his son returned, and the sheriff followed behind him. "Ah, I see now what hast happened, but I thought ye said there were two?" The sheriff asked them.

Frozen with the spoon in the air, Thomas stared at the sheriff and saw his salvation instead of incarceration. Samuel informed the sheriff that the other man had left and was probably long gone by now, but this one man remained.

"Why did ye not follow your friend, pirate? Aye, I know thy trade by thy look and countenance."

Thomas shook his head, put the spoon into the bowl, and then pushed it away from him. With skill an actor would envy, Thomas told them the tale of his capture and pressed into service for Black Samuel Bellamy, captain of the ships that had wrecked in the storm. No, he did not know if Sam had survived and had no idea if it was the same Samuel Bellamy who had once lived in the area.

After his tale of woe was finished, Thomas sat quietly, bowed his head, and waited for the sheriff's judgment.

"I just need to take ye in, but with such a tale, I am sure the magistrate will release ye forthwith." The sheriff bade Thomas follow him outside after he thanked the couple for their find of the man. Outside, Thomas was placed into a wagon with a guard watching over.

The other seven men found their way to a tavern in Eastham and went inside with only their wet clothing and some gold in their pockets. They hoped the occupants would believe they were simple fishermen marooned on the coast after losing their fishing boat.

There were a lot of curious looks as they entered and sat at a table near one of the corners. Soon, a tavern maid came by and took their orders, bringing them ale and some stew left over from the day's meal.

"What do we do now?" asked John Brown in a whisper as his eyes fell upon the many tankards of ale around him.

Hendrick looked them all in their faces, and, using the same tale as Thomas Davis, he told them, "We are just unlucky fishermen who were cast out of our canoe when the waters turned rough, and now we are seeking another ship at first light."

"Ye think ye that they will believe that? Look at ye, unless ye can clean up and suddenly have a wife who can vouch for ye then ye are surely meeting the hangman's noose with the others." John Brown told him, then looked around at the others and told them, "I will make my way back towards the south and find a ship to take me back towards The Bahamas."

Peter Cornelius Hoof wiped his mouth and looked over at John Brown, then scoffed and said, "As if ye would not stand out, lad. How far do ye think ye could get before someone sells ye out?"

A slight scrape of a chair nearby alerted the men that others were around, and they had best finish their ale quickly. Unfortunately, a tavern maid cleaning the tables nearby had run out to fetch the sheriff's men.

As the other patrons cleared out of the way, Justice Doane, who had presided over Maria's fate, stood in the doorway. It was not long before the men found themselves clapped in chains and added to the wagon with Thomas Davis. Once they were on their way to jail, Justice Doane went down to investigate the wreckage himself and consulted with Colonel William Bassett, who stated he would write the governor of the Massachusetts colony.

In the distance, John Julian had slowly and silently melded into the woods, thanking whatever spirit was aiding him. He saw the arrests of the other men from the branches of a tree in which he was hidden. After their departure, he climbed down quickly and turned to run.

He heard a noise and crouched into a fighting stance only to stand quickly when a gorgeous young woman came into view from the shadows of another tree.

"Are ye one of Sam's men?" she asked.

"Aye, *senorita*, I was his pilot at the wheel. Ye are?" he asked.

Smiling, she told him, "I am Maria."

John Julian could not believe his fortune. To be saved by the very woman who held his captain's heart. He then felt she may not know Sam's fate, so he told her about seeing Sam briefly before John was cast from the wreck before he could jump clear.

Her eyes clouded, and a tear tracked down her cheek. "I know as I have come from there, and my heart aches, but I knew I had to help out his men; he would have wanted me to do that."

"'Tis truly my fortune and my blessings upon you for such benevolence! Ye should know he spoke of you in love and reverence. If we meet again, I will strive to tell you the tales of our adventures together."

"Here," she told him, handing him jewelry from her pocket. "These should help you get home or wherever ye wish to go."

His fingers felt gold links and beads with heavy gold chains. *"Gracias, mi bella."* He walked backward until he was once again shrouded in darkness and took off running with as little noise as a deer.

***

Loyd told the kids, "There are many versions of what happened to Sam, but most say he perished. Some tales, however, say he survived and joined up with Maria to live in secret. Some say he showed up on her doorstep, and she nursed him to health. My favorite is that he somehow had amnesia and wandered around town with a head full of white hair and an unending supply of money and was later found dead with a bag of gold around his waist.

"There are also many versions for John Julian, but I like the one I made up better. It is thought he might have been sold into slavery and even ended up working for John Quincy Adams's grandfather."

"I'm going to believe Sam survived, and he and Maria ran away together and were never heard from again. And I agree John Julian ran off and had a whole new life somewhere." Clarissa stated as her phone began to ring.

Clarissa jumped up and ran into her room to take the call. Laura looked over at Loyd and shrugged.

"I don't think John King made it, Grandpa," said Charlie. "The team who found the ship have displayed a kid's leg bone, stocking, and shoe at their museum."

Loyd nodded sadly and told him, "Yep, they are sure it is his, and we all hope it was quick for the little firecracker. You also have to remember the waters around here in April are still very cold, so they were thrown into with other debris being slammed against them. Even if they managed to survive the rolling of the ship, most of them probably couldn't escape that minefield."

Charlie looked down at the ship in his hands, nodded to himself, and set the ship on the coffee table. "What a way to go," he said with tears in his voice.

Running back into the room, she cried out, "he's okay! He dropped his phone in water at school during practice, and then his truck caught water in the intake and flooded out, so he walked all the way back towards the school before he found someone to give him a lift home!" Twirling around in a happy circle, she ran back into her bedroom, and they could hear her talking to him.

"I guess her 'Sam' got to come home to her, huh?" asked Charlie.

"Seems like it," Loyd said, ruffling Charlie's hair.

"Does this mean the story's over? Kind of anti-climatic, doncha think?"

"Don't you want to know what happened to everyone?"

"Yeah, I guess it would be good to get some kind of 'closure,'"

Charlie told him in an adult voice, his fingers making air quotes around the last word.

Clarissa came back in, positively glowing and with a renewed interest in finishing the story. "Okay, so what happened to the guys that were arrested?"

"Funny you should ask, as that is the last part of the tale, ready?"

Both kids yelled, "Aye!"

Chapter 21: Maps and Wrecks

Boston, Massachusetts, May 1717

Massachusetts Governor Samuel Shute sat behind his large, heavily carved desk and read the report in his hands from officials off the coast of Cape Cod about the wrecks of *The Whydah Gally* and *The Mary Anne*. News of shipwrecks were not uncommon but reports from the survivors of the staggering amount of cargo caught his attention. Seeing the following message spurred him into action:

"The Pyrate Ship commanded by Capt. Samuel Bellamy was Shipwreckt [on shores of Eastham] whereof about 130 Men were drown'd and none saved except two Men, an English Man and an Indian that were cast on Shore…A great many Men have been taken up Dead near the Place where the Ship was cast away."

Yelling for his assistant, he immediately began crafting orders for someone to go down and take control of the wreck before it was thoroughly looted and to "encourage" the townspeople to part with whatever they may have already salvaged. The rough estimate of over $140,000 worth of items plus exotic goods (in modern pricing) was too good to pass up and would definitely fund his colonies.

"Aye, Governor?" answered his assistant.

"Make haste and find me someone to go down and take charge of the wreck in the harbor near Eastham. I want someone there as quickly as possible!"

Cyprian Southack heard of the summons and answered it with haste. A knowledgeable map maker and sailor, he knew the waters and would later be one of these maps that would lead to *The Whydah Gally's* last resting place in 1984.

By the very next day, Southack was aboard *The Nathaniel* and was in Eastham by May 2nd, just a week after Sam's shipwrecked so close to the shore. Everything was chaos upon his arrival as the townsfolk took what they felt was their due and proper right. They stated that it came from the beach, not the wreck itself. His work to secure the Crown's cargo would prove difficult.

Soon after his arrival, he took charge of the officials and directed them to stop all salvage immediately and to report any findings to him for the good of the Crown. He could give instruction but was definitely more comfortable sailing the waters and mapping the topography, and to him the lack of order was abhorrent.

Upon his arrival, Southack expected some courtesy due to his office and appointment but did not receive anything but furtive glances and closed doors. Judge Doane and his family were the only ones to offer him any hospitality.

A few days later, he penned a letter to the governor apprising him of the situation. Later records of this particular letter would highlight his frustration and an example of writing before Webster's Dictionary.

Cape Cod Harbour, May 1717

Maye itt Pleass Your Excellency,

Sir, may 2 at afternoon I Came to the Anchor here, finding Serveral Vessells, Visseted them and on board one of them found a Yung man boling to the Ship the Pirritt Took 26 April in South Channell, Lading with West India Goods, Sloop or Master I no not as Yett. At 7 After noon the Pirrett Shp with her Tender, being a Snow a bout Ninty Tuns they Took in Latitude 26, 15 days agoe, maned with 15 of Pirritts men, wine Ship and Sloop all to gather Standing to the Northward. At 12 Night the Pirritt Ship and wine Ship Run a shore, the Snow and Sloop Gott off Shore, being Sen the Next Morning in the Offen.

Sir, 29 April Came to Anchor sum Distance from the Pirritt Rack Ship, a Very Great Sloop. After Sending his boat to the Pirrit Rack Thay Came to Saile and Chassed several of Our fishing Vessels, then stod in the Sea which I believe to be his Cunsatte.

may 2 at 2 After noon I sent Mr. Little and Mr. Cuttler to the Rack. They Got their that Night and Capt watch till I Came the Next morning. At my Coming there I found the Rack all to Pices, North and South, Distance from one a Nother 4 Miles. Sir, whear shee Strock first I se one Anchor at Low water, sea being so Great Ever sence I have ben here, Can not Come to se what maye be their for Riches, nor aney of her Guns. She is a ship a bout Three hundred tuns. She was a very fine ship.

all that I Can find saved Out of her (the Whidah) is her Cables and som of her sailes, Cut all to Pices by the Inhabitances here. their has ben at this Rack Two hundred men at Least Plundring of her. sum saye they gott Riches Out of the sand but I Can not find them as yett. Sir, what I shall Gett to Gather will be to the Value of Two hundred Pounds. If Your Excellency Pleass to send the sloop to Billingsgatt for itt, is Carted Over Land to that Place...If their be aney News by the Pirritts at boston whear the money is, I humbley Desier Your

He was very displeased and took the power given to him by the Crown to invoke patriotism in the hearts of the townsfolk and prompted them to bring any and all of their loot. After closing his letter with wax and his seal, he handed it off to be carried to the governor with the next delivery to Boston.

A few days later, after drudging around in the cold and wet weather using the whaling vessel to investigate the wreck, Southack came down with a cold and, while convalescing, he learned of who might have taken loot from the waters. Gleefully, he had a plan to advertise to the townfolk that they needed to turn in any who had looted along with any loot obtained.

Unbeknownst to Southack, as he vented his wrath with a pen, his rescue ship was on the way. *The Swan* sailed through the waters only to be captured and boarded by none other than Paulsgrave

Williams, who had received word of the wreck from Richard Nolan and the eighteen other men aboard *The Anne*. After plundering the ship, Paul let *The Swan* continue to its destination as he sailed to another part of the cape, hoping to find survivors and Sam, that may have eluded authorities. *The Swan* would make it to the harbor, where later Southack would use it to return to Boston.

Finally finished with his advertisement, Southack had it copied and posted around the cape.

> *Whereas there is lately Stranded on the back*
>
> *of Cape Cod a Pirate Ship & His Excellency the*
>
> *Governor hath Authorized and impower'd me the*
>
> *Subscriber, to discover & take care of s. wreck & to*
>
> *Impress men & whatsoever Else necessary to*
>
> *discover & Secure what may be part of her, ...with*
>
> *orders to go into any house, Shop, Cellar,*
>
> *Warehouse, room or other place, & in case of*
>
> *resistance to break open any doors, chests, trunks &*
>
> *other package there to Seize & from thence to bring*
>
> *away any of the goods. ...And all of his Mjoesty's*

officers and other his loving Subjects are Hereby

Commanded to be aiding and assisting me, my

Deputy or Deputys In the Due Execution of S.

warrant or they will answer if Contrary at their

utmost peril. These are therefore to notify all

persons that have found or taken up any thing of S.

Wreck on what was belonging to or taken out of S.

Wreck vessel that they make discovery thereof &

bring bring in the same to me at Mr. William

Browns in Eastham or where else I shal order Or

they will answer the Same at their Utmost peril, and

then all officers and other persons will give

information of any thing of S. Wreck taken up by any

persons of Suspicion thereof, that they may be

proceeded with and a Discovery made pursuant to

my power & Instructions. Eastham, May 4th, 1717,

Cyprian Southack.

Needless to say, the townsfolk were glad to see the back of Southack when he finally departed.

***

The men sat in misery in jail for at least six months, awaiting their trial. In a separate trial, Thomas Davis had successfully convinced the magistrates that he was coerced into serving aboard a pirate ship and was, indeed, acquitted. However, the men who remained to stand trial had help in the form of Cotton Mather.

Cotton Mather was a local minister who was a type of prodigy minister for the Puritans in Boston, giving his first fiery sermon at the age of sixteen after graduating from Harvard when he was only twelve. Over his lifetime, he would publish many works, making him one of the most prolific writers of his time. He made daily visits to the incarcerated men and urged them to denounce piracy and say they were pressed into service. He is one of the prime examples of fire and brimstone preaching.

The clanking of iron bars at the front of the jail announced Cotton's arrival, and he breezed in dressed in his black raiment's and powdered wig. "Good morn, gentleman! How fares ye the night?"

Hendrick had been unofficially voted the speaker for them, so he answered Cotton, saying, "About the same as the night before that

337

and the night before that since we were arrested.”

“Fear ye not, for God is with ye and abides within this very cell with His guiding hand ever o’er you,” Cotton told them. “I pray ye and thy companions to heartily repent of any sin and wrongdoing committed in the service of the man led by the devil to commit such heinous acts upon the persons of those ships.”

“He t’were not a sinner, good minister, but gave all that joined him hope and provided us a way to feed our families when we returned to them…had we returned,” Hendrick told him.

Peter Cornelius Hoof, John Shuan, John Brown, Thomas Baker, and Simon Van Vorst had gathered around Hendrick and Cotton and agreed with Hendrick’s assessment of Sam’s character.

“The only one who sinned was meself,” said John Brown. “I let the burn of liquor douse my mind and enfeeble it so my thoughts were focused only on the next drink. Let me tell ye, six months of abstinence has cleared me mind, and I see now the error of my ways, but ye shall not besmirch the good name of Sam Bellamy, for he was a righteous man. He did not take lives, nor did he let those suffer before he set them free or welcomed them into our family. I pray that God watch over and give him peace, for he has joined Him by now."

The rest of the men nodded and spoke of their own affirmation that Sam was above reproach in his dealings as their captain. Was Sam guilty of unlawfulness as a pirate? Yes, but he was an honorable pirate.

"What of the young boy, no more than ten winters, that this so-called captain captured and forced into service?" Cotton gestured to Hendrick and said, "Did ye not flog the boy and others for what you saw as shirking their duties? A man was found without guilt and sin and was acquitted but told of the maniacal dealings while in the crew."

Hendrick shook his head, smiling, and said, "Nay, if me whip did crack, it was in the air and for a cause to give encouragement where t'was needed. The whip never tasted human flesh and is clean of the taint of blood, although it is now resting beneath the waves along with many of our mates."

Thomas South stood and said, "Captain Bellamy was a good leader, but I would gladly renounce Satan and anything else if it would free me to go home to my family as I was coerced into signing the articles."

The crewman did not judge him for, in their hearts, they felt the same longing, but it was still a blow to their morale to hear it.

"Do ye other men feel the same? Would ye profess against your sins and come to God with a clean heart and conscience? I will put forth your words, Thomas South, and God be with ye." Upon saying that, Cotton left, and the men knew he would be in the courtroom the next day.

Never one to pass up notoriety and a chance to preach and hear his own voice, Cotton attended every day of their trial in October, especially when it came time to hear the verdicts. The courtroom was packed with men curious about the outcome or for revenge upon the deeds done to them by other pirates and the loss of goods they caused them. Women stood outside the courts as they were not permitted inside, so they waited for word of the events and decisions of the magistrates.

Standing behind the desks facing the thirteen judges, which included Justice Doane and Governor Samuel Shute, the prisoners awaited the verdicts that would decide their fates. Some prayed silently and promised all sorts of things to God if He would but help them now. Future records would record the court testimony as said in the following passages, which are written in modern language terms.

"Stand ye for the pronouncement of charges and testimony of the accused!" called the bailiff to the prisoners. Once everyone had stood, the principal magistrate began reading the following description of offense and charges. Historical documents record the charges as follows in this excerpt from legal papers and Cotton Mather's writings at the time:

"Nevertheless so it is, that the said Simon Van Vorst, John Brown, Thomas South, Thomas Baker, Hendrick Quintor, Peter Cornelius Hoof and John Shuan, to the high pleasure of Almighty God, in open violation of the rights of nations and humanity, and in contempt and defiance of his majesty's good and wholesome laws aforesaid, willfully, wickedly, and feloniously, all and each of them, being principal actors and contrivers, associates, confederates, and accomplices, did, perpetrated, and committed on the high sea sundry facts of piracy and robbery, distinctly specified and expressed, and qualified with respect to time and place, and manner, when, and where, and in which the said facts were so done, perpetrated and committed by all and each of them...

1. *On or about the twentieth & sixth day of April…in hostile manner with force & arms, piratically & feloniosly, did surprise, assault, invade and enter on the high sea, between St. Georges Bank and Nantucket Shoals, a free trading vessel or pink, called The Mary Anne of Dublin.*

2. *The defendants having in a manner foresaid, entered the said vessel or pink, and at the same time and place, aforesaid, piratically and feloniously seize and imprison Andrew Crumpstey master thereof, and him the said Crumpstey did force & constrain with five of his crew to leave and abandon The Mary Anne to go on board a ship named The Whido [one of the many ways The Whydah was spelled], which employed the defendants and others in continued acts of piracy & robbery on this, and other coasts of America.*

3. *The defendants piratically and feloniously embezzle, spoil and rob the cargo…consisting chiefly of wines, and also other goods and wearing apparel of the said master and his crew.*

4. The defendants over powered and subdued the said master and his crew, and made themselves masters of the said vessel...then and there piratically and feloniously steer and direct their course after the above-named pirate ship, The Whido, intending to join and accompany the same with the intent to oppress the innocent and cover the sea with depredations and robberies."

Each prisoner was called upon to give their testimonies and pleas to acquit themselves; however, the court was stacked against them. Though they tried to use Cotton's instructions and say they were pressed into service, or the articles did not bind them, it was to no avail. The only one for whom it worked was Thomas South, who praised God and wept copiously. The judges determined he was, indeed, pressed into service and was a victim.

"Hear ye! Hear ye! It is the will of this court and that of our Lord God Almighty that ye six men shall be taken to the gallows and hanged from the neck until ye are dead. May God have mercy upon your souls."

Hendrick bowed his head as the decree was read and looked at his hands. Weather-worn with many scars, much like his soul. Silently, he closed his eyes and trembled, knowing his time on earth was about to come to an end. His shipmates also wept silently as their throats were sore from months of arguing and shouting at guards and anyone who would listen. There had also been a small hope, but there, that Sam would somehow appear and rescue them. They wondered if Paul had survived the storm and if he would speak on their behalf or maybe spirit them away from the jail cells. Jeers and exultations of deviltry followed them as they were escorted back to the cells to await their execution.

Chapter 22: Legacy of a Prince

Coast of Wellfleet, Massachusetts May 1717

The Anne anchored off the southern coast of Cape Cod and the crew kept its lanterns turned low to save their night vision. Paul knew there were survivors who were captured, and he grieved the loss of them as well as the ones claimed by the storm, for he knew he could not save the prisoners, and they were as good as dead. It was a given that piracy was a dead man's game as none survived for long, even if they gave it up and tried to live a quiet life.

Still, he sent a man dressed as a townsman to the local tavern to glean what information could be had on who survived and if Sam was one of the ones taken. He knew that Southack was thereafter relieving the captain of The Swan of some things that looked very disconsolate and lonely amid his belongings and hearing the captain swear Paul would "rot on a rope on the gallows when he told Southack what happened."

Paul still grinned as he remembered the captain's face as Paul looked through the cabin and rifled through the drawers and trunks. The sheer shock was payment enough for the baubles Paul took as payment for letting the captain go. Paul could swear the man's wig ends curled.

The spy returned and climbed aboard the ship, scaling the ropes like a monkey with expertise and a lifetime of skill. Once inside the cabin, the spy informed Paul of what he had already suspected.

"Aye, c'pn, 'twas Hendrick Quintor, John Brown, Thomas South, Thomas Davis, Thomas Baker, young John Julian, that Swedish feller…umm…Peter Van Hoof, John Shuan, and Simon Van Vorst. They say Thomas Davis is loudly proclaiming his innocence to anyone who will listen." The spy, none other than Richard Nolan, downed a shot of rum and then wiped his brow.

"'Tis as I feared, my friend, our captain, and his shipmates are lost to us. E'vn we could get to the prisoners, there are too many ways the watch could catch us, and we are already wanted men. It grieves me to say that we must go away for richer waters, but first, I want to find Sam's Maria and see how she and the babe fare." Paul tied his doublet closed, threw on his frock and hat, and strode to the deck.

Quietly, Paul gave orders as Richard took temporary command. Then he climbed down into a dinghy and made his way to the shore. He knew tales of a witch nearby, and he had seen the light dancing near a hut.

As he drew closer to the hut, his booted feet silent in the shifting sands, he noted there were no sounds of a child, and the hut had none of the usual things around it, such as he gave his own children to play. Something was off, and he crept closer. Inside, a woman was stooped over someone on the pallet, and, for a moment, Paul thought it was Sam.

He rapped on the frame, and the woman gave a start and then turned. Though it had been almost two years, he knew it was Maria. Her flaxen hair had dulled, and there were circles beneath her deep blue eyes. Those eyes were filled with pain and grief. She immediately recognized Paul and ran to throw her arms around him before leading him to the pallet.

The man's face, however, was bloodied and gashed, so there was barely anything recognizable and held the pallor of death. Maria gained control of her tears and bade him sit as she bent over the wounded man.

"'Tis not our Sam, though I have wished it true," she said in a voice husky with emotion. "I could take no chances, however, so I tried to give this man some type of comfort amidst his pain, but he passed not long after I dragged him here."

Leaning over, Paul confirmed it was one of *The Whydah Gally's* crew, and he reached over to place a hand over the man's eyes. "I cannot give the cannon salute in honor of this man who gave his soul to the sea, but I can say a quick prayer and then ensure his body is sent down to live forever with his brethren.

"For as much as it hath please Almighty God of His great mercy to take into himself the soul of our dear brother here departed, we, therefore, commit his body to the ground; earth to earth, ashes to ashes, dust to dust, insure and certain hope of the resurrection to eternal life through our Lord Jesus Christ, who shall change our vile body, that it may be like onto his glorious body, according to the mighty working whereby he is able to subdue all things to himself."

Paul removed his hand and then dragged the body down to the water. He made sure to cover the drag marks as he made his way back up to the hut.

"Maria, where is thy child?"

At that simple question, Maria's strong facade broke, and she wept with the grief of her soul overwhelming her. She told him of the events that had befell her the past two years and, when she finished, felt wrung out like the linens in her bowl. It felt good to her to finally have someone with whom to share it, even if it was not Sam.

Paul was silent throughout the tale, and when she finished, he closed his eyes and said a quick prayer for the soul of the child that never knew the love of its mother and father.

"Mayhap Sam will find his child in the kingdom of Heaven," he finally said.

Sniffing, Maria nodded her head in agreement. "'Tis the fondest wish of my heart and soul."

"What shall ye do now that ye have no one left here to need

you," Paul asked.

"Nay, I have been playing on the fears of the people of the sea witch, know ye the tale?"

"Aye, but do you have red-soled shoes?" he joked, then closed his eyes as he knew it was not the time to jest.

"I also have ones who still look after me. Do ye remember Gladys?"

"Aye, I do. She was tough in body and soul, so ye shall be well kept. Do ye need anything?"

"Nay, I am not proud that I pillaged what I could from the shores and have gone out each night to see if more have landed in the form of gold or jewels. Have ye heard of Cyprian Southack?"

It was all Paul could do not to grin and instead said, "Oh, aye, I think I have heard of him."

"He had advertised that no one is recover anything more and whatever has been taken need be given to him 'for the crown,' he states." She shook her head and then said, "'tis unfair a practice as folk here barely survives on what we can forage and trade and depend on this bounty to provide for their families. I grieve I must take from my

Sam's stores, but I know he was bringing them to me, so I feel they are mine to keep."

"Aye, he always remained true to you, Maria, never doubt his love for you. I imagine 'twas why he braved the storm as his need to see you and prove his worth to you far outweighed his own safety. His crews were mostly a loyal lot and agreed to try for these shores. That storm had to have been sent from the devil with the speed it hit and the velocity of the winds." Paul put a finger under Maria's chin and tipped her face up to look at him. "Sam proved that only the devil could keep ye apart as he was but five hundred feet from shore."

Closing her eyes, she hugged Paul and hurried him from the hut while the night was still on them and before the sun's glow tinged the horizon. "Go, Paul, live ye the life ye wish and never take your family for granted. Visit them often until your soul is sated with your lust for adventure, and then retire to them."

Paul nodded and left as quietly as he came and, once aboard his ship, departed Cape Cod and its waters. He could not tell her his wife had taken the children and left him once she learned of his pirating. He knew he would never return to his home and hoped to find a new life back in the Caribbean. Soon after arriving, he accepted a pardon by King George, sold *The Marianne*, and served as second to La Buse, who was still hunting those waters. He would indeed retire and die at his new home in the Bahamas of old age.

After Paul had left, another person rapped once on the door frame. Maria opened it and could not contain her tears.

***

Cotton surveyed the six prisoners slated for execution as they were lined up to walk to the gallows. He knew it was no longer a matter of redeeming their souls, but Cotton was determined to repent, so he turned to other sermons to invoke the men's faith.

"I exalt ye to think now of thy souls and their path down to the fiery hells as ye stand now. Thy souls are weary with the weight of thy sins, and ye must give them to Almighty God so ye may have everlasting peace at His hand." As they walked, cotton continued to exhort the men to give themselves to God. "Suffering gives thy soul reason for forgiveness; now is the time to give it voice."

November 15, 1717, had dawned dreary as if setting the funereal stage for the participants. The condemned walked to the

352

gallows, attached with ropes to their shackles, so they formed a single file line. With despair and sadness, they climbed up the steps, Cotton trailing them the whole way until a guard had him stand to the side to wait until the last rites were given.

Simon Van Vorst began singing softly under his breath, a Swedish psalm continuing to rise in volume as the hoods were shoved over their heads and the nooses tightened. John Brown, realizing this was his end, was determined to go out the same way he had lived, loud with curses and angry at the world. Peter Van Hoof and Thomas Baker remained stoic and still repented for their actions. Hendrick Quintor, his large head, and dark frame standing him taller than the others, required special consideration for his noose, and he kept his eyes only on the judges until a sack covered his head, then he prayed softly to himself. Poor John Shuan could only mutter prayers and invocations in French as tears filled his eyes.

Finally, all was ready, and the decree was once again read. The motion was given to the hangman, and, there on that hill, six men died.

Cotton bowed his head and gave a speech exalting God and praising the men for repenting their souls. In his later writings, he wrote about his views.

The crowd satisfied that "dirty pirates gained their comeuppance," departed back to their lives. Some of the children darted forward, trying to get some type of gruesome souvenir or something they could sell then they faded back into the crowds.

A lone man stood cloaked in dark clothes and hiding in the shadows on the edge of the field, out of sight of prying eyes. He only gave a sharp jerk when the hangman released the trap door, causing the prisoners to fall and strangle on their ropes unless they were fortunate enough to have their necks snap instantly. Silent tears tracked down the man's face as he rotated a golden bracelet on his wrist and then turned and walked deeper into the forest, disappearing.

***

Off the Coast of Wellfleet, Massachusetts, October 7, 1985

"In tonight's news, we bring you the story of a remarkable find in New England today from the expedition team led by Barry Clifford on the shipwreck he found once belonging to the pirate Black Sam Bellamy. First, we'll show you footage of the team bringing up what appears to be a bell!" A newscaster said with her hair teased high and heavy makeup accentuating the neon pink of her top with large shoulder pads. "Local news sources state that this find is significant in proving the ship is the one which Mr. Clifford has sought for many years and against many obstacles. We'll bring you more as the story develops!"

Chapter 23: Love Never Dies

Wellfleet, Massachusetts Present Day

"I think this whole thing is the saddest thing I've ever heard, especially since I know parts of it actually happened. Here I was expecting some romantic, heroic tale of swash-buckling, but, let me tell you, I don't think any buckles were swashed in this story," Clarissa observed.

About this time, the doorbell rang, and Clarissa jumped up to throw open the front door, revealing a man with short, curly blond hair and eyes blue as the sky and an athlete's body. He had the collar up on his team jacket and huddled against the rain pouring off the roof. Clarissa threw herself into his arms, laughing and crying happily, then led him inside, where he removed his sodden shoes and coat then joined them.

"Hey, all, that's a wicked storm going on out there, but I think it's moved on," Reggie told them. "Why does everyone look a little glum?"

"Because Grandpa decided to tell us a really sad story about some dude that became a pirate, so his girlfriend's parents liked him more, and then he died before he could reach her even though he was, like, hundreds of feet from shore," Charlie told him.

"Ah, the story of Sam and Maria, eh? It really is sad, but I just hope they are all together now," he said, hugging Clarissa closer. "Maybe 'Goody Hallett' brewed up this storm as she was rumored to have done back then in vengeance for Sam leaving her."

"Do you believe she would have done that?" asked Charlie.

Reggie thought about it for a few seconds, then shook his head. "Naw, they had one of those loves that last a lifetime, so I never could see her doing that. I'm sure she found a way to prank those townspeople since she was a saucy little thing."

"Grandpa, who was the figure on the hill?" asked Clarissa.

"No one knows, and that was just added flavor for the story.

But remember, it might have been any number of guys.”

“Maybe it was John Julian! He disappeared!”

“Could have been, but in some of the folk tales, he was actually sold into slavery to John Quincy Adams’s grandfather and later hanged in 1733.”

“I like your version better!”

“Or, maybe it was Sam, and he didn’t really die, and he and Maria actually lived together in solitude and happiness,” Laura chimed in, smiling at William.

Clarissa laughed and told Loyd, “I’m gonna have to give you zero stars for this story, Grandpa. Do not recommend it.” Reggie laughed with her, and they went into the kitchen to talk as he only had a few minutes and just wanted to let her know he was okay and check on her.

William and Laura told Charlie it was time for bed, and he hugged them and Loyd then headed towards his bedroom. Halfway down the hallway, he turned back to ask them a question. “Wait, didn’t Blackbeard get hanged like soon after? Is this what happened to all the pirates, and why you don’t hear more stories about them?”

Loyd nodded and told him, "It was definitely a huge blow, and since everyone was being hanged, many other pirates took pardons, turned privateers, or simply retired, so you could say it was the beginning of the end."

Charlie nodded and then went on to do his bed routine. Clarissa walked Reggie to the door, and they said their goodbyes, and then she also went to bed.

William and Laura told Loyd they were exhausted from the store and the storm, so they were also headed to bed. Soon, Loyd sat in silence, watching the fire crackle and pop in the fireplace, and thought back on the story.

Loyd had observed Reggie's blond hair and Clarissa's raven black hair mingling together on their shoulders and shook his head silently at how everything came full circle. He took his necklace in one hand, fiddling with the gold beads and figurines of a sea turtle, a lobster, and a piece of eight that had always been passed down as a good luck charm in his family, and smiled. He knew where the necklace would go when it was time.

THE END

AFTERWORD

This book was written over almost fifteen years due to my crazy life and my need to gather all the information to present as factual a work as possible. My degree is in American History, as I have always been obsessed with anything to do with pirates and their motivations, and it gives me access to amazing resources.

Many of the facts and timelines are given as close to the truth as possible. However, a poetic license was taken to make the story flow. As with many historical stories, primary sources are hard to find, so sometimes we must fill in the blanks, so to speak.

Much research was used, such as works by Karen Brunelle and her book "Bellamy's Bride." The two most used works were "Real Pirates" by Barry Clifford, Kenneth Kinkor, Sharon Simpson, and

Kenneth Garrett, which provided the timeline's basis, and "Expedition Whydah" by Barry Clifford and Paul Perry. Also used was the book "Pirates Then and Now: Notorious Outlaws of the Sea" by Kathy Campbell and Michael Fleeman. And, of course, "The General History of Pyrates, vols. I & II", by Daniel Defoe under the penname Captain Charles Johnsson.

Many characters existed; however, some were invented or told differently to help fill in the gaps. The inherent problem with history is that there are many views and sides to a story, so I've taken the most accepted views on historical figures and events and done my best to keep fidelity to the lives of the people whom I wrote. I used the quotes, as best I could, whenever Sam gave a speech, so you may be able to search for them and find exact wordings or sources. Again, I used the following facts that are as much a majority opinion as I could find as a basis for my book based on the above-mentioned works and my own research. Some characters are real; however, I placed them in Sam's path for better storytelling. I hope you enjoyed this look at the life of a man whose fame has lasted over three hundred years!

1. Samuel Bellamy was born in 1689; his parents were Jonathan

and Elizabeth. He possibly had siblings named Rose, Hirnana, little Elizabeth, and Joan, but I could only find that in one place.

2. Sam's mother died giving birth to Sam or soon after, so I filled in that entire scene with knowledge of birthing practices of that time and created Goody Tate.

3. The entire scene of Sam's teen years with the fight in the field and their little club was completely fictional but fun to write.

4. Sam enlisted and served in the War of Spanish Succession from 1701-1714.

5. Sam came over to Cape Cod, and the dates I've found have varied as to whether it was 1714 or 1715. To make the story flow, I've had him arrive in 1715.

6. He possibly had an uncle named Israel Cole, and I made up the rest of the family as I could find no further verified relatives.

7. A low percentage of sources state they believe Sam had a wife and child he left back in England, but I have found nothing to back up that story. Mr. Kinkor confirmed it was highly unlikely.

8. Maria Hallet was only 15 or 16 when she met Sam. You must remember, in those days, girls who were above 25 were considered "spinsters" or in danger of never marrying, and 15-16 were considered of marriageable age. You must also remember the average lifespan of people in those times was very short. Some sources report her first name was actually "Mehitable," but I preferred Maria.

9. Maria's family was wealthy and Puritan, but I made up the details about them from the context I could find.

10. At some point, Sam and Paul find out about the Spanish wreck. The details vary as to the sequence of those events, whether Sam knew of Maria's pregnancy before he got the news of the wreck, and if it was a major deciding factor as to why he wanted to make a living for them. Or if he heard the news and left before discovering Maria was pregnant. I adjusted the timelines to suit the story as most of the information was generic and usually only read as "sometime in the fall" or "early spring," so I deduced the months and went with those for the book.

11. There are many corroborating reports that Maria was not a good inmate and often escaped her numerous incarcerations through various means, from trickery to a deal with the devil. The description of the devil and the "deal" was obtained from Kathleen Brunelle's book, the passage she used from Elizabeth Reynard's book The Narrow Land, and the dialogue the devil uses in this book. I based him on pirate Edward Low, who was known for cruelty but seemed to settle when he married in Boston, Mass so that he would have been around the area at this time. Unfortunately, he didn't stay settled down once he lost his wife in childbirth, but he was kinder towards women afterward and loved his daughter though he left her with family to resume his pirating life.

12. I've tried to keep the timeline and fidelity to the order in which Sam captured the ships and the people he met along the way.

13. According to documentation, most of the names are correct for the others who journeyed Sam; however, I embellished their characters with the context clues I found on them.

14. Sam served Captain Benjamin Hornigold, who also had

Edward Teach (Blackbeard) as crew. At some point, a vote was taken, Sam took over, and Blackbeard went his own way.

15. There are conflicting reports on why Sam decided it was time to sail north to Maine. Some sources cited his wealth and the fact he felt Maria's parents would finally accept their match. Others state he never intended actually to stop there and was headed further north. I prefer to think he was on his way to claim his love and for them to live on an island they dreamed of together.

16. In most sources, John Julian was recorded as part of the crew with Sam and the pilot of The Whydah Galley. However, two different hypotheses are given for what happened to him. Some say he was sold into slavery to John Quincy, the grandfather of President John Quincy Adams. Others say he escaped, which is the idea I used, and was never found. However, there are accounts he was hung in 1733 after running away multiple times and killing a bounty hunter. I like happy-ever-after's, though it is contrary to most pirate biographies.

17. Cyprian Southack's missives and advertisements were taken

directly from the sources listed at the beginning of this

foreword and given as it was written in those sources.

18. The magistrate presiding over the trial of the men's

pronouncement of charges and descriptions were taken directly

from Barry Clifford and Paul Perry's book Expedition

Whydah. The lines were edited for modern pronunciations.

LIST OF CHARACTERS

1. Loyd Jones – *Fictional*: grandfather telling the story. His name is spelled correctly and not as the typical "Lloyd", as I took it from my own father's name, who passed away in 2015.

2. Clarissa & Charlie Jones – *Fictional*: Loyd's grandchildren.

3. Reggie – *Fictional;* Clarissa's boyfriend.

4. Julie Jones – *Fictional*: Loyd's deceased wife (cancer).

5. William & Laura Jones – *Fictional*: Loyd's son and daughter-in-law, parents of grandkids. They own a comic shop.

6. John & Elizabeth Bellamy – *Actual*: Sam's parents.

7. Rose, Hirnana, little Elizabeth, Joan – *Actual*: Sam's sisters.

8. Goody Martha Tate – *Fictional:* midwife who helped with Sam's birth.

9. Jacob Tierney – *Fictional*: Sam's childhood friend.

10. The Scalawags – *Fictional*: Sam and Jacob's gang as teens:
Port (oldest and leader), Jib (youngest), Rudder (quiet and 11),
Helm (Sam), Stern (Jacob).

11. The Hammers: *Fictional*: opponents for The Scalawags.

12. Friar "Cox-Comb" – *Fictional:* monk at the local monastery
that constantly gave them chores.

13. Israel Cole, Dorothea Cole, Ephram Cole (17), middle child
(5), baby – Sam's uncle and family, mostly all *fictional* except
for Israel Cole's name and relation to Sam.

14. Paulsgrave Williams – *Actual*: Cape Cod goldsmith and
jeweler, son of attorney general John Williams.

15. Maria Hallett – *Actual:* Sam's soulmate and lover.

16. William Shakespeare – *Actual;* Everyone knows this guy.

17. John Hallett, Mother's name unknown – *Actual*: prosperous
Puritan farmers, they liked Sam but did not believe he could
support their daughter.

18. *The Whydah Gally* – *Actual*: Sam's ship that wrecked in a
hurricane in 1717 leaving behind great treasures.

19. Sir Humphrey Morice – *Actual*: Financier of *The Whydah
Gally* for his slave trade.

20. Captain Lawrence Prince a.k.a Laurens Prins – *Actual*: Retired
captain called back into service for *The Whydah Gally.*

21. Lily – *Fictional*: The best multi-tasking cow that ever lived.

22. John Williams – *Actual:* Father of Paulsgrave Williams,
attorney general for the area.

23. Edmund Halley – *Actual & Fictional:* inventor of the diving bell and discovered Halley's Comet.

24. Captain Henry Jennings – *Actual*; captain who raided a Spanish fort when the sunked treasure was already recovered upon his arrival.

25. Charles Vane – *Actual*; part of Jenning's crew who later became a pirate himself known for his brutality.

26. Captain Benjamin Hornigold – *Actual*; captain that mentored Sam and refused to attack English ships. Crew would mutiny and put Sam in charge.

27. Edward Teach, a.k.a. Blackbeard – *Actual*; Hornigold's quartermaster who would later find his fame as a pirate in his own right.

28. Goodman James Carver – *Fictional*; Maria's parents promised her to him for an arranged marriage and he would claim her child as his if she accepted.

29. John Julian – *Actual*; a Miskito Native American from Central America, pilot of *The Whydah Gally.*

30. Justice Judge Doane – *Actual*; Mean-tempered official who presided over the town where Maria and her family lived and would also assist Cyprian Southack when he came to salvage. Part of the court magistrates that tried the seven men from Sam's crew.

31. Gladys – *Fictional*; Maria's nanny who remained loyal to her and tried to help Maria during her pregnancy and incarcerations.

32. Thomas – *Fictional*; Maria's jailor who was sympathetic to her.

33. Edward Low, a.k.a. Ned Low – *Actual*; Pirate captain that was written to be in the area at the time of Maria's incarceration.

34. Richard Caverly – *Actual;* One of Hornigold's men that would join Sam later.

35. Peter Cornelius Hoof – *Actual*; Swedish sailor that would join Sam later and one of the hanged men.

36. John Fletcher – *Actual*; One of Hornigold's men that would also join Sam's crew.

37. Jeremiah Higgins – *Actual*; One of Hornigold's men that would also join Sam's crew.

38. Hendrick Quintor – *Actual*; African American that joined Sam's crew and would later be one of the men hanged.

39. John Brown – *Actual*; African American that joined Sam's crew and would later hang.

40. Oliver Lavasseur "La Buse" – *Actual*; Pirate captain that teamed with Sam and Hornigold and helped Sam get started in his pirating venture. Affiliated with John Taylor and Captain Edward England.

41. Simon Van Vorst – *Actual*; Joined Sam with Thomas Baker from one of the captured ships and one of them men later hanged.

42. Thomas Baker – *Actual*; Joined Sam from one of the captured ships and also one of the hanged men.

43. James Ferguson, Edward Moon, Joseph Rivers, William Osbourne – *Actual*; Joined Sam from one of the captured ships.

44. Abijah Savage – *Actual*; Captain of *The Bonetta.*

45. John King; *Actual*; Youngest pirate in history who joined Sam's crew after Sam captured the ship he was on with his mother.

46. John King's mother – *Actual & Fictional*; Her description and dialogue are fictional since she is only briefly mentioned in historical documents.

47. Captain Sylvanus Rich – *Actual*; His story is in one of the sources used for this book but his location at the tavern is fictional.

48. Thomas Davis – *Actual*; Press ganged into service as a carpenter by Sam and would use that as a defense when he was on trial as a pirate. He was exonerated.

49. Thomas South – *Actual*; Press ganged into service by Sam and used that as a defense when on trial. He was exonerated.

50. Richard Nolan – *Actual*; Took over as Sam's quartermaster when Paul was given command of *The Marianne*. He would later take command of *The Anne*.

51. Captain Beer – *Actual*; Captain of *The Tanner Frigate* that lost his ship to Sam when the crew voted to scuttle it. Sam, angry at the vote, gave one of his famous speeches to Captain Beer.

52. John Shuan – *Actual*; Member of Captain Beer's crew that joined Sam and would later hang.

53. Captain Crumpstey – *Actual*; Captain of *The Mary Anne* that held the rich trove of Madeira wine.

54. John Spincks – *Actual*; Actor who played Alexander the Great in the play "The Royal Pyrate" and was wounded when some of the crew mistook the play for an actual enemy boarding party.

55. Captain Ingolls – *Actual*; Captain of *The Fisher* who is recorded as leading *The Whydah Galley* and *The Mary Anne* to their doom when the storm hit instead of helping them navigate the rocks and shoals.

56. Samuel Harding & Family – *Actual*; Owner of the home Thomas Davis and John Julian found once they reached shore. He would turn them over to the authorities.

57. Colonel William Bassett – *Actual*; military official over the town and would inform the governor of the wrecks.

58. Governor Samuel Shute – *Actual*; Governor of Massachusetts colony who would contract Cyprian Southack to take control of the salvage mission.

59. Cyprian Southack – *Actual*; Sailor and cartographer contracted to take control of the salvage mission by the governor. He created the map that would later be used to locate the wreckage in 1984.

60. Cotton Mather – *Actual*; Famous preacher who was a child prodigy following in the footsteps of his father, Increase Mather. He ministered to the men while in prison and was with them when they hanged.

61. Barry Clifford – *Actual*; Famous salvage archaeologist who found *The Whydah Gally's* final resting place, established Expedition Whydah, and created *The Whydah Gally* Museum with his historian and partner, Kenneth Kinkor.

BIBLIOGRAPHY

BOOKS

Brigham, Albert Perry. *Cape Cod and The Old Colony*. New York

City: The Knickerbocker Press, 1920. (.pdf version)

Brunelle, Kathleen. *Bellamy's Bride: The Search for Maria Hallett of*

Cape Cod. Charleston, SC: The History Press, 2010.

Campbell, Kathy and Michael Fleeman. *Pirates Then and Now:*

Notorious Outlaws of the Seas. New York City, NY:

Centennial Books, 2021.

Clifford, Barry and Paul Perry. *Expedition Whydah: The Story of the*

World's First Excavation of a Pirate Treasure Ship and the

Man Who Found Her. New York City, NY: Cliff Street Books,

1999.

Clifford, Barry and Kenneth J. Kinkor, et al. *1717 Real Pirates: The Untold Story of The Whydah from Slave Ship to Pirate Ship.* Washington, D.C.: National Geographic, 2007.

Fox, E. T. *Pirates in Their Own Words: Eye-Witness Accounts of thee "Golden Age" of Piracy, 1690-1728.* Troutdale, OR: Fox Historical, 2023.

Goldman, William. *The Princess Bride.* Bloomsbury Publishing PLC, 2008.

Johnsson, Captain Charles. *A General History of the Robberies & Murders of the Most Notorious Pirates,* (Vol. 1, 1724; Vol. 2, 1728). Edited by John Franzén. Turku, Finland, 2017.

McClaine, Matt. *Piracy Papers: Primary Source Documents from the Golden Age of Piracy.* Troutdale, OR. 2020.

Reynard, Elizabeth. *The Narrow Land: Folk Chronicles of Old Cape Cod.* 4th ed. Foreword by Andrew Oliver (1978). Chatham, MA: Chatham Historical Society, 1934.

Sandler, Martin W. *The Whydah: A Pirate Ship Feared, Wrecked & Found.* Somerville, MA: Candlewick Press, 2017.

WEBSITES

Brittanica. "War of the Spanish Succession".

www.britannica.com/event/War-of-the-Spanish-Succession

Brittanica. "Whig and Tory". www.britannica.com/topic/Whig-Party-

England

Brittanica. "Separatist". www.britannica.com/topic/Separatists

Brittanica. "Cotton Mather". www.britannica.com/biography/Cotton-

Mather

Brittanica. "Sir Francis Drake".

www.britannica.com/biography/Francis-Drake

Cartwright, Mark. "An A to Z of Pirate & Seafaring Expressions".

World History Encyclopedia, 27 Aug 2021.

www.worldhistory.org/article/1823/an-a-to-z-of-pirate--

seafaring-expressions/

Chard, Donald F. "SOUTHACK, CYPRIAN," in *Dictionary of

Canadian Biography*, vol. 3, University of Toronto/Université

Laval,

2003, http://www.biographi.ca/en/bio/southack_cyprian_3E.ht

ml.

Crystal, David. "Listen to a Demonstration of the Original

Pronunciation of Shakespeare's English and How it Differs from Modern English".

www.britannica.com/video/187707/David-Crystal-pronunciation-Ben-Elizabethan-English-British

Expedition Whydah. *Whydah Pirate Museum.* www.discoverypirates.com.

Frommer's. "History in Cape Cod, Nantucket and Martha's Vineyard". www.frommers.com/destinations/cape-cod-nantucket-and-marthas-vineyard/in-depth/history

History.com Editors. "Glorious Revolution". www.history.com/topics/european-history/glorious-revolution.

History.com Editors. "What's the Difference Between Puritans and Pilgrims?". www.history.com/news/pilgrims-puritans-differences

History.com Editors. "William and Mary Proclaimed Joint Sovereigns of Britain". www.history.com/this-day-in-history/william-and-mary-proclaimed-joint-sovereigns-of-britain

Marsden, Alan. "Humphry Morice, Prince of Thieves". 20 Aug 2022. martintop.org.uk/blog/humphry-morice-prince-thieves

Mitchell, Matthew David. "Humphry Morice: Slave Trader, Embezzler

of the Bank". 01 Jul 2022.

www.bankofengland.co.uk/museum/online-

collections/blog/humphry-morice-slave-trader-embezzler-of-

the-bank

NASA. "1P/Halley: The History of the Halley Comet".

science.nasa.gov/solar-system/comets/1p-halley/

National Park Service. "Hampton National Historic Site Maryland:

Indentured Servants".

www.nps.gov/hamp/learn/historyculture/indentured-

servants.htm#:~:text=All%20indentures%20were%20bought%

20for,substantial%20food%20and%20clothing%20provisions.

New England Historical Society. "Black Sam Bellamy, The Pirate

Who Fought Smart, Harmed Few, Scored Big".

newenglandhistoricalsociety.com/black-sam-bellamy-pirate-

fought-smart-harmed-scored-big/

PBS History Detectives. "Indentured Servants in the U.S.".

www.pbs.org/opb/historydetectives/feature/indentured-

servants-in-the-us/#:~:text=Indentured%20servants%20first%20arrived%20in,

one%20to%20care%20for%20it.

Phelan, Ben. "Explainer: What Was the Triangular Trade?". *PBS*, 11

Jan 2016.

www.pbs.org/wgbh/roadshow/stories/articles/2016/01/11/trian

gular-trade

STARZ. "The Making of Keelhauling". *Black Sails*, 24 Feb 2017.

www.youtube.com/watch?v=s_CSGfOTsaw

UShistory.org. "Witchcraft in Salem".

www.ushistory.org/us/3g.asp#:~:text=As%201692%20passed

%20into%201693,crime%20of%20witchcraft%20in%20Salem.

The Colonial Williamsburg Foundation. "Ouidah".

slaveryandremembrance.org/articles/article/?id=A0120

The Way of the Pirates. "Famous Pirate: Samuel Bellamy".

www.thewayofthepirates.com/famous-pirates/samuel-bellamy/

Town of Wellfleet. "History of Wellfleet". www.wellfleet-

ma.gov/about-wellfleet/pages/history-of-wellfleet

Wilson, David. "The 1715 Plate Fleet and the Rise of the Pirates".

History Today, 30 Jul 2015. www.historytoday.com/1715-

plate-fleet-and-rise-pirates

ACKNOWLEDGEMENT

Special thanks to Barry Clifford for his hard work and perseverance to find the final resting place for this ship and crew and for enabling the Whydah Pirate Museum of Cape Cod to thrive. He and his team at Expedition Whydah made all of this research possible through their discoveries!

Thank you to Kenneth Kinkor for answering my random questions back in 2009 and clarifying some of the events. Mr. Kinkor passed away in 2013, but his legacy of research and preservation lives on.

Lots of appreciation goes to Cielo Bellarose for tackling the beta reading and giving such a great summary of where I needed to clarify things and create a better flow.

And, last but definitely not least, my thanks to my editor/proofreader, Kara Travis!

ABOUT THE AUTHOR

E. H. Casteele was born and raised on a small farm in White House, Tennessee, and her dream was to travel the world as an award-winning archaeologist after she graduated in 1993. Then reality set in, and she decided to pursue a degree in American History. Always an avid reader, she was a frequent library patron and knew that someday she wanted to see a book she wrote on the shelves! She married her high school sweetheart in 1996, and then he joined the Air Force, where writing was challenging between stations in remote locations and eventually children.

While stationed in Charleston, South Carolina, she obtained her BS in American History/Secondary Social Studies and teaching certification in 2006. Her studies there gave her access to primary and secondary resources and a renewed longing to dig into the past and

discover why people made decisions. Charleston was unique and rich

in culture and pirate lore! She could take field trips and visit local

areas of interest and history to build on her knowledge of the world

where the pirates and their crew lived and played.

Her husband retired from the Air Force in 2018 at their last

duty station, Joint Base Elmendorf-Richardson (JBER) in Alaska, and

they decided to stay in the frozen north even after their children

graduated. You couldn't ask for a more remarkable and beautiful

environment in which to write!